Her City of Dreams

By Sarah PB

For my T.A.G Team

xxx

Chapter One

I could cry. The pest control guy has just vacated the, what is apparently, a "Zoo" in my new bedroom. I grab my bag and don't hesitate to escape from the room let I signed up for two weeks ago, rushing to my job to earn the minimum wage, which has landed me in this small space with just enough room for a single bed and a shelving unit. It's a creature, bug-ridden abode, in Central London. In fairness, bites aside, it was the best of an interesting and awful bunch of accommodation options. There was the house behind Holloway prison who I would be sharing with a lap-dancer and seemingly helping to babysit her daughter most evenings. Or the creepy guy who had a supposedly artsy photo over the kitchen sink, of a man getting up close and personal with a very 70's inspired bush, not the garden variety. I had started to give up hope until I met the fellow flat sharers in this Farringdon apartment and thankfully, so far, seem very normal and more importantly, not serial killers. Which is always a bonus when you move to the capital city.

Leaving Brighton was a huge step. I had made a life there over the past few years, after moving there for University. Originally from a small village in the Cotswolds, I grew up in a bubble. Albeit a beautiful bubble of country life and simple pleasures. I have always craved the big city lights and our trips to anywhere with a population larger than 7,000 inhabitants got me excited throughout my youth. Growing up with two sisters, one younger and one older, also with a mum and dad who seemed very content in their lives, I have always dreamt of returning to the countryside to settle down, but before those days come, my heart draws me to a faster pace of life and that includes travel and adventures all filled with excitement.

My Brighton days had experienced it's fair few ups and downs and with the breakdown of my relationship, which, with nearly a decade of age difference and his constant jealousy, plus the lack of career prospects on the South Coast, I jumped at the chance of a TV job in London. I say "TV job" loosely, in fact, I would be answering the calls for a live show, but it was that or a Runner's role and this paid slightly better, still barely minimum wage, but it was a stepping stone.

As I walk down the streets from Farringdon to the TV studios at Charlotte Street, even though, since moving to London I could only afford one meal a day and my back continually itches from at least a dozen bedbug bites, the bounce in my step is palpable. Here I am at 25, newly single and at the start of my career, living in one of the fastest and most exciting cities in the world. The smile beams from my face and the fresh October breeze chills my blushed cheeks. I feel giddy, this is exciting and who knows where life will take me... who knows?

The TV studios are renowned in the industry and even though the show is a little entertainment chat show, far, far up the digital channels, I was surrounded by greatness on a daily basis and the buzz is as exciting as I always dreamt. Even in the lifts, the daily show ratings for all the top UK shows are displayed with pride and it feels amazing to walk through the security barriers and know I am part of this world.

'Hi Sophia.'

'Oh, hey.' I reply coyly as I scurry off to the phone room. I scurry, closing the door behind and collapse into my seat. How does he know my name? I sit and wonder momentarily, until the door crashes open behind me, which encompasses the subtlety of sound engineer Lucy and Craig, one of the Cameramen as they bound in. Both in their mid-twenties and both looking like they have walked off stage from performing at a rock concert and both, more importantly, making me feel welcome and at home in this intimidating new world.

'What are you doing after work?' They both ask full of excitement. I look down at my £4.50 meal deal, which will be the one, 500 calories worth of food I can afford today, which I probably have already worked off bouncing down the London streets to work.

'Well, I can't really afford much, so I was going to just head home,' I missed out the fact I had zero funds due to a £50 bill to the pest control guy and actually, that bedroom is the last place I want to rush back to.

'I will buy you a drink.' they say, jinxing each other, I open my mouth to thank them but also politely decline their kindness, but before I even get a chance,

'No arguments, you are coming out.' Lucy orders and I already know not to argue.

'Thanks so much. Only if you are sure though?' They both nod in unison.

'I promise to buy you a round in return when I can.' I say, hoping finances will take a turn for the better sooner rather than later.

'No worries Sophia. Right, I better go and soundcheck, see you after the show.' Lucy heads off with Craig following close behind her and I twizzle in my office chair to face the monitors which display all the action being broadcast from the studio adjacent. I can hear the excitement of the Producer and Director plus a whole crew through the wall in the Gallery. The Gallery where it all happens and the main cogs of creativity spin, I listen on in awe, hoping one day I will earn my spot there.

'Hey, are you OK? You seemed a little upset the other day?' I feel my cheeks burn. Standing in a bar around the corner from work, I have my first gifted drink of the evening, courtesy of Lucy. She's off talking about all things music with some fellow colleagues and I find myself suddenly a little overwhelmed and feeling incredibly awkward. I really need to snap out of it and act a lot cooler if I intend to survive in this city. Miles stands with a questioning look on his face and I know exactly when he is talking about.

Miles is a presenter, he is tall, blonde, handsome and he used to be in a boyband. I feel giddy and shy just being in his presence, let alone having a one on one conversation with him. The moment Miles is referring to is a call with my ex, which I made the mistake of answering in the work corridors a few days previous. I personally thought I had done a great job of disguising my upset from the barrage of abuse I had been receiving from a very angry ex-boyfriend, but clearly, Miles had clocked on to it, as well as my name.

'Yes, I was a little. Nothing important, just ex issues.'

'Oh, I had hoped it was something like that,' he gives me his best teeth whitened grin and sparkly blue eyes and I smile back, struggling to know how I should respond. He "hoped", what had he hoped? That it was an ex? Why was he hoping anything to do with me? Before I get to respond, Lucy and Craig bound over like excitable puppies.

'Oh, what's going on here, flirting much?' subtle guys, really subtle I think to myself, rolling my eyes to disguise my embarrassment and I cannot even bring myself to look in Miles' direction.

'Sophia, it's shot time.' Craig explodes with tipsy excitement.

'No, no. No, honestly I think I might head back home,' is what I should have said, but I didn't.

As I slouch in one of the billion coffee shops in the city, first paycheck in the bank and sipping on a totally overpriced Chai Latte, I'm surrounded by meetings, tourists and tapping laptops. I relax and ponder the night before. A throb pounds from each of my temples, back and forth. I should have stopped at the shot, but peer pressure got the better of me. Two Tequila's later and we had moved on to an underground club, dancing our socks off and smiling like it was the best night of our lives. From the group of the crew who partook in the evening, we had been whittled down from the married and sensible parent members of the production team to just Lucy, Craig, Paul, Lisa and of course Miles.

'Living our best lives,' I recall in my head the moments that Miles had shouted over the music into my ear and also, how he was pleased my ex was out the picture and he had noticed me the moment I walked into the office. I also recalled the jealousy I felt when two very attractive fellow dancers recognised Miles from the TV and as if they knew him, they flung their arms around his neck. They were both glamorous from head to toe, they probably had wardrobes the size of my bedroom and definitely far less bug-like inhabitants. They towered over me in Louboutins and LBD's, while I stood by in my knee-high boots, skinny jeans and black roll neck. In fairness to me, they did look like they took a wrong turn and should have been in a far more upmarket establishment. However, this didn't stop me feeling completely inadequate and questioning why anyone like Miles would pay a second more attention to me.

I guess I'm OK looking, 5'7 size 10 but dramatically decreasing to an 8 due to funds for food, not a diet I would ever recommend. Bluey grey eyes and light brown long hair that falls over an average bust. I've been told I am pretty, but usually by people who are biased. I see all my faults, but then, don't we all? My mum always reminds me that when I am struggling to accept a compliment, that in years to come, I will look back and be envious at how I once looked. I hope that when I reach that point, I will have achieved so much in my life, the least of my worries will be how aesthetically pleasing I am. Or maybe that's just my youthful naivety getting the better of me and I should pay more attention to my mother's wisdom. However, the evening before, all the self-doubt rushed through my intoxicated brain and I did what I always seem to do, I grabbed my coat and rushed out of the club like my life depended on it. It was rash, I know, but what were the options? I had to do what any good, independent woman should do and leg it, rather than stand by and feel two inches tall. Well, that was mine or the Tequilas logic anyway.

I scroll through my messages of-

Sophia, worried, where you at?

YOu OK, WORRIED?

Drunk messages from Lucy. A Pang of guilt runs through me for concerning my new friend but also feeling grateful that in this huge city, I had already had at least one kind human looking out for me.

'Hey, hey, Sophia.' Miles shouts out from the Studio doors. Dammit, the aim was to hide in the telephone room and avoid all contact and more importantly, any questions of my disappearance.

'Where did you go last night? I managed to shake off those overly chatty, drunk girls and I turned around and you had vanished!' What a tit I feel. I probably look like the ridiculous, insecure girl that I obviously am.

'Sorry. I noticed I missed some calls and had to ring them back.' I lied.

'Oh OK, it wasn't more hassle from the ex, was it?' Wow, how I managed to turn that from me looking the fool, to now Miles showing concern about the potential ex being in the picture. I feel bad and relieved in equal measures.

'Oh no, nothing like that, I think he finally realises it's over,' Miles' eyes light up.

'Excellent, well as long as you are OK?'

'Absobloodylutely.' I say and then panic, hoping Miles has never seen Sex and the City and this reference is lost on him.

'Great, well can we finish our drinks soon? The night ended far too quickly.' Phew, reference missed and he wants to go out again, maybe I didn't totally screw it up after all.

'ON AIR IN 5,' the Producer shouts over the monitors, Miles squeezes my left arm gently, smiles and runs off to the studio doors, ready to show his face on TV and make more women and men feel as gooey inside as I do right now.

'SOPHIA.'.. Oh no, I'm totally in for it now, did I mention Lucy is a feisty Sound Engineer Scot? Honestly, there are some men I would take my chances in a fight with, rather than her!

'Sorry, sorry, sorry. I had to quickly leave and I couldn't find you.' more lies.

'Sophia, just come here quickly please.' Lucy loudly whispers, dragging me into the sound room, she urgently closes the door behind me and pulls over a chair.

'Sit.' She orders, so I sit. 'I screwed up, I went back with Craig last night and totally SCREWED UP.'

'Oh Lucy, what happened? Surely it can't be that bad.'

'Will you come to the Chemist with me?' Oh right, it really was that bad.

'Yes, of course, there is a Chemist around the corner. Let's go after the show.'

'Thank you Sophia, thank goodness you started working here, I literally didn't know who to turn to and really can't bring myself to go alone.' Lucy's eyes start to fill and she bows her head. I never expected to see such a strong and tough woman, standing so vulnerable in front of me. I stand and walk over, giving her a silent, but hopefully reassuring hug.

'Don't worry, we will have it sorted in no time.'

I always imagined being in my mid-twenties, I would feel like a fully-fledged adult, so why, when Lucy and I leave the Chemist with her "solution" to the previous night's misdemeanours, do we walk out with our heads hanging low, feeling like at any point we will get told off? I am even feeling some kind of shame and I'm just doing my best to be a supportive friend.

As we walk into the studio, we catch Craig's eye, Lucy lifts the brown paper bag and he shrugs and responds nonchalantly, 'well it's cheaper than a baby.' What the hell! We both stand, gobsmacked in shock. Who in their right mind, thinks that is a respectable response? I direct Lucy through to the green room in the hope that it is empty.

'I can't believe he said that,' Lucy's eyes glaze over.

'No, me neither, but I think we have the answer as to whether you should pursue a relationship with him.'

'Sophia, can we get a drink before I take these?' My glare answers her question. 'OK, fine, fancy dinner at mine? Pretty sure you can't live off a BLT and Quavers your entire life.'

'Many true words are said in jest.' I laugh.

'Sophia, I wasn't joking, if ever there was a woman who needs a good feed, it's you.'

We arrive at the Limehouse Docks on the Thames and it's not exactly the surroundings I had expected Lucy to live in. 'It's amazing. That view down the river is beautiful. How did you manage to land a place like this? I can barely find a room with basic hygiene standards.'

Although Lucy is a bonafide Sound Engineer, she has only been qualified for a few months and I had imagined a flatshare in trendy Shoreditch or Dalston, this is far more glamorous than I had ever anticipated. She has bright red, straight hair to her shoulders and the fashion style of a Roady who had taken on a few festivals in her time. She looks the part and acts it too. I am a little in awe, she has London at her feet. I, on the other hand, do not.

Lucy laughs off my comment and walks me around the two-bed, plush third-floor apartment with a balcony and views of all the London evening lights you could dream of, illuminating the Thames and horizon.

'Ignore the mess babe, my flatmate is packing up, he is off on a new production in South America, lucky git has totally blagged the best gig.'

'Oh wow, that really is amazing.' It suddenly occurs to me, 'Lucy, if you don't mind me asking, how much do you pay for this place and I don't suppose you are after a slightly peckish work pal, who is house trained and REALLY needs a decent place to live?' Pretty sure my expression is now on par with a begging dog, desperate for a treat, or a wee, whichever.

'YES babe, that would be the best idea. I hadn't realised you are looking for somewhere, otherwise it would have saved me wasting lots of laborious hours, interviewing really annoying and weird people. It's £850 a month, how does that sound to you?' Well, that sounds like I would be even skinter if that was possible, but at least I would be skint and actually like my home.

'Can you give me a few days to work it out please Lucy? I would absolutely LOVE to live with you.'

As I look out the window of the DLR, with a tummy full of food and wine, heading back to what I hope is now my very temporary home. I try to figure out how I can manage to earn more money and get myself out of this current rut I find myself in. I could ask my parents, but they have done so much for me already and now is the time I need to prove I can do this alone, I have to be proactive.

I seem to have settled into work really well, my manager likes me, I know that, because she smiles at me, which is more than what anyone else gets apparently. I will be open and honest, explaining my situation. Offer myself for more hours of work, which was near impossible, but take on extra duties if needed. I feel good, I feel like this could work and positivity is bubbling in my tummy. As the multitude of street lights merge and create a colourful rainbow blur out of the train window, I know this is where I should be, I have to make this work, failure is not an option.

Chapter Two

'Sophia, so nice to see you. Please sit down. What can I do for you today?'

I suddenly feel incredibly tiny and nervous. I am sitting in my bosses office, asking for a pay rise for a job I have been in for a month. A month. I take a breath.

'Thanks for seeing me Jo, I really appreciate you giving up your time. I wanted to come in and be honest with you.' Her eyes widen, which doesn't help to ease my nerves. 'I absolutely love my job here and feel like I have settled in pretty well. The problem that I have is, I cannot afford to live in London and I am struggling financially. I totally understand this is a starting role and salary....'

'Let me stop you there Sophia. Thank you for coming to me with this and not sitting back and struggling. Your salary is very low and I understand it is difficult to live in London on a starter wage. I have had nothing but fantastic feedback from the team and we have discussed where we see you going in the company. Your qualifications and work experience at the BBC mean we have you down for a potential Trainee Assistant Producer role.' I get sudden butterflies and Jo continues, 'the fact you have the motivation to come to me and have this conversation, proves that you are the right candidate for the job. It comes with an instant 3k pay rise, which will hopefully be the amount you need to continue working with us.' This conversation could literally not have gone better.

'Jo, that really is the best news I could have wished for. Thank you so much and I promise to not let you all down.'

'I know you won't. You start Monday. Be in the office at 9 am and I will email you an updated contract.'

YES! I inhale the largest, most satisfying breath as soon as the lift doors close. I would fist punch the air, but I am more than aware of the security camera gazing down on me. Who to call first? Lucy, I must ring Lucy and confirm I will rent the room of my dreams. Then my Mum and Dad, the people who believe in everything I do and would probably sell a kidney if it helped me to fulfil my dreams. I know they will be equally excited and probably relieved I won't be moving back home anytime soon! Not far down the list was letting my current flatshare know I would be vacating as of immediate effect. I won't be missed, I was barely there to build any kind of relationships with them and due to them subletting, there is very little they could legally do to stop me leaving the infestation. Before all this, however, I have my final show in the telephone room to complete and I am going to sit back and enjoy it, in the knowledge that this will be my last stint in this role.

As I partially skip/walk through the studio doors I swing it open a little too far and of course, just my luck, I nearly wipe out a very taken aback Miles, 'blimey, I thought we were under attack for a second,' he grins.

'Oops, sorry. Clearly more power in these little muscles than I thought,' I smile like a Cheshire cat and realise I must look like a crazed woman, 'Oh and I just have had some good news, hence the expression of a nutter.' I point manically to my face and my cheeks start to rouge as I realise what a dickhead I must look.

'Yes, I heard through the grapevine that you will be finding a place in the gallery to sit your little muscles. Congratulations, I look forward to working closely with you. I really feel a drink, post-work is in order. I'm sure there will be a few others in tow, sound good?'

'Wow, the news really does travel fast around here!'

In one day I had secured a new, much better role at work and will be shortly confirming a move to a much nicer home. Now I also get to spend the evening with possibly my version of Aiden or Mr Big, either would suit me just fine.

'YES,' I spurt out, a little less eloquent than intended.

'Great, it's a date then.' Before my overthinking gets a chance to kick in and even question the use of the word "date", the gallery door is swung open,

'PRODUCTION MEETING.' The producer shouts from the gallery, Lucy appears out of the sound booth.

'Hey Lucy, I have some fab news, do you still fancy a new flatmate?'

'Hell to the yeah babe,' she grabs me and twirls me around into the gallery.

'Cheers to Sophia, our new colleague and who, if we are not careful, might end up being our boss soon!' Everyone laughs, I smile and mouth 'thank you' to Miles. He clinks my glass of Prosecco and winks at me. I feel instantly protected and looked after when I am in the presence of him, which is ridiculous as I barely know him. There is something so confident and warm in his manner which I find totally alluring, I feel like a moth drawn to a flame, which feels dangerous but also impossible to prevent.

'Sophia.' Lucy breaks my train of thought. She's visibly angry and downs a shot as though it was a breath. 'He's chatting to that tart,' Lucy nods to the right of her.

'Who is Lucy, what's wrong?' I look around, trying to figure out what has made her so angry.

'Him. Craig. The tosser.' I look over to see Craig with his focus on another colleague.

'Lucy. Seriously. He's a huge prick and I don't mean in the good way,' she chuckles and then sighs.

'He has really pissed me off,'

'I know, but better to find out earlier on, right?' She reluctantly nods, rolling her eyes as if I was a mother to her teenage self.

'Anyway, you will have a new wing-woman next week, just let me know what time on Saturday and I will Uber myself and my few bags of belongings to yours.'

'What's all this about wing-woman and belongings?' Miles glides next to me and I jump, I was convinced he was out of earshot.

'I'm moving in with Lucy, to a more sophisticated residence,' I grin.

'Excellent, you will have to let me know where to send the housewarming gift.'

'Oh for god sake.' Lucy walks off in the direction of the bar.

'Was it something I said?' Miles tilts his head and grimaces.

'No, don't worry, just a little bit of man trouble in her life, not Miles trouble. I can't imagine you causing anyone any problems,' I say, far more flirty than intended. Oh gosh, I really need to rein it in, my focus is my job, my focus is my job, I repeat in my head. Do not get distracted by the handsome guy, standing in front of you and directing lots of attention your way which is doing huge amounts to boost your ego. Oh crap.

'I try my best not to Sophia. Let me get you a top-up,' Miles winks at me, taking my glass and walks to the bar. I watch him walk through the crowd and struggle to see how I am going to resist him and all his charm.

We head into the November evening, Christmas lights are already up and the streets are as busy as ever. The bar at the studio is handy as an easy post-work drink venue, but it closes at 7 pm and the sensible among us head home to families and to the warmth and comfort of their homes. I currently have none of those waiting for me, so with a linked arm to Lucy, we giggle down Oxford Street, closely followed by a few more colleagues who are equally not in any rush to head home. We are en-route to a bar with Garlic in the name near Soho Square, I can't exactly remember what Miles said the name was, but it didn't sound particularly enticing.

'Sophia, here's a seat,' Miles ushers me in to sit next to him and once everyone has settled, a waiter is called over and looks less than impressed. I get the impression this is bar service, but after Miles' slyly exchanges a few notes, the bartender seems more than happy to take the order of some disgusting sounding garlic-infused shots for the table. Lucy nudges me, right in the ribs,

'Ouch, what was that for?'

'Oops, sorry Soph, I was trying to be subtle.'

'Well you failed and now I am most likely bruised' I say dramatically rubbing my side and teasing her.

'Please just do us all a favour and snog him, the sexual tension is too much for us all to handle,' Lucy loudly whispers in my ear.

'Lucy! Jesus, I hardly know him. Anyway, he is just being friendly.' Lucy glares at me and I try to give the most convincing expression of innocence, even though I don't even believe what I am saying. Before I get to faux protest my obvious attraction to Miles, the waiter returns from the bar with a tray full of shots.

'Here you go Sophia,' Mile's hands me a very garlicky smelling clear liquid and I regret drinking it even before it touches my lips.

'Here is to the fabulous Sophia and for bagging herself a promotion, cheers.' Miles lifts his glass and with a chorus of 'cheers' and 'well done' from the table, everyone downs their shot, which tastes as rank as I imagined it would.

'Right all, it's crap in here, we need music. Follow me.' Lucy stands and without hesitation or argument from any of us, we follow her lead.

I don't want to leave, I could stay with Miles all night. It was like something out of a film. The laughing, the jokes and the dancing.

We had moved on to a popular Jazz Club in Soho, which is very upmarket and different from our previous nights out. Having seemingly jumped the very long queue to get in and having protested a number of times to Miles, he was refusing to let me pay for a drink or anything for that matter. He was totally pulling a Mr Big on me. I feel swept off my feet and the most wined and dined I have ever experienced, it's proving very difficult to not be sucked into the whirlwind that is Miles. It's quite a contrast to my ex, when on the last Valentine's day we spent together, he decided we should "go Dutch". I'm all for feminism and equality, but really? I still crave the idea of a man who can whisk me off my feet and make me feel like the only girl in the world. The old romantic in me is succumbing to Miles charms quicker than I had hoped and planned.

We are sitting in a small booth, surrounded by a loud mix of laughter and Jazz music and there are only a few of us left. Lucy, one of the runners and a camera guy called Paul, they wave a pack of cigarettes from across the table, announcing their smoke break and we watched them fight through the crowd and out of sight. Just Miles and me, alone. A strange mix of giddy verging on sobering at the reality of the two of us left here alone hits me. Lucy was right, the chemistry between us is off the scale. I look up to make some inane conversation about the decor, to attempt to detract from my discomfort, but Miles is just looking at me with his head tilted slightly and a smile. 'I really wish I could read your mind Sophia,' and without another breath, his hand was suddenly at the bottom of my neck as he gently leans in and his soft warm, Bourbon flavoured lips kiss mine. It went from zero to a hundred in seconds and all the build-up over the past month was obvious, I could have potentially levitated and I wouldn't have known. The noise of the room faded into the background, that was until a loud clapping brought us to an abrupt halt. The rest of the group have returned from their cigarettes and are now standing gleefully smacking their hands together and cheering us on. Not exactly the impression I wanted to give, but honestly, in my current daze the kiss feels worth it.

'Soph, we are off. Hey Miles, make sure my girl gets home safe and when I say home, HER home,' Lucy laughs and directs the others towards the door, Miles mimics a salute in her direction.

'Well I have been told, right?' Miles laughs and kisses my cheek softly.

'You certainly have,' as I move my lips to his and continue kissing.

It could have been hours. All awareness of time fell into the black hole that is Miles' lips, it was only when the lights were slightly brightening courtesy of closing time, we knew that was our cue that we have outstayed our welcome. We stumble out onto the busy streets of Soho and it's 3 am, but the hustle and bustle never seems to diminish.

'Sophia, I literally live there,' he points to what looks like a flash penthouse apartment. 'I'm not a weirdo trying to lure you in, but it's Friday and unless you have plans tomorrow, it seems a shame to not have at least one more drink?'

'If you had asked me up for coffee, it would categorically be a no, but if there is a glass of wine available, then that is definitely more tempting.'

'Sophia, for you, anything.'

'This is seriously amazing,' I gasp, looking around at the floor to ceiling windows, which overlook the London streets. The decor is how I imagined after walking through the plush foyer moments earlier, the apartment is clean, white and minimalist, the ultimate bachelor pad.

'How long have you lived here?'

'Well, I bought it while I was still in the band, as an investment. The plan was to rent it out when the band went their separate ways, but it's so handy for work and I just love being in the heart of it all. Obviously it won't be forever, I can't imagine there are any schools in a five-mile vicinity.' I've no idea of my drink count by this point, but I am pretty sure he just mentioned schools. 'Hehe, don't worry, I'm talking about a five-year plan, certainly no children for a while.'

'Hmmm, I will be 30 then, I might well be on board,' I say without even thinking.

'OK Sophia, I will certainly keep that in mind,' he laughs, passing me a large glass of red wine as I blush, wishing I had my non-intoxicated filter intact.

As we sit and look out at the night lights and the passers-by, for what feels like hours. We chat and laugh with intervals of kissing and it feels pretty amazing. It was all I imagined London to be when I was packing up my bags, mid-argument with an overbearing ex, desperate to escape his grasp. The freedom and romance is feeling exciting and after a slightly rougher start in the city than I had anticipated, bed bugs and all, I take a sip of wine and glance over at a very handsome Miles as I slowly rest my head on his arm, feeling a whoosh of content flow over me.

Ouch. As incredible as these windows are, waking up with the sun beating down on a hungover and dehydrated head, really makes you want to crawl down the nearest, darkest hole. 'Morning,' Miles says with far more enthusiasm than required when I am feeling this crappy.

'Morning,' I manage to whisper as I rub my eyes and wonder how much mascara has smudged down my face, I can imagine how utterly unattractive I look right now.

'We must have drifted off on the sofa. Do you fancy pancakes?'

'That would be fab, thank you. I just need to go and freshen up.'

'Bathrooms to the left, I have left a new toothbrush out for you.' A new toothbrush? He is either very prepared and never wants to get caught out with bad oral hygiene, or this is not the first time he's brought a woman back after a night out. WHAT AM I TALKING ABOUT, his credentials scream "player". I roll my eyes at myself, of course, I am probably just a statistic now. A foolish stat who thinks she's smart and has a decent understanding of the male form, to now a dopey 25-year-old, lured into a smooth-talking, players flash pad. Although we didn't actually have sex, I remember, feeling redeemed, even if it is only to myself. I look at my tired and drained face in the illuminated mirror.

'Wow, I look shit!' I say louder than intended to my reflection.

'What's that? Are you OK Sophia?' Miles calls from the kitchen.

'Yes, fine thanks,' which was actually, no, I need to get out of here and regroup my thoughts and not feel like one of the, possibly, million women he has fed pancakes to. Jeez, what a cliche. I splash freezing water in my face and use my travel concealer to cover most of the dark circles under my eyes. The tinted lip gloss makes me feel a little more put together and I'm hoping the journey home doesn't look too much like a dreaded walk of shame. Thankfully it was straight out after work, so with low heeled leopard ankle boots, black skinny jeans and simple white shirt and black winter coat, I can easily get away with walking half a mile back to the grimy room let and look like I am actually off to brunch. Hair in a top knot and as long as nobody gets too close, they won't smell the alcohol seeping from my pores.

'Coffee? I can make a better Cappuccino than any Barista you can find,' Miles says with a cheeky grin.

'That would actually be amazing, thank you,'

'... And here's a pint of water, that will soon sort out your head.' I down the water as if I had crawled across the desert for twelve hours and fallen upon a puddle.

'So tell me, Miles, how is a good-looking, talented guy like yourself, single? Surely you have had women falling at your feet,' I pry and he laughs.

'Well actually, more men. If I am being completely honest. They assume because of the jobs, the hair, living adjacent to Soho, come to think of it, on paper I probably should be,' he shrugs and smiles. 'A lot of women also assume they are just a notch and that I have a long list of conquests, so that doesn't do me any favours.' Miles looks at me, almost through me, I feel instant guilt that it had crossed my mind and it's clearly something that bothers him.

'Well, I guess that's all stereotypes, better to get to know someone to find out who they are.' I say, attempting to cover up my hypocrisy.

'Wise words for such a hungover, tired young woman. This is getting far too deep for this early and such little sleep. Fancy some homemade compote with your pancakes, or Maple Syrup?'

'What about both?' I say cheekily, feeling certain that my initial instincts about Miles were correct.

'Stay. We can swing by the shops and get you something fresh to wear. I'm not talking about Pretty Woman standards, I'm thinking somewhere highstreet,' I nearly snort out my final bite of breakfast.

'Well, that's not the kind of reference I was anticipating over pancakes' I laugh, not really sure how else to respond. Thoughts rushing through my brain and I'm weighing up the pros and cons of taking Miles up on his offer. Having always verged on the more sensible and not to take too many chances and quite possibly over analysing everything, this offer of Miles' is sending my, already hazy brain, into a spin.

On a few occasions that I have really gone wild, it was thanks to my childhood best friend, Cary. The Thelma to my Louise. Apart from the murdering part, the comparisons are incredibly similar. I am the friend who will make sure you get home OK, the least drunk one at the party and the one who can instantly sober in a time of trouble. The friend who will go looking for you around a holiday resort, if you leave a club with a guy and haven't reappeared for breakfast. The times I have let others be the sensible ones and do the thinking, let my hair down and did less worrying and more living, I look back on with fond memories. Possibly not the ethos I would condone my future children to live by, but I definitely need to find a healthy balance and at 25. Sod it, I am blowing caution to the wind.

'Yes, let's do that. On one condition,' I stipulate 'I really need a shower, I feel gross.' Miles smiles.

'Your wish, my fair maiden, is my command.' He takes a bow and I feel a little happy glow hit my cheeks.

We take a long, cold December walk with hot chocolates in our hands, through Green Park, past the Royal residence and through to Kings Road. It must be miles, but we take it slow, laughing and chatting, never missing a heartbeat in conversation. I have learnt about his upbringing in Rural Wilshire, how his parents are still madly in love after 30 years and he has an older, married brother who is a Lawyer. I also found out that Miles is 28, which with three years age difference, feels perfect, but as I link arms and cosy into him, anything he said would feel perfect right now.

'Gap, that seems like a good place to get a cosy knit and some jeans?'

'Did you really just say "cosy knit"?' I mock.

'Yes Sophia, that's right. I did. because men can like fashion too,' he rolls his eyes and shakes his head in fake despair.

'OK, OK, I'm sorry, that was very small-minded of me, you just continue to surprise me Miles. In good ways, of course.'

After ten minutes of looking at all the price tags and trying to justify if I REALLY need a new jumper and jeans, or I should just get the bus back to my room let and avoid the unnecessary expense or dipping into my overdraft, Miles bounds over with a gorgeous oat coloured, chunky roll neck and black faux leather leggings.

'I think you would look amazing in these.'

'They are lovely Miles, but I probably can't stretch too far right now,' I say, pretty sure I am blushing. 'I have to start my new job on Monday and then my finances will improve. Thanks so much for looking though. It's really sweet to see you bounding around a shop, excited about women's clothes,' I tease him, hoping to distract from my money woes.

A shop assistant walks over with a bag, 'sorry for the delay sir, I have found a more suitable size bag for your purchase.' Purchase, hang on, wait, what? Miles pulls a, "I'm sorry for being too generous and now I feel like I have done something wrong" face. I decide not to risk embarrassing him in front of the shop assistant and graciously accept the bag.

'I'm sorry Sophia, I hope I haven't overstepped the mark, I just really want to spend the day with you and thought these would be fab for a casual meal out with a few of my friends. If you will do me the pleasure?' I pause for thought as we navigate our way to the exit of the shop. His eyes have a slightly watery glaze from the cold December air hitting him, as we leave the warmth of the indoors back out onto Kings Road. I take a look at the life around me, all the excited shoppers on the run-up to Christmas, the dusky bluey pink skies with Christmas lights gently twinkling against them. I feel so lucky right now, to have met this man standing here, offering to take my potentially lonely situation and making me feel like the only girl in the world. The luckiest, only girl. A bus speeds past breaking my thoughts and I smile at him, curling my arm under his and linking in, tight next to his body.

'Nothing would make me happier right now Miles. You are very generous and I am very grateful. Thank you,' I look him in the eyes and he smiles, then he gently kisses my forehead, I squeeze his arm and we take the long walk back to his home.

I'm slightly giddy with excitement and nerves. I sit, peering out the window while Miles "throws some clothes on" as he describes it, but he never looks like anything has been thrown on him. He is 6'1, broad shoulders and obviously fit. Not a gym fiend kind of fit, but he does look like he takes good care of himself. He walks out in a plain white Tee with a brand logo on the chest, indigo jeans which look like they were tailored for him and dark brown suede Chelsea boots, he grabs a dark brown leather jacket and I can't stop staring. I don't want to meet his friends and go out for Sushi, I want to turn him around, march him straight back into that bedroom and undo all his hard work, but I won't because I am not that girl and I will not give into lust that easily. If I think it enough, maybe it will be true.

'Heelllooo, Sophia,' Miles mock waves at me, as though I had been in a trance. 'The Uber is downstairs. I would love to know what's going on in that head of yours,' I grin.

'Maybe you will find out soon enough,' Gah, I've failed at the first hurdle. Miles flashes me a questioning but playful look and I follow him out of the apartment into the lift. The lift is one big mirror and I admire the choice of clothes picked out for me. The Oat roll neck is perfect over the faux leather leggings with my black Pea Coat over the top. The leopard print ankle boots give enough of a dressed-up look to make me worthy of a fancy Sushi restaurant in Kensington. I feel good and together, we look like a pretty decent couple.

'We look good together, don't we?' Miles says, as if he is reading my mind.

'Yes. Actually, we do,' I smile, like the cat that got the cream.

Air kisses are being thrown around the table and there are far more people at this casual meal than I had anticipated. There are ten of us, three couples who I think, if

I recall correctly, are Darren and Susie, Paul and Sarah, Matt and Simon then two people, who I am pretty sure are not together are Emily and Martin. I get an instant bad vibe from Emily. She blatantly looks at me head to toe and then barely acknowledges my existence, which clearly is not down to her being shy, as she throws her arms around Miles' neck. He is forced to take her weight in his arms and she lifts her feet off the ground. I immediately dislike her, he is not yet mine, but he is currently more mine than hers.

'Milllles, I've missed you my darling,' Emily says with a private school educated drool.

'Emily, it's been a week, I'm sure you can't have missed me that much,' Miles laughs, glancing at me and putting a reassuring hand on my shoulder. It's obvious he has clocked that her behaviour is odd. There is clearly a back story to this, I am intrigued and will find my moment to dig for information when dearest Emily is out of earshot.

Emily is blonde, petite and pretty. Wavy shoulder-length, just off the beach kind of hair and minimal makeup, I feel instantly in competition with her. Her aura tells me she thinks she is better than me, my unconfidence tells me the same, but the way Miles' looks at me tells me otherwise.

'Miles, I'm just nipping to the loo,' I decide I need a moment to compose myself and check my makeup is still in place.

'What drink would you like if they come before you get back?' Miles puts a caring hand on my knee and I can see out of the corner of my eye, that Emily is watching us.

'Hmmm, surprise me' as I give him a peck on the cheek. A very territorial peck.

As I stare at myself in the fancy toilet mirror and wash my hands, I remind myself that I start a new job on Monday. My career is on the right path and I will be moving into a fab apartment in a week. My life is coming together in only six weeks and the progress is quicker than I ever imagined. I mess with my hair, flick it over the right side of my face, giving my locks a little volume boost and a coat of gloss to plump my lips and here goes, 'back into the lion's den' I say to myself, I take a deep breath, I have got this.

'Emily, please go back to your seat, Sophia is sitting there and she will be back in a second.' I can't see Emily's response as her back is to me, but I can see she has no intention of moving.

'Oh hey, sorry Emily, do you mind if I could have my seat back, please?' I say with a large grin, killing her with kindness. There was a childlike grunt and she slowly moves her derriere back to her side of the table.

'I'm so sorry,' whispers Miles as he places his arm around my shoulder and pulls me into him. 'She can be such a brat, I've known her since childhood and she is a family friend. I will explain later when we are alone.' I grab his face with both hands and plant a gentle kiss on his lips, knowing full well that we are being watched from across the table.

We laugh the evening away, eating some of the best Sushi I have tasted and sharing our life anecdotes, from the times each of the couples met and their jobs. Excluding the few spikey comments from Emily, it went far better than I had imagined and we all left and headed home in our separate directions.

'Do you fancy walking?' I say, totally oblivious to the cold three degrees, December night.

'Yes, I know a fab little bar we can nip into for one last drink if you fancy?'

Chapter Three

We walk into a blue-fronted bar called "Mr Fogg's residence", it's one of the most beautiful establishments I have been to and is quaint and full of charm. We find a small table tucked into a corner and the barman walks over, 'Good evening, can I take your order?' I look at the menu and they all have witty Phileas Fogg titles.

'What I fancy is something like a Whisky Sour, please.'

'Ah madam, the Bitterly British Bailout would be an ideal choice,' I feel like I have just walked into a tardis and time-warped back several decades. I'm not complaining, I would take this over any packed tourist bar off Leicester Square any day.

'Make that two please sir,' Miles passes back our menus and we sit and absorb our surroundings.

'This is such an amazing spot, I love it.'

'Yes, it's my favourite place to come. It's civilised, quiet and they do an excellent cocktail. Sophia, did you enjoy meeting my friends? I am so sorry about Emily, she acts like a spoiled brat if she feels anybody is invading her territory.' I think for a second, I work out how to ask Miles to dish the dirt, but in a more subtle way. I couldn't think of one so I just blurted out,

'what's the deal with her, she obviously feels like she has some hold over you?' OK, a bit crass, but he laughs and actually, honesty is the best policy as they say, whoever "they" may be.

'Well, we have known each other all our lives, we are essentially like cousins. Holidayed as families, spent Christmas' and New Years together. Our parents used to joke that my brother, Harry, would marry Eliza, Emily's older sister and I would marry Emily. I have always had the impression that she somehow thought it was a done deal and at some point, the childhood jokes would actually become a reality. I just don't see her like that.' Well that all makes sense to me now. Her territorial instincts and instant disparaging comments and her nasty looks thrown my way, I relax back in relief that there is a simple explanation as our drinks arrive.

'Cheers to my pretty Sophia and a success meeting my friends,' Miles raises his glass.

'Cheers,' we clink our drinks together and I take a long, relieved sip.

Before we know it, we are kindly asked to leave the closing bar and we make our way back to Miles', zig-zagging our way arm in arm through the freezing sleet. We fall through the front door of his apartment, cold and sodden but giggling. 'Sometimes in life, when I face life-threatening conditions, I think to myself, what would Bear Grylls do?' Miles exclaims dramatically.

'Oh, really and what do you think he would do in these terrible conditions?'

'Well, as I am sure you are well aware, Inuits use body heat to save themselves from the freezing temperatures, but as we have the luxury of central heating and a shower, I suggest that is our form of survival.' He wraps his arms around the lower part of my back and carries me into the bedroom, laying me down on his bed and then kissing me tenderly from my neck to my lips. My whole back arches as I feel him edging down my leggings, over my knees and off to the floor. Hands quickly returning and sliding his hands up my jumper, gliding it over my head.

He has already managed to remove his jeans and pulls his white t-shirt over his head, revealing the body which I had imagined on more than one occasion. There is an unexpected tattoo of what looks like a ram's skull on the inner of his upper arm in bright colours, but I soon lose focus as he glides my bra off with ease, kissing my neck and then continuing down my body.

I wake, wrapped in bedsheets and Miles' arms. A slight glimmer of sun rays shoot through the blinds and I realise it must be late morning. We slept in, having said that, we still had minimal sleep. I grin at the memories of the evening and roll over to see the tattooed inner bicep. I trace the lines gently, trying not to wake him. He starts to stir and smiles, whispering 'good morning pretty,' without even opening his eyes. I kiss his nose and nuzzle into his warm chest.

After a slow Sunday start and a hearty brunch a la Miles, I realise I should get home, plan my outfit for my first day as Trainee Assistant Producer and get my head out of the clouds. Miles is insistent on driving me home. Firstly, I explain, it's barely two miles away and it will ironically be quicker to walk than drive. Secondly, how and where does he even keep a car in central London? Last but by absolutely no means least, I will be mortified to take him back to the dingy room I have to suffer for five more days. Thankfully he takes the hint, on the agreement he will walk with me to the closest coffee shop and arm me for my travels with a Flat White. He has also managed to secure himself the privilege of being the first person to visit me when I move to the much more presentable apartment with Lucy.

Flashing my pass against the security gate, I head to the lifts, 'Sophia!' It's Lucy and she is rushing into the lift behind me. 'How are you? Busy weekend, getting ready for the new job?' As she gives me a playful, yet slightly hard dig the ribs.

'I have, thank you, excited and a little nervous too.'

'Argh don't be silly babe, you are going to nail this! So excited for Saturday, anytime after 10 am I can let you in the apartment and we can celebrate. I was thinking, shall we invite some work peeps over, preferably not tosser though?' Craig is "tosser", understandably after his behaviour towards Lucy and I am happy to refer to him as that and also exclude him.

'Yes, sounds like a good plan to me.'

'What about Miles? VIP invite?' She beams with knowing eyes, even though I hadn't in fact divulged any information to her.

'Yes of course, why not?' I say, keeping it cool and giving my best Poker face.

'I can see this line of questioning will get me nowhere, I will use my other tactic and ply you with Tequila until you talk,' she laughs, I nervously inhale, pretty sure that would end up being the case.

The first meeting in the new role went well and I walk out of the studios feeling positive. My initial fear was the idea of sitting around a meeting table, across from Miles, seeing the other females flirt outrageously with him and remaining professional and calm. In fact, this was not an issue at all, in reality, I barely noticed he was present and every second of my focus was directed to the job in hand, my career took the lead role and that's exactly how I like it. I did, however, catch Miles from the corner of my eye, looking for a reaction from me, but it wasn't happening. I was not going to be the trainee with a reputation for hooking up with the "talent", he would get a pat on the back, I would potentially look like a silly, naive little girl, foolishly getting involved with colleagues.

'Sophia.' Miles jogs up behind me, as I speed walk down Tottenham Court rd. 'How did your first day go? You seemed totally on top of it already. Very impressed indeed.'

'Thanks Miles, that's very kind of you to say, I really enjoyed it.'

'Fancy a drink and a debrief of the day?' The offer is difficult to refuse but having not even spent twelve hours apart in two days, I am in need of some me time and a good night's sleep.

'As tempting as that sounds, I really need to have a catch up with my parents, I have slightly neglected them since moving to London.'

'Oh, so they haven't heard about me yet then?' He winks.

'Erm no, definitely not' I laugh, but his expression looks a little more hurt than I had anticipated.

'No problem,' he says, a little less upbeat, 'I will see you at the Production meeting tomorrow, see you laters.' He jogs across the road and vanishes into the hoards of commuters who are like lemmings, following each other into the black hole of the tube. Well that felt odd, he seemed more sensitive and distant than the normal Miles that I have come to quite like. Now the little bounce I had, has been taken out of my step. I feel like I just gave Miles some bad news or insulted him, not just requested an evening alone. Scrap that, I argue with myself, I'm not REQUESTING for an evening to myself. If I need some me time, I will take it. I am a single independent woman, I remind myself, regaining a little bounce as I head home to start packing for my move at the weekend.

'Lucy, it's your new roomy.'

'YAAAAAY' she screeches down the intercom.

The week had gone really, really well at work and I was settled as though I had been in the role for a few months already. The team had been fabulous and taught me all the ropes and I feel like I have fully landed on my feet. I have spent the week keeping a distance from Miles, for professional reasons and actually, he had also been doing a good job of staying clear of me. I'm not sure if it was me turning down his offer on Monday, but if there is one thing I do not require, it is another needy man on my hands. That being said, I have missed him a little.

'Wow, you travel light?' Lucy laughs. She was right, I do. I left Brighton so quickly, I hadn't wanted to go through the arguments of who bought what between my ex and me. I had packed a capsule wardrobe to cover my needs and it felt freeing not having too much baggage, literally and metaphorically speaking. My Ex, Richard, had kindly and somewhat out of character, offered to store the rest of my belongings until I was settled in a more permanent abode. Whether or not my possessions would be in one piece and not incinerated would be a miracle, but I would be finding out in a couple of hours, as he had agreed to drive the belongings up. My first instincts were 'oh, that's decent of you,' then realising, actually this was most likely a ploy to see where I was living and check up on me. I wasn't really in a position to turn down the offer with my current funds and lack of transport, so even with my reservations, I accepted his offer.

'Coffee?' Lucy peered through into my new room as I unpack the few bags I currently possess.

'Yes that would be fab, thanks,' but before I made it to the kitchen, my phone is ringing, it is Richard and he's early. I answer with trepidation and hope for the best version of my ex to be present.

'Sophia, I'm downstairs.' He sounds miserable and I sigh at the next few minutes of my life in the knowledge from past experiences, that this is not going to be any fun whatsoever.

Richard is 33 and at eight years my senior, I had gone into the relationship assuming, wrongly, that he would be mature and have his life together. He had a great job and his own place and it all seemed so alluring for a 22-year-old. That was until the lies and petty jealousy kicked it. I couldn't go anywhere or talk to anyone without some form of mental abuse, but I had moved in with him after only a few months of dating in a rash decision and while it was all happiness and rainbows to begin with, I soon felt trapped and worn down.

'Hey, where's your room?' Richard grunts, barely looking at me. His eyes are red and he looks upset. I feel a pang of guilt, but try to remember the absolute nightmares I went through with him. It wasn't all bad, of course, but the bad memories definitely outweigh all the good.

Not having said another word to me since walking in, Richard puts down the last box and looks up at me, seeming more tired and vulnerable than I have ever seen him. 'I'm sorry it ended like this Sophia. It was a toxic relationship and I'm sorry it couldn't have been better for us. I was actually going to ask you to marry me.' WHAT?! There it is, taking me straight back to the lunacy that was our two-year relationship.

'You were going to ask me to marry you? At what point did you think that was a good idea? The point where you lied about your best friend's girlfriend hitting on you? The point where you made every evening out an argument because, apparently, somebody looked at me? The point where our relationship was clearly and utterly SHIT?' I have far more anger towards this recent history than I thought and it just all fell out of my mouth, sentence after sentence. Just seeing him reignites my anger and even though I feel like a brat, considering he had just done me a huge favour, I just want him gone and not face all his crap anymore.

'Right, I will go then,' he stands in front of me and I'm pretty sure he is waiting for me to stop him leaving, because that's the sort of rubbish I would have done in the past. Not now though, now I need him to leave and move on with his life like I am with mine.

'I wish you the best Richard. I really do and I hope you find happiness. Thank you for doing this for me, I am very grateful for going out of your way.' He looks at me, defeated and walks to the front door.

'Knock, knock, is anybody there?' For fuck's sake, it's Miles. On one hand, this was the worst timing possible, yet on the other hand, he could well be the person to distract me from the ten minutes of sheer hell I have just experienced with the ex.

'Oh hey, there you are,' Miles brushes past Richard and kisses me on the cheek.

'You have got to be fucking joking?' Hisses Richard, 'him? Really Sophia? It's been five minutes. You have really taken the piss out of me.' This could not have gone worse.

'It's not been five minutes and honestly Richard, it has nothing to do with you anymore, so I suggest you leave.' Now I feel like a bitch, kicking the sad pup while he is down, but I'm not Bridget Jones and this is not going to end in a sexy scuffle in the street. This will turn into Richard, ripping my personality apart and mentally torturing me, I am just not dealing with him anymore. He leaves, muttering all kinds of profanities about me and I grip Miles' arm as he opens his mouth clearly about to defend my honour. As sweet as it is, no good will come of it. The whole saga reminds me of why I was prepared to live in a dingy room for those months with bed bugs and the odd mouse, anything to get away from him.

'Wow, what an arsehole,' Miles' face is red and his fists are clenched. I grab his face and give him a thankful kiss, relaxing his shoulders he gives into me and kisses back.

'I know, but I guess that saves us having "the ex" conversation?' I shrug hoping to lighten the mood and Miles finally cracks a smile.

'Erm, your coffee is getting cold!,' Lucy stands casually leaning against the kitchen door, coffee in hand and looking like she is just catching up on an episode of Eastenders in her own hallway.

'Oh hey Lucy, I'm just popping by to bring you these....', Miles hands me a bunch of flowers and a bottle of Prosecco '... And also, I'm hoping to steal you away for the evening Sophia. I know it's your first night here, but I managed to get some decent tickets for a show and I remember you mentioning you hadn't been to a West End theatre before, so thought it would be a nice treat after a successful first week at your new job.' Lucy looks at me with eyes that scream, "OH MY GOSH HE IS AMAZING", she makes me laugh without even meaning to, 'I'm guessing that is a yes?' laughs Miles. I give a really cheesy thumbs up and regret it whilst thumbs are mid-air, I must look like a total moron and it clearly doesn't go unnoticed, when Lucy and Miles simultaneously copy, obviously mocking me.

'Piss off you two. Yes, it's a yes from me and also, thank you so much for the gifts, it's very generous.'

'You are welcome', as he kisses me on the cheek and I can hear mock kissing sounds coming from Lucy's direction.

'Right, I'm going to carry on unpacking and regain my cool' I say, walking into my room. I hear my phone ting, ting and more tinging, I don't even want to check the screen, because I know full well it's a barrage of abuse from a reeling Richard. I check, I quickly delete without even reading them and then I block him, for good. The wonders of technology, making us so well connected but equally being able to shut people out of our lives just as quickly.

'See you at 6.15. I will pick you up from here,' Miles shouts walking past my room and I hear Lucy letting him out.

'Fab, looking forward to it' I holla back, now time to pick an outfit fit for the theatre.

'Are you sure this is suitable,' I say, arching my body back and forth in front of Lucy. I picked out a plain black, midi shirt dress, ankle boot, leather jacket and a clutch.

'For the fifth time, YES, you look fab and you don't look like an obvious West End first timer! When is Miles' getting here? He needs to hurry up ,' she smiles, but I am realising Lucy won't be my go-to for fashion advice, she's far too cool and lives in black Tees, jeans and the one biker jacket she seems to own. She scoffs at fashion magazines and it just isn't her thing, which makes my line of questioning very annoying, I'm sure.

There is a strange-sounding beep from outside, we both rush to the balcony, there stands Miles, arms resting on the soft top of what looks like a classic car. Not at all what I expected, but more Bridget Jones flashes before my eyes, driving through the countryside attempting to exude 1920's glamour and failing miserably. Still, there is something incredibly romantic about it.

'Come on then, we have a show to see,' Mile shouts up and laughs, clearly realising he has left us both lost for words.

As we drive through the streets of London, passers-by turn to look at the roar from the engine, it's not exactly the most comfortable ride, but it's the first sports car I have even sat in and I love it.

'I would never have pictured you in this car!'

'Hmmm, I'm not sure how to take that, too sophisticated for me?'

'Yes, something like that,' I tease.

'Oi, I was fishing for a compliment madam,' he laughs.

'It's fab and very cool, just like you. Is that good enough?' I look with fake despair.

'Well I guess it will have to,' he sighs with a grin.

We walk into the theatre and the buzz is exciting. This was the best surprise after what could have been a totally crappy day. Saturday night at the Theatre and we are getting escorted to our seats, we don't follow the crowd and instead get taken down a small corridor. A door is opened and we get ushered into a box, with what I can only imagine must be the best seats in the house. There is a bucket with champagne and the young man shows me to my seat and passes a glass filled with bubbles. I look at Miles and he gives me a little grin,

'Nice hey?'

'Really nice, this is so exciting, thank you.' If it wasn't for the fact we had only been dating for a matter of days, I would be half expecting a proposal any second now. I had always imagined being romanced and Miles was all over it like a pro. Even if doubts about him had already crept in, I decided on the car drive over that I was obviously being hasty and judging him too quickly, based on my past experiences with boyfriends wouldn't be fair. After all, nobody has swept me off my feet the way Miles has, he feels too good to be true, but I'm sure he's not. I have to have more faith in him, as the curtains rise and my overthinking is drawn to a halt for the show.

The Actors take a bow and the audience jumps to their feet, covered in smiles and full of the joys of the theatre. 'That was amazing, I never imagined I would like Monty Python quite as much as that, but I'm a total convert' I beamed.

'I'm so pleased you liked it, I have been wanting to see this for a while, but waited to bring someone special,' he slips his hand into mine and kisses my cheek.

'Right, I'm hungry, I know the perfect Vegan Restaurant that I'm pretty sure you will love and there just so happens to be a table with our name on it.'

We arrive at a small, cute restaurant in Soho and we take a seat tucked away in a corner, a perfect spot to assess our surroundings. The place is packed with very fashionable and cool clientele, but I wouldn't expect anything less in such an establishment in the heart of Soho.

'Sophia, this might sound a bit odd, but was everything OK this week? I felt like we had such an amazing weekend and I don't want to sound over sensitive, but...'

'All is great. I was just focusing on work. I don't want to be the new girl, hooking up with the presenter. That could quickly make me a handful of enemies with half of the team.'

'Well, that's a relief and I'm pretty sure you are wrong, the team are all lovely and just genuinely a friendly group.'

'Yes, I'm sure. That's until someone steps into their territory, you may not realise how many admirers you have. To be on the safe side, I would rather keep whatever this is, to us for now.' He stares into the distance thoughtfully.

'Well I'm going away for a week anyway on Wednesday, to Miami with a couple of the old band, so that will give you some time to focus.' Miles says with a smile and puts his hand on top of mine, but I get the feeling there is a slight passive-aggressiveness in his delivery. I guess I could have potentially damaged his ego, not wanting to shout from the rooftops of our fling, relationship, whatever status we were at. I feel like it's the mature thing to do and after the dramatics with my ex earlier, I thought it would be clear why I need to take it slow.

'That's great. How exciting, have you been before?' I say, trying to remain cool and not show any signs that this news could bother me. Although the idea that he will be in one of the sexiest cities in the world, himself and a group of good looking guys, I am fully aware that the attention will not pass them by.

'Yes, we do a trip like this every year, just to let our hair down and have fun, it's always a good laugh.'

'What happens on tour, stays on tour,' I playfully wink.

'Something like that.' He grins.

'Miles, I just need to be honest with you. You saw my ex earlier and you witnessed the kind of crap I have dealt with. I'm not ready to jump into a relationship and at this stage in my life, honestly, my focus needs to be my career. Although, I love spending time with you and tonight has been amazing, I hope you understand where I am at. I really do have so much fun with you, I just don't want to get in too deep too soon.' I feel good, I've been honest and I have laid my cards on the table, surely that is the best you can do in any kind of relationship?

'Sophia, I'm not asking for that, it's fine with me. I'm never going to tell you I love you, or anything like that. The moment I do, it all goes wrong anyway,' he shrugs his shoulders.

'Right,' I say, feeling a little confused and like I have taken a metaphorical punch to the stomach.

'Well, I guess we are more clear on where we both stand then?' Miles doesn't even look at me and is too busy gazing around the room.

'I guess we must be.' All I want to do now is grab my things and head home. Maybe I'm being oversensitive or maybe the idea of yet more rejection and a failed relationship is just making the urge to run for the hills the best option right now.

'I'm not feeling that great actually Miles. I think I need to head home and get some sleep. Thanks for this evening.'

'No problem. I will catch up with you soon.' Miles barely looks in my direction as I put my coat on and grab my bag, edging my way out of my seat, 'don't worry, I will get the bill,' he still doesn't look up at me, but instead is now staring at his phone, I reach for the cash I very rarely, but conveniently have in my bag and I put £25 under my wine glass.

'No that's fine. See you soon.'

Fuck him, I keep thinking to myself as I wait for my DLR train. I can't deal with that bullshit, fuck him. I try to be honest and open expecting some understanding and all I get is the news he will never say he loves me. FUCK HIM. I wasn't asking for that, it didn't even cross my mind so early into whatever the fuckity fuck this is anyway. The thoughts run through my head the entire journey home. I don't even have my headphones to drown out my own brain with music, as I had just assumed stupidly that he would be driving me home or we would end up back at his. That whirlwind of being romanced just suddenly took a left turn to Shitsville and the only redemption of the evening is the idea of returning to my new home, new bed and a bottle   of   wine   with   my   name   on   it.

Chapter Four

Friday evening and I find myself in a very plush Soho House, this really could not be any more "media" if I tried. Another evening out straight after work and it seems to be an unhealthy pattern in my life currently. The peer pressure is intense and it's a choice of coming out and taking part in the fun, or sitting in the office and listening to all the fun they had and the FOMO is strong.

The week had gone pretty well at work, a few little stumbling blocks as I settled in, but all in all, I am feeling happy and content that I can handle the new role I have taken on. I had also managed to avoid Miles as much as physically possible and kept a pleasant demeanour even in his presence. Even if, inside, I am still annoyed how our evening ended and the lingering idea that someone could write-off loving me so early on in a relationship. It seems to have dug up my insecurities that I might just not be cut out for actually meeting "The One", maybe that person just doesn't actually exist for me. I keep reminding myself to be that strong independent woman I have always wanted to become, but then, the thought that might come at the cost of not having the husband and family package I have always assumed would be a given, scares me.

Miles had left for Miami with his pals and I was avoiding Instagram like the plague, wishing all social media would fall down a black hole and people were unable to display how fabulous their lives are.

'Earth to Sophia,' Lucas waves a mocking hand in front of my face, as I am lost in my thoughts and misery, 'something on that mind of yours?' Lucas is another presenter, he has all the credentials for this role, I'm guessing 26, tall and fair short hair with a slight wave. He's undeniably good looking and whilst being given the lowdown also known as gossip, regarding all the talent on the show, I remember someone mentioning his long term girlfriend who he lives with and is devoted to.

'Oh sorry, I was on my own planet for a second then,' I feel myself blushing, grateful that nobody can actually read minds and see the muddle of thoughts that are currently jumbled in my head as I sip on an overpriced cocktail at the bar.

'Daydreaming about how much you love your new job and the amazing presenters you get to see every day?' He teasingly elbows me.

'Yeah Lucas, that's exactly what I was thinking,' I laugh but keep to myself that he is not far off the truth.

'Here you go,' as Lucy passes Lucas and myself our second shot of the evening and having already made my way through two cocktails in quick succession, I try to argue whether it's a good idea. Unfortunately I'm weak to her Scottish charm and she promises it would be the last and we would definitely be leaving for home very soon. Which I should have known was just her way to keep me out and her intentions were to actually end up in a club that had soon become our regular haunt. I decided it was the club or going home and I'm not convinced I would be able to stop myself from checking up on Miles' Instagram, so I quickly decided the hangover and the distraction of continuing the evening was a much better option.

Before I know it, I am propped up against the bar trying to get the attention of one of the many bar staff who is running around like blue arsed flies, trying to fulfil the needs of the drunk and impatient.

'Hey, I think this is my round,' Lucas shouts over the music, as he slides in next to me and makes the tiny personal space I had even smaller.

'I'm pretty sure it's mine,' I say, attempting to keep my face a respectable distance away from his, as we get pushed even closer together.

'Well even if it is, please allow me the pleasure of getting you a drink Sophia?' It's fine, I remind myself, he's just being kind, he has a long term girlfriend who I am pretty sure he lives with. I shouldn't be so arrogant to think any guy who wants to buy me a drink is hitting on me, especially when I can hardly get one guy I like to see a future with me.

'That's really kind of you, a Vodka and Tonic please.'

We take our drinks to the table, where all the remaining colleague's coats have been piled high and we perch ourselves on the last two stalls available.

'You know, you really are the sort of girl who would make an ex jealous.'

'What? Sorry, I didn't catch that.' I am pretty sure I heard it wrong as the loud music and chat is fairly deafening in the club.

'YOU ARE THE SORT OF GIRL WHO WOULD MAKE AN EX JEALOUS,' he shouts in my ear, making it ring and I wish I hadn't heard right. It becomes clear to me that Lucas has split from his girlfriend and he is now, in fact, chatting me up. Suddenly the reality of the past few hours have all become obvious to my naive brain, him being overly attentive, a few looks and whispers from the rest of the team. Lucas must be oblivious to my fling with Miles or if he isn't, he clearly doesn't care.

'I'm sorry, I hadn't realised you had split up,' I say, trying to play down the comment.

'Nobody does, it's very recent, but I kept it to myself. I thought we may sort it out, but it's obvious we won't, she's moved on already. Clearly, there must have been an overlap at some point.' Poor Lucas, he really does seem very genuine and I can see his sadness as he tries to brush it off as "all fine", "a bad experience" and "onwards and upwards". He is throwing me all of the cliches of breaking up, but I am still not convinced he means any of them.

'Come on you, there is only one thing for it,' as I grab his hand, almost dragging him onto the dancefloor, where we kept dancing into the early hours.

Don't tell me you slept with him.

My phone lights up. It's Miles, it must only be 5 am and I'm squinting and confused. I see another notification from Instagram, oh fuck, what have I been tagged in? I open the App and the first image I see is, however innocent it is in reality, I am receiving a piggyback through Trafalgar Square, courtesy of Lucas. It's actually a great photo, we are laughing and with the gorgeous backdrop, all it represents is friends having a very fun, drunk night out. The truth behind the photo was actually that my feet were sore and we were all freezing cold and desperate to get home. To our own homes. But you can't let reality ruin a good Instagram post! I see Miles has liked it and commented,

Looks nearly as fun as Miami

Lucas has responded almost instantly.

It's better, mate

I chuckle to myself. You were asking for that Miles. I look back at his message and however annoyed I probably should be, I also feel a slight relief. He is obviously bothered by the image of me having fun with another guy. I don't know why, I know I should probably write any idea of a relationship with Miles off. The alarm bells are clearly ringing very loud and resonating in my head that this isn't ever going to work out. However, the knowledge that he is still possibly concerned over me, is making me feel less disposable than being told he will never love me, which definitely helps to soften the blow to my ego. Even though I should put my phone down and go back to sleep, I can't.

It's none of your business, like what you are up to is none of mine.

I send and see the dots pulsating to acknowledge that Miles is typing almost instantly.

OK, point made Sophia, but just so you know, nothing like that is happening here and I am missing you. I understand I upset you the other night, but I have issues with relationships and I didn't want to scare you away with it so early on. Sorry, it's just how it is x

It's just how it is. So definite. Although it does feel nice to be missed, but then after two years of being worn down by a relationship which ended up so toxic, which saw me focusing all my efforts on trying to make my ex feel secure at the expense of my own sanity. I now feel the urge to be with someone who is as equally concerned about my emotional needs as well as their own.

You did upset me, but it's all good, because maybe now is just not the right time for either of us. You know I am here as a friend, but let's just keep it like that. Take care x

I tap the send button and I feel like I'm making the right choice, maybe a hazy and sleepy choice, but nonetheless, the right one. I have enough emotional baggage of my own to work through.

Wow, cold, thanks for your brutal honesty. See you at work.

That's it then, it's done. I have a sick feeling in the pit of my stomach and I cannot work out if it's the text conversation with Miles, or the drinks from a few hours before and the impending hangover. I switch my phone off and roll over, hiding under my duvet. The only answer is to fall back to sleep and hopefully wake up with all my life's woes magically solved.

Morning Soph, sorry if I caused any problems with Miles with the photo. He's actually never liked or commented on my posts before, so I assumed it's because you were also in it. Hope your head doesn't hurt, Lucas x

Hey Lucas, no worries at all. There are no issues and yes, my head does pound a little this morning. Hope you aren't suffering, thanks for the piggyback!x

Obviously there were quite a few issues caused by the photo, but won't be explaining them to Lucas. The less I discuss my private life with colleagues, the less it will creep into my work life. There are enough informants around the office, who are eager to latch onto any hint of rumours or tittle-tattle and I certainly don't want to be the topic of any water cooler gossip if I can possibly help it.

Oh good, in which case, can I please take you out for dinner after work tomorrow? Just as friends and colleagues, of course. I really enjoyed our chats and it was a much needed distraction x

Sod it, I have zero other plans and Lucas is a really easy person to chat to. This could be just what I need, two newly singles, chatting through their troubles over food and wine.

Yes, I would very much like that. See you then x

In any case, I would be leaving the city in a couple of days for the Christmas break, back in the Cotswolds with my family. So I may as well enjoy my time in London before I leave.

'Right, are you ready?' Lucas raises his arm for me to link on to.

'Yes, let's do this,' as we stepped out into a flutter of snow. It is slightly slippery on the ground and I am grateful to have him to cling onto and thankfully it is not far to the row of upmarket restaurants and bars on Charlotte Street.

As we walk into an Italian, I suddenly realise how fancy it is. I gave myself a quick once over to check I look suitable, I only threw on a jumper dress and boots, thinking it would be a less classy affair.

'You look great,' Lucas helps me take off my coat as we wait to be seated.

'Thank you. I hadn't realised how fancy this place would be.'

'Don't worry, you fit in just fine.' He shoots me a huge white grin and we are escorted to our table.

We spend the first hour chatting about work and he catches me up with the office goings-on and essentially, gossip. Which, although I dread being the topic of, it's actually fun to hear the misdemeanours of my new co-workers and being in the knowledge that I am not alone in blurring the lines with colleagues. The wine and food are flowing and I am really enjoying it. I'm actually enjoying it far more than I imagined I would. I hadn't looked at Lucas the way I am now, before he was a taken guy in a serious and long term relationship. Now he is a very handsome, charming and single man sitting in front of me and I can't tell if it's just the wine, but I catch myself looking at his lips. They are slightly plump and incredibly kissable, I daydream to myself.

'Have I got something on my face?' he says, tapping his chin with his napkin. Oh fuck, my moment of lusting has been noticed.

'No, sorry I just got distracted for a second,' Oh for fucks sakes, that is the lamest excuse for gawping at his lips. Before I even get to make up a better story, he moves his seat next to mine, cups my chin and with zero resistance we kiss. The softest kiss. His hand runs down my back and I pull away, conscious of our surroundings.

'Right, let's get out of here,' Lucas says, grabbing my coat and holding it out for me to put on and then leading me out of the restaurant. After a short goodbye kiss in the slow flutters of snow, Lucas stands with his nose touching mine and his arms wrapped around my waist pulling me in close to him.

'Well, that was much better than I had even imagined,' Lucas kisses me on the cheek and I look up and suddenly the thought that he is not Miles crosses my mind and not for the first time this evening. A pang of guilt hits me and something just isn't sitting right.

'It was lovely, thank you so much and it was very sweet of you to invite me. I better head home as it's getting late,' I look at my watch, not even reading the time, just using it as a prop to back up my sudden urgency to leave. After Lucas spends a few moments offering to escort me back, I insist I will find my own way and agree to the potential of another date after Christmas. I genuinely had so much fun with him, but the fact that Miles has popped into my head on more than one occasion throughout the evening. Good old, unobtainable Miles. I feel like it's a disservice to Lucas. We part in our separate directions and I feel overwhelmed that of my own doing, I have already got involved with two colleagues, exactly what I had promised myself that I wouldn't do. 'What is wrong with me,' I scorn myself under my breath as I head in the direction of home. The only saving grace is time away in the confines of my parents home over Christmas, will give me the space needed for any complications or dramas to die out. Hopefully giving Lucas the time to lose any interest in me and for me to stop thinking about Miles and that fleeting relationship.

Walking into the studios with a spring in my step, I am excited this will be the last day at work for a week. Although I am beyond happy with my new role, so much has happened in the past few months and I feel so ready to take a break from the city and its rollercoaster ride. The spring in my step grinds to a halt, as I walk into the gallery to take my assistant position and see Miles on the monitor, 'crap,' I mouth. I had totally forgotten it was the last show of the year and Lucas and Miles are co-hosting a Christmas special. This is not ideal. As a five-minute countdown is called out by the Director, I see Lucas rush past the Gallery and into the Studio. He walks in and straight over to his position on the studio floor, which just so happens to be next to Miles. Lucas holds his hand out to greet Miles, 'Hi Mate, nice to have you back. Good holiday?' I can see the reluctance in Miles' face as he slowly puts his hand out to acknowledge the gesture.

'Yes, we had a great time. Not as good as you by the looks of your Instagram,' Miles responds coldly and Lucas smirks. I can see the realisation has hit him, that actually, there had in fact been some fallout after his Insta post of us together.

'Well, if you go away on a boys holiday, the mice will play,' Lucas responds, clearly enjoying the fact he has somehow had an impact on Miles. They both walk to opposite sides of the studio and I am pretty sure I am yet to take a breath since seeing them both together.

It's not gone unnoticed and the Producer turns to the Director, 'what the hell is wrong with them now?' she peers around the room, looking for insight from the crew. Everybody is shrugging and people start making up their own guesses. The Producer doesn't turn to look at me and why should she? I'm just a newbie in the corner, doing what I am told, seemingly totally innocent. I'm doing my best to calm the rouge glow that I can feel creeping and heating my cheeks and say a silent prayer to myself that Miles can keep his cool and get through the next hour on air.

We manage to end the show and there have been no more uncomfortable moments between Miles and Lucas and I sigh with relief. However, the moment I see an escape out of the gallery and back to the office to quickly grab my belongings, I am going to take it. The presenters usually end up in the gallery having a small debrief after the show and my chest feels tight with the idea of being trapped in this dark and confined room, in a corner, with the Producer questioning any issues the pair have. I head for the door, in the hope that I am no longer needed and will not be missed. 'Sophia', the Producer shouts after me as I am two seconds from exiting the gallery. Shit, she has caught me.

'Yes?' I turn around to find the entire room focused on me.

'I just wanted to say what an ace job you have done today and hope you have a fabulous Christmas. See you in the new year.' I breathe in deeply with relief that my lip hopping between presenters is still not public knowledge and I am not about to be scolded for my unprofessionalism.

'Thank you so much, I have really enjoyed it. I hope you all have a brilliant Christmas too,' as I turn on my heels and dodge the Miles and Lucas bullet.

Chapter Five

I grew up on the outskirts of Chipping Norton which is a quaint and pretty Cotswolds village. It was an idyllic childhood and my dream, as much as I longed to escape from there when I was younger, is actually to return one day and give my own children the same simple and country upbringing that I got to enjoy.

My parents are the most patient and loving couple, they would go to the ends of the earth for their daughters and sometimes they have come close to it. We definitely had a bubble surrounding our childhood and after living in Brighton and London and having a more rounded view of the world, I would imagine most people would probably describe us as privileged. Don't get me wrong, we were by no means spoilt, but we also never went without. My mother is very soft and tactile and both my older sister, Charlotte and younger sister, Margo take after her. They are all very nurturing and although that is so welcomed and needed on occasions, I am more like my father, who feels a little smothered after a while. I am pretty sure I stepped into the role of the son he never had for the majority of my life, until a few years ago when Charlotte, or Charly as she likes to be known, married Harry, her first love who she met in Uni. He now seems to have taken over the role and has far more interest in Golf than I ever will, which keeps my Dad happy and saves me listening to stories about a game I literally know zero about or have zero interest in.

'Sophia, darling, could you please, please call us at least once a week, just so we know you are OK?' My mum says, dabbing her tears as she stands at the family home to wave me goodbye.

I have been home for only three days over Christmas, partially because I have work to return to, but also because I love my independence and as much as I enjoy returning to see my family, I am ready to get back to my life and into the thick of the city pace.

'Of course mum and sorry I haven't been in touch more, it's just very busy at the moment and I am not home until late most days.' I hug her goodbye, trying to ease her worries.

'More like you are out getting pissed until late,' Margo pipes up, grinning. Even though she is only a couple of years younger than me, she still uses the youngest sibling card to annoy me, way too often.

'Don't be jealous, you just enjoy living with Mum and Dad a bit longer,' I hug her, knowing the jab at her still living at home will wind her up enough for payback.

Sitting on the train, with a Chai Tea in hand, squashed into a window seat on a typically packed train to London, I catch up on my messages and plans for the remains of the Christmas holidays. Just before leaving for Christmas, Lucy had managed to convince me that a house party would be a great idea for New Years Eve and even though I instantly had some massive reservations about the idea, I metaphorically had my arm twisted and ended up agreeing. The main selling point was the extortionate costs to go anywhere in London that evening and also we have prime views down the Thames, meaning we get an excellent seat for the fireworks. Unfortunately, before we even finish the call about the party, Lucy has created a WhatsApp group and invited a whole host of people. I didn't get the chance to have a say in the guest list and before I even get an opportunity to object, I see two responses in close proximity,

I would love to, thanks ladies x

from Lucas and,

Count me in xx

from Miles. Fantastic, what a shit show this could turn out to be.

Lucy had zero idea about the meal with Lucas, so I can't blame her for not knowing. I had decided to keep it to myself in the hope that Lucas would also be in the same mindset, he understands the gossip dynamic better than me and appreciates the potential fallout of inter-office dating.

'Hey Sophia, is that you?' It was Lucy, I hadn't expected her to be back already, I had anticipated a cold empty flat, so it was comforting to hear her dulcet tones as soon as I walked through the front door of the apartment.

'Yes it's me, one second,' I shout, as I drag my suitcase, dumping it in my room and walk into the kitchen, where Lucy who was already putting the kettle on, almost reading my mind.

'Sophia, I've got some really exciting news, Paul has been in touch and offered me a sound job, on location in South America with him. So, I handed in my notice a few days ago and due to all the holiday I'm owed, I only have next week and I am off,' she says, barely taking a breath or making eye contact with me. I stand a little bewildered, this information hit me out of nowhere. I had literally been in the flat for a matter of weeks and now what?

'That's really exciting Lucy, will you be coming back?' I say, feeling selfish for worrying about my living situation when this is clearly a huge opportunity for her.

'Yes, of course, I will be there for three weeks, then I will be back and use this as my base. I'm not moving for good, just means you get this place to yourself for a few weeks at a time, are you OK with that?'

'Well it will definitely feel a little lonely,' I sigh, still feeling selfish but also relieved that I won't be flat hunting again for awhile.

'Not with Miles about it won't, I'm sure he will keep you company,' she teases.

'Hmmm, well, I am not so sure about that Lucy.'

Having stocked up and spent far more than I had hoped to on Prosecco and Tequila, the apartment is ready for the New Years Eve party and the way Lucy is acting, anyone would think it was a production of the 'Jools' Annual Hootenanny,' rather than the simple party with decorations, nibbles and copious amounts of alcohol.

My mind is more focused on seeing Miles and Lucas together, in my home with no obvious escape plan. The best thing I decide, is focusing on looking good, feeling confident and hitting the Tequila, a plan I run through in my head as I give myself a once over in my full-length mirror. Skinny black jeans, black silk shirt which was a fancy Christmas gift from Charly, tousled hair and some obligatory bright red lipstick to at least add a little party glam for the occasion. Deep breath, as I look at my phone to see the time is 8 pm and any second now, the guests will be arriving. I head out of my room to top up my prosecco glass and the intercom buzzes, but before I even get a chance to acknowledge this, Lucy has already leapt off the sofa and bounds towards the door.

'It's Lucas and Simon,' she announces to me moments later. I inhale, reminding myself that I actually haven't done anything wrong and owe neither of these guys anything.

Lucas strolls over after double air kisses with Lucy at the front door, 'Sophia, I've really missed you, how was your Christmas?' He lifts me, feet off the ground and kisses my cheeks. I see Lucy over his shoulder, pulling a "what the actual fuck" face and I realise, I probably should have mentioned my little encounter with Lucas to her.

'It was fab thanks, a really chilled out one with the family, but happy to be back home. How was yours?' As I walk into the kitchen and Lucas follows, I hold out a choice of beer or Prosecco for him.

'Beer would be great, thanks. Christmas was OK. First time I have been single for years, so it was a bit odd.' He says, focused on pouring his beer into a glass. It's obvious he is not over his ex, which helps ease my guilt that I have absolutely no interest in him and part of me really wishes it had been Miles who had turned up first.

The apartment is getting busy and there must only be about ten people I recognise. Everyone is mingling and the music is playing with the murmur of chats and laughter filling the apartment. I head to top up my drink and I feel a tap on my shoulder. I turn to see Miles standing behind me, he puts his hand up and salutes me, looking as awkward as I instantly feel.

'Can I get you a drink?'

'Yes, please Sophia.'

'Anything in particular?' As I spin on my heels to show him the selection of booze that seems to have multiplied dramatically as the guests have arrived.

'I will just grab a cold beer, thanks.' I grab Miles a beer out of the fridge and part of me just wants to pretend nothing has happened, grab and kiss him. He's looking particularly cute with his Miami tan.

'Do you mind if we have a quick chat in private,' Miles says, looking around and obviously trying to be as subtle as possible.

'OK, meet me in my room in a minute.' I head to my room, trying to act as casual as possible and not drawing anyone's attention.

Two minutes later and Miles edges around the bedroom door, 'sorry, Lucy started chatting and I couldn't get away. I swear I can't understand half of what she says.' I laugh at how flustered he is,

'Her accent doubles in strength after a few drinks, I wouldn't worry, I am the same.' Miles perches on my bed next to me and we sit in silence for a moment.

'I just need to know, did anything happen with you and Lucas?' Then it becomes clear to me, he doesn't want me, but he doesn't want anyone else to have me either, I sigh.

'We kissed,' I say honestly and Miles rolls his eyes at me.

'Oh Sophia, did you have to?'

'Miles, you have made it quite clear there is no future for us. You have done your own thing in Miami. I don't even want to know. I didn't even hear from you over Christmas.'

'I didn't hear from you either!'

'No, you didn't, because as far as I am concerned there is no reason to get in touch. You are the one who is at my apartment and wanting to talk, what do you want Miles? What?' He stands, looking out of my window and is looking a little sullen.

'I really, really care for you Sophia, we have an amazing time together, in every way,' he glances at me with a glint in his eye and I try to stay strong. 'I can't promise what the future holds, but can we just be casual and maybe just date exclusively and see where it goes with no pressure?'

'It's a strong statement to say you could never love me. You have to understand, that isn't a pleasant thing to hear. I have had my head messed with enough by ex. I would be an absolute idiot to even try and be with someone who feels like that from the very start.' Miles sits down on the edge of my bed and puts his head in his hands,

'I know and I totally get it. I am just crap at this stuff and I thought I was in love once and she went off with someone else. It took me ages to open up to her and the moment I did, she was gone.' It must be the bubbles kicking in, his vulnerability or the fact he is looking gorgeous, because I move Miles' elbows off his knees and sit on his lap and kiss him with all the pent up frustration that is running through me. As much as he drives me crazy, I have missed him. He grabs my hips and pulls me further on to his lap, so our chests are touching and we kiss.

'She must be here,' the door swings open and Lucy strolls into my room. There is no time to compose ourselves and there stands Lucy with Lucas right behind, frozen, looking at us.

'Erm, knock much?' Miles breaks the silence, but I can see from the twitch of his smile, he is pleased his territory has been reinstated, as Lucas looks on, clearly as embarrassed as I feel. I stand up and grab my drink,

'Sorry Soph, I hadn't thought that you might be busy. Fancy getting a top-up?' Lucy does her best to break the awkwardness. I know I don't owe Lucas an explanation, we had been out for one meal and had a kiss, I don't even know why I feel as guilty as I do. Maybe because Miles is lapping it up, far more than he should.

'OK Lucas, you can leave Sophia's room now if you don't mind.' Miles says cuttingly. It's nice to feel wanted, but this is ridiculous and I have never envisaged myself being worthy of this kind of attention.

'Lucas, let me get you a drink,' I say, walking him out my room, looking back over my shoulder and letting Miles know with a furrowed brow that I am not impressed with his need to mark his territory so smugly.

'I hadn't realised you two are seeing each other,' Lucas says with genuine surprise.

'No, nor was I until around the same sort of time you found out,' I joked, hoping to lighten the mood.

'It's a shame as I really had fun with you Sophia, but when he screws up, keep me in mind,' he grins and I prod him in the side jokingly.

'You should take some time anyway, get over that ex of yours. Play the field a bit more, you must have women throwing themselves at you.'

'Well now you come to mention it,' he smiles, looking off in the direction of one of the cute runners. I instantly realise that Lucas could well have been dating a few of us and maybe Miles winding him up was more deserved than I had realised and I shouldn't feel too bad for him.

'You go get her Lucas,' I cheers to him, clinking his glass, as any guilt I first felt, fades quickly away.

It's 11.55 pm and Miles taps me on the shoulder and silently directs me out of the apartment. Holding my hand, he walks me to a raised promenade overlooking the Thames. Standing behind me, he wraps his arms around my waist and kisses my cheek as we look down the river. 'I just want to see in the new year with you and be able to kiss you out of sight of the others.' Suddenly the fireworks illuminate the sky and there are murmurs of cheers and celebrations from all directions. I turn in Miles' arms and we kiss, the perfect ending to the year.... and an even more perfect start to the new one

Chapter Six

'What do you mean, YOU ARE NOT COMING BACK?'

It's mid-January and as far as the most miserable month's reputation goes, this one has been great so far. Lucy went off to her new exciting job and Miles and I had been

flitting between each other's apartments with some fun evenings out, consisting of meals and drink dates. All was well, until this call with Lucy.

'Sophia, I'm really sorry to drop this on you. They have offered me the role to stay in South America for six months and I just don't fancy the City anymore. I won't be paying my rent for the final month, so they can just use my deposit to cover it and then you can find someone to move in or you move out.' I can't believe she is dropping me in it like this, what an absolute, total, full-blown bitch move. London is the worst place to find somewhere to live or someone to live with and I certainly can't afford this apartment alone, let alone risk losing my deposit because she doesn't fancy paying her rent anymore.

'Fine Lucy, thanks a lot. You have really dropped me in it,' I say, seething.

'One thing Sophia, I have left a load of my sound kit in a bag in my room. Do you mind packing it and keeping it for me when I get back? Everything else you can get rid of.'

'Maybe, I might just throw it out with all of your other mess I am left to clean,' I hiss down the phone as I hang up before I lose it with her and end up getting into an argument over something, totally out of my control. I'm so pissed off and the cheek to ask me to do her a favour too. The thought of putting her precious sound kit on eBay crosses my mind on more than one occasion as I reach for the open bottle of red wine and pour myself a large glass.

'What a shit thing to do, I knew she was flakey, but that is just totally out of line.' Miles confirms my rage and offers to come over and bring pizza and more wine to ease my stress. As much as I would love to hibernate under my duvet and hide from the world, full of self-pity, his distraction would be a real bonus right now.

Miles arrives half an hour later with a huge bunch of flowers, pizza and Serendipity, one of my favourite films of all time. 'I thought this might put a smile on that pretty face of yours,' he grins and I can see he is enjoying being my knight in shining armour.

'Well you thought right and thank you, I really appreciate it Miles. I literally cannot believe she would drop this on me. The bit that really gets me, is refusing to pay her rent. She is leaving me here to lose my deposit and clear up the mess with the agents. I'm so pissed off, I genuinely hope I never see her again. As for her sound kit, she can piss right off.' I look at Miles as he leans against the kitchen counter, watching on as I serve the pizza on to plates and pour us a glass of wine each. I pass him a glass and he looks deep in thought.

'Please do not take this in any other way than me offering help,' Miles says, looking a little resistant, 'but you could move in with me until you save up a bit of money and find somewhere more permanent to live. I'm not asking you to move in with me, so don't panic. I just want to help you and it's not like you don't spend loads of time at mine now, anyway.' I think for a few moments, weighing up my options, which takes no time at all, as currently, that is my only option. It would certainly get me out of a difficult situation and it is only temporary. I can't afford to lose my deposit and I definitely don't fancy ending up in a mouse infested room again.

'If you are sure Miles? It really would be a temporary option until I figure out my next move and it really would be a huge help.'

'I am sure, I wouldn't ask otherwise. I just want to help you out Sophia. So it's a yes?' He smiles, holding out a glass of wine to cheers.

'Yes, it's a yes, thank you. Cheers.'

'We will be there in ten, make sure you have absolutely EVERYTHING.'

The last couple of weeks have flown by and now I feel like the time in my amazing new apartment was cut far too short, thanks to the incredibly selfish Lucy, who I haven't heard from again since she dropped the bombshell, not a single word from her. Not to check I had found a home or how the agents had handled the news. I had, under the advice of my parents, rang the agents and explained to them the situation and how I had been dropped in it by Lucy and I couldn't afford to stay in the apartment. It seemed the agents were more relieved that I wasn't going to resort to squatters rights and considering they could rent the place out in a day, they agreed that I could pay up to the date I stayed and then use Lucy's part of the deposit to cover her unpaid rent and I would get my rightful money back. From being an absolute shitshow, it has actually restored my faith in fellow humans and Miles has been my absolute hero. From being totally supportive throughout the whole saga to now hiring a small van to collect my belongings and move me into his apartment.

'Right, this is the last box and this is a bag full of Lucy 's crap she asked me to look after,' Miles looks at me with raised eyebrows. 'I know, I know, but I can't just leave it. The chances are I won't see her again anyway and I'm sure they will end up in the charity shop or something.' He grabs my face and kisses me really hard on the lips.

'And that Sophia is why you are the best human being. Anyway, dump it in the back, hop in and let me get you back to mine and all to myself.'

I dramatically throw myself onto the large grey sofa in the lounge of Miles' apartment with the feeling of relief that the moving day was out of the way. Trying not to worry this is not actually a permanent solution and viewing it as just a little holiday home, while I work to save up a little more money and find a place that will actually last more than a month. It also just so happens to be owned by a very good looking guy, who I intend to enjoy for however long this situation lasts.

'Right Soph, lets order Chinese now, it will be a 45 minute delivery and that gives us time to do the environment proud & both jump in the shower,' he grins and it's obvious what he has on his mind.

'Good to hear you are considering the planet in this scenario,' I giggle.

We sit with damp hair and in dressing gowns, slouched on Miles' sofa and tucking into my favourite Chinese takeaway, watching Saturday night TV. I gaze over at

Miles as he is mesmerized by a talent show with a dancing donkey and I feel like we could have been together for years. Some rocky years, but still, I feel so comfortable just being with him. I literally don't know where I would be right now, had he not taken me out of a really shitty situation and here I am, living my life like a princess in his penthouse and lapping up all the luxuries of life with Miles.

'I can tell you are watching me,' he puts his food down on the coffee table and turns to face me, 'well that's a lie, I was actually watching you in the TV reflection,' he rests his hands on my thighs.

'Well, that's a bit creepy,' I grimace at him, trying to detract from being caught out ogling him.

'Erm, well you were just staring at me eat. Now THAT is creepy. What were you thinking? You looked very deep in thought.'

'I was just thinking how much I appreciate you helping me out and that, well, I feel like we have known each other for so much longer than we have.'

'I feel the same and you are very welcome, I am already loving you living here, there is no rush to find somewhere else,' he picks up his food and returns back to the TV in one swift movement.

'Are you SURE you are going to be OK?' Miles grabs his weekend bag and launches it over his shoulders. He is off, back down to visit his parents in Wiltshire as his mum is unwell and although he has been promised it's not serious, he seems nervous and eager to return to his family. Which I find adorable and I feel myself falling for him the more time we spend together. I also realise I am slowly losing grip of the idea that this is not a permanent solution to my future or housing crisis. With a couple weeks of living together completed, it's been nothing but fun and happy times together and I'm more than aware it's potentially vulnerable territory I can feel myself creeping into.

'You absolutely do NOT need to worry about me. I will be fine,' I reassure him.

'You know how to contact the caretaker or just call me and I can sort if anything goes wrong? Also, if you lose your keys, remember there is a set...'

'... With the couple at number 205. Yes, after two weeks I think you have probably mentioned that at least twenty times already,' I sigh dramatically, teasing him.

'OK, I'm sorry, I'm being an overbearing boyfriend, aren't I?' He looks at me, with a look of surprise and I am pretty sure he didn't mean to drop the 'b' word. 'Anyway, I better go.' and before we even got a chance to acknowledge his slip of the tongue, he had vanished out of the door.

I'm not even going to read into it, we have been getting on so well and even though both of our little quirks were appearing day by day, so far, his habits all seem to be pretty kosher. No foot fetishes, no safe words and no skeletons hidden in his wardrobes. I go to the window and watch Miles jump into his Uber and that's it, he has gone and for the first time in a long while, I have a TV and a place to myself. Although it's Friday evening, there is a show airing at work tomorrow, so I decide to stay in, wash off my makeup & slob out in my pyjamas. I haven't got around to admitting the amount of trash TV I am addicted to, to Miles as yet. So, the plan is hours of catch up, a glass of wine and a chocolate fix. Bliss.

'Don't worry, he won't mind,' suddenly the front door crashes open and I am pretty sure I'm about to be attacked when I see three women, no older than me, stumble through the front door.

'EXCUSE ME.' My shock suddenly turns into anger, 'Who the hell are YOU and what are you doing in HERE?' They all freeze and then a blonde woman with bright red lipstick and a gorgeous body clinging, clearly designer dress & what I am pretty sure are Louboutins, steps forward.

'More like who the FUCK are you?' She looks me up & down and I'm now feeling pretty unattractive. Before I even get to say another word, she seems to be dialling someone. 'Miles, babe, there is some girl who looks like she is squatting in your Pent, do you want me to chuck her out?' I feel speechless and the other women stand giving me looks of glee that I am being completely humiliated. I can hear the bass tones of Miles' voice over the phone and then I realise, this must be his ex. It suddenly occurs to me that we have never discussed his past relationships, although he alluded to the one woman, but never went into any detail and in my attempt to be cool, I had never broached the subject.

'Right girls, we have to go,' she looks at her friends as she hangs up her mobile, dropping it into what looks like, Gucci bag. 'No fun with my Miles tonight. Bye hun, enjoy it while it lasts,' she glares at me and then walks out, taking what must be her set of keys with her. I run to the door and slam it closed, whoever that woman was, had clearly left it open for effect and a reaction from me. I latch it shut, run to the bedroom and I feel like crying. I feel worthless, pathetic and I don't even want to know the answers to all the questions I have, as I know I won't like them.

My mobile starts ringing and of course, it's Miles and I switch it off, absolutely nothing good will come of me answering that phone. I'm upset, he is most likely with his parents and I will end up looking like a needy girl who has been embarrassed enough for one evening. I grab the laptop and start looking for new jobs. The only way I am going to get out of this situation, is to find a new company to work for and cut the cord from Miles. He is so amazing in so many ways, but then there are these reminders that come and metaphorically slap me around the face ever so often that this is "Miles the Unobtainable". I slump back into the sofa and gaze at the laptop, reeling in self-pity.

I feel so proud of myself as I wake up and remember how I have managed to go the whole evening and night without checking my phone and getting in touch with Miles. He did this, he allowed that woman to have his apartment keys and he didn't warn me of her or tell her about me. I feel so stupid and angry but rather than dwell on it, I decided to throw that energy into my next step and found a handful of amazing jobs online. Some a little out of my league, but I went for it anyway. I remind myself that I am at my best under pressure and last night was the kick up the backside I was needing. The next thing I'm in need of is a hot shower, a good outfit and makeup to put the skip back in my step and return the confidence that was totally drained from me last night. Work would be the perfect distraction I am craving.

'DRINKS?' shouts Izzy from the studio doors.

'Yes,' I call back, 'I'm just dropping the production notes back to the office and will meet you out the front.' I didn't fancy rushing back to someone else's apartment and as the thought of the previous night's misdemeanours has only crossed my mind a couple of times throughout the day, my plan is to go out and carry on distracting myself for the rest of the evening. Not make myself a sitting duck and wait for the potential return of that woman.

Izzy is the Studio Manager and our paths had started to cross a lot. She knew there was something happening between Miles and me, but I hadn't confided in anyone since Lucy and I have decided, since my choices of who I can trust have to date been somewhat questionable, I am going to keep the current saga to myself.

I latch onto Izzy and the rest of the group of colleagues who are making their way to the nearest waterhole. Apparently it was one of the lighting guys birthdays, but there isn't really any excuse needed for drinks after work, especially on a Saturday. It seems more the norm rather than the exception and today I am certainly not complaining. The instant social circle of similar minded and aged humans is exactly what a girl still relatively new to the city needs to drown her sorrows and let loose.

Whilst enjoying the first sip of Dirty Martini which Izzy ordered without even consulting me and said I "MUST TRY," I hear a faint 'Oh hey Miles, what are you doing here?' Over the loud murmurs of the bar, I turn to see him patting backs and shaking hands, but I can see he is only being polite and is quickly making his way over to me.

'Can we talk outside now, please,?' He tries to be subtle in my ear but failing as everybody has clearly clocked onto the fact that something is wrong. I follow him warily, hoping this isn't the start of a full-blown argument. We step outside and cautiously move out of sight of prying eyes.

'Please do not say a word and let me explain. I am so sorry you faced that bitch alone. I should have warned you sooner, but I had no idea she would pull a stunt like that.' OK, I calm instantly, I feel like we are on the same page and my shoulders relax. 'She responded to my Insta story about my train ride home and I said I was visiting family. She asked if you were going to meet them. I can only presume she knows about you via Emily, as I haven't spoken to her since way before I met you.' Hmmm, I should have known that Emily had a part to play. 'How the hell she has keys to my apartment, I don't know. I can only assume she had a copy cut as I did take her set back when we broke up. She's a lunatic, which is one of the main reasons I currently have a locksmith at the apartment making sure she can never get in again.' I throw my head back in relief, but a part of me wants to cry. I should have given him the benefit of the doubt, I should have trusted there was more to this story. 'When she called me and pretended we were on any sort of talking terms, I knew she was there to upset you. She knew you would be in the apartment alone. Again, I'm assuming the news of you moving in was kindly forwarded via Emily. Sophia, she's angry because all she ever wanted to do was move in with me, for months it was a constant argument. Now she sees my new girlfriend is living with me and she is losing the plot by the looks of it.' I'm not sure if it's the sheer relief of what I am hearing or being referred to as his girlfriend, but I put my glass down on the nearest surface and throw my arms around him.

'I'm sorry for doubting you,' I say, trying my best not to cry all over his shoulder. 'Her and her posse made me feel two inches tall and I was so confused by it all. Clearly, you need to fill me in with more detail of your recent relationship history, so I don't get caught out again by any other crazy women.' Miles looks relieved and smiles.

'Of course. I think I can manage that, especially if it stops events like last night. Thank you for being understanding, it means a lot. I was so worried when you wouldn't answer, I just told my folks I needed to get back to London ASAP.'

'Oh, no, they are going to think I'm a total pain in the arse now!' Miles laughs and strokes my cheek.

'How sweet you are to worry about that, but not at all. I explained it all to them and actually they told me to come back. I think my mum's words were "go and save Sophia from that horrible madam". They know full well what you had to deal with.'

'You have told them about me?' I ask surprised,

'Of course I have, I can't have my first girlfriend living with me and not tell them!'

There it is again, it's confirmed, I have myself a boyfriend.

Chapter Seven

Sitting back with a morning coffee overlooking the busy streets of Soho from the comfort of Miles' apartment, I am feeling a little gleeful. A day off in the week and life is feeling really good. Miles has gone to the gym and my plans only include catching up on some emails and having my daily look at the potential new room lets available. Although, having the new label as girlfriend and with new locks on the apartment door, the stress of finding a new abode doesn't feel like a top priority right now. My phone rings and it's a London number, 'Hi, this is Sophia speaking.'

'Oh hi Sophia, my name is Angela and I am calling from Freedom Productions about the role of Assistant Producer you recently applied for,' Oh wow, I had totally forgotten my rageful job applications at the weekend and nerves instantly hit me.

'Hi Angela, nice to hear from you.'

'So, we like your CV and would love to get you in for an interview with the Head of Production this Friday, if you can be available? We are looking to fill this role very quickly, so the sooner we can see you, the better.' My stomach churns with excitement as this was the job I had instantly fallen in love with, but thought it would be out of my league being such a newbie to the industry.

'That is great news. I can definitely make myself available at 10 am if that works for you?' I say, trying to keep my cool and not sound as giddy as I currently feel.

'Fabulous Sophia. I will send a confirmation email shortly with the address details and the name of the person to ask for on your arrival.'

'Thanks so much and I look forward to it.' We echo our goodbyes and I hang up and I sit staring out to Soho from my makeshift office at the breakfast bar. I start to daydream and remember reading somewhere, that in life we are always looking to change something in our lives; our jobs, our homes or our relationship. For the first time in a long time, I think to myself how content I am with all those three aspects of my life, but it also occurs to me that none of them is realistically permanent. Miles and I are such early days and although life is fun right now, I can't imagine us in years to come with a house in the suburbs and two children. This is his home and I am purely crashing here for a while. My job is great, but I need to do what's best for my career progression. I find my emails and skim over the role I had applied for at Freedom Productions, reminding myself what I had applied for and start some serious prep for my interview.

The finest research for such a role such as this surely is to sit down with a coffee and watch the show they produce, which just so happens to be a very popular primetime hit, "Cooking with Dominic". Dominic is renowned for his good looks, attitude to healthy eating and the perfect recipes for evenings with family and friends. He's created numerous cookbooks and his empire is huge and international. So, the idea that little old me with only one TV credit to my name and a not a great deal of experience so far, has a chance to be a part of that team is sending my nerves into a frenzy.

The front door opens and Miles walks in, I don't break from the screen as he grabs a drink and crashes down next to me on the sofa, 'not your usual viewing Soph, usually it's some crap about housewives of whatever!' Oh dear, clearly he has clocked my infatuation with reality TV.

'Well actually, I had a call earlier about a new job for the production company behind this Cooking with Dominic show,' Miles recoils instantly.

'Oh right, I didn't realise you were looking. When did you apply for that?'

'Well, last Friday when lunatic turned up. I had this urge to get a new job and, well, you know...'

'Get away from me?'

'Yup, I guess.' I shrug and I may as well be honest.

'So you might end up working with this guy?'

'Maybe, I mean, they might not even like me!'

'They will Sophia. They will. As long as he doesn't like you too much.' I nearly spit out my tea and try to contain my laughter.

'Well, I definitely wouldn't worry about that. I have thought about it quite a bit since the call and I am thinking it won't do us any harm to work somewhere different. In fact, it's probably better for us.' Miles gazes out to the cool blue sky and I can tell his brain is working overtime.

'Yes, true. Or this Dominic guy, whoever he is, will fall madly in love with you and steal you away from me.' I'm pretty sure he is just joking, but I can't be a hundred per cent.

'Firstly, you know full well who the world-renowned chef is, even if you want to pretend you don't. Also, he is a happily married man and even if he wasn't, he will have a queue of women, probably a few Victoria Secrets models among them, who would jump at the chance if he becomes single. So no, you have nothing to be concerned about, I'm more than satisfied with my very own TV hunk.'

'So he's a hunk?' Miles' eyes widen at me.

'Seriously!!' I sigh, getting frustrated by his sulk and the dampening of my good news, 'that's what you took from that compliment I gave you? Jeeezzzz I give up.'

As I walk into the very swish production offices in Kentish Town, I feel the buzz of excitement. The walls are covered in TV show stills which pretty much all include Dominic and there is a large projector, playing a constant loop of the companies showreel. I knew as soon as I had the call that I need to do some serious impressing to land a job here and now standing in the foyer, the nervous sickness in my stomach is confirming how much I really, really want this job.

'Hi, it's Sophia, right? I'm Anna, the Head of Production for Freedom.' A very cool woman holds out her hand, she's wearing a black roll neck under a very expensive looking houndstooth blazer with black jeans and Burgundy Doc Marten boots. She must be in her late thirties and has a simple dark brown bob with thick black-framed glasses perched on her head. She oozes confidence and I take an instant liking to her. I shake her hand back and try to mimic her poise, but pretty sure the slight nervous shake in my voice gives me away,

'Yes, I'm Sophia. Lovely to meet you Anna.'

'Please, follow me, Can I get you a coffee, tea or water?'

'No, I am fine thank you.' I would rather be dehydrated for the next hour, than risk adding needing the toilet, to my list of mid-interview fears.

I follow Anna into a glass-walled meeting room just off the foyer and take a deep breath while I sit down.

After about five minutes of explaining my very short career thus far and education, it all feels positive and Anna is lovely and comes across as very encouraging.

'So, Sophia, all that sounds great and you certainly have gained some very good experience in the past few months. At the risk of sounding very cliché, where do you see yourself in five years?'

'In five years I will be 30, so anticipate being married. I also envisage being exactly like you, amazing job, totally cool and you seem to have pretty much nailed life, you also mentioned you have two kids? Yeah, I would like a couple of those too.' Is what I would have said, if I were being totally honest, but instead I give the appropriate answer,

'I would really like to see myself as a Producer at a renowned company such as this one, making shows that I love and am proud to be part of,' which got the nods and smiles that I was aiming for.

'Well, as we have such a tight deadline to get this position filled, I don't want to hang around and waste time we just don't have. I think you would be perfect for the job and fit in here at Freedom Production. So, I will drop you an email on the return to my office and if you could let me know by the close of business today whether you accept the terms of employment, that would be great.' Somehow, it seems that I have managed to wangle a job and now I just have to make my way out of the building and accept the contract, before Anna realises she has just hired a total novice.

'That's amazing news, thank you so much for this opportunity' I spurt, trying to remain vaguely cool, even though my heart feels like it's going to explode out of my chest with excitement.

'Hey Miles, I got the job!' He was the third person I phoned, after letting my parents know the news.

'That's great Sophia, well done,' Miles says with what sounds like false enthusiasm. I was hoping for a better reaction, but as I am basically skipping and delighted at my current success I choose to overlook it.

'Fancy drinks tonight after work?'

'Erm, well, Some of the crew asked if I wanted to go to this new bar, but you are welcome to come if you want?' Miles sounds reluctant and is clearly distracted.

'Do you want me to Miles?'

'Well yeah, if you still have time for us old lot here.' For fuck's sake, he is totally making this about him, I'm not letting him ruin this moment for me. I instantly remember an old Uni friend, Poppy, had mentioned she is up for the weekend, I will message her. I'm sure she will be delighted and more than happy to celebrate my good fortune with me.

'Actually, forget it Miles, enjoy your evening,' I hang up and before I even get a chance to stew over Miles' lack of excitement. My phone pings and I check my email. My contract is there and I give it a quick skim and if anything could prepare me for a night out, it was reading my 4k pay raise and all the added benefits including, "will require shoots abroad and on short notice", it's written as if it is a bad thing whereas I feel like pinching myself.

HER CITY OF DREAMS

I walk out of the studio building and with the skip still in my step, having read through my contract and it being even better than I could have ever imagined. 'Yeah, bye Sophia, guess I'll see you at home,' it's Miles and he is shouting after me. After he has basically ignored me from the production meeting through the entire show, it now seems by the tone in his voice, that he anticipates me hanging around for him. However, Poppy is at Soho House and she has a cocktail waiting for me and I just can't deal with Miles being in a sulk with me, again. I will pretend I had earphones in and didn't hear him, lying so early on in a relationship to avoid confrontation is not feeling like an ideal strategy, but I really, really just want to celebrate my success for a moment.

'HEEEEEEY.' Poppy throws her long, long arms around me. She is stunning, tall with long wavy auburn hair and is built like a supermodel, she had in fact been up in London for a casting.

'How did your meeting go?' I ask, wiggling myself onto the fancy barstool.

'Standard casting crap. Stand around, keep my mouth shut and be judged, but it's a big payer, so it will help fund my final year.'

What I didn't mention is that Poppy is also in the process of completing her Masters in Law, using her beauty is a mere money-making exercise to help her reach her career goals. She's one of the smartest and most gorgeous women I know and I have always been in total awe of her.

'Fuck.Him.Off.' I roll my eyes at Poppy's response to Miles' reaction to the news of my new job.

'Your ex was an arsehole. I called that from the night you met him. Remember Sophia?'

'Yes, you were spot on. In every way. Unfortunately.' I say in annoyance that her instincts always seem to be incredibly accurate. 'Oh, can you please just move here, life is so much better and more fun with you around,' I grab her hands and plead with her, half-joking, half not.

'Give me a year and I will be here to stop you from wasting your precious time on these men and stupid flatmates,' she promises and we cheers our Espresso Martinis and continue our evening putting the world to rights. Which was absolute bliss, in between the constant barrage of men trying to hit on my friend.

I tiptoe into the apartment and the plan is to not disturb a, most likely, peed off Miles. I had missed a few of his calls innocently whilst out with Poppy, as the bar had been noisy and we were so wrapped up in conversation, I had only noticed Miles' attempts of contact as I was five minutes from his apartment. I peer into the bedroom, juggling my heels and bag and trying to maintain my balance. He's not there, I'm the first one home which is perfect. I quickly get ready for bed and in my slightly hazy, cocktail induced thoughts have concluded that the best idea is to get to sleep and the chances are, Miles will be in a better mood in the morning. He may even be ready to sincerely congratulate me on my success by then.

I wake up to the sound of my alarm resonating through my brain and instantly roll over to Miles. He's not here. I walk out to the lounge and there is no sign of him anywhere, his shoes aren't by the door, his keys and wallet are not on the sideboard and I come to the realisation that he didn't return home last night. Running back to the room to check my phone there is nothing from him and I instantly start to worry, after all, this is London and bad things happen all the time here. I call him and it goes straight to voicemail. I try to think logically and call Simon, one of the crew's phone numbers, they were bound to be out together so he may have an idea where Miles is.

'Morning,' a very husky and tired sounding voice answers.

'Hi Simon, it's Sophia from work, I'm really sorry if I woke you.' A sudden feeling of embarrassment washes over me, as I realise I am hunting down my so-called boyfriend. 'Just wondering if Miles is with you? He's not at home and I'm just a little concerned that something has happened.'

'Erm, no sorry Soph, he's not here, he was with a friend. E, E, E, erm, what was her name. EMILY, that was it. Not sure if he is with her?' Surely he's not with her after the way she was with me and sending the lunatic, Miles' ex after me. Or is he? Is he playing a horrible game because he knows that would be a shitty move and is bound to ignite a reaction from me. I feel instantly sick.

'Oh OK, that makes sense. Thanks Simon,' and I quickly hang up the phone, trying to not sound as infuriated as I feel.

What I want to do is call him and shout at his answerphone to release my anger, but there is a good chance Emily will get to hear it and I just don't want to give her the satisfaction. The feeling of being trapped overwhelms me right now. I'm in his home and he is not happy with me, so I will pay the price and he will humiliate me by going to stay with her, or someone. Wherever he is, he is not here. I take a deep breath, my plan is to make a coffee and work out how to get out of this situation. I will not play games like this. If this is the way he deals with me having a little success in my life, then how can this ever work? When success and my career is my main goal right now.

Checking my emails as I inhale my coffee, I see I have a response to the letter I wrote, handing in my notice. I had signed and returned my contract instantly when I received it after lunch yesterday, knowing how much Anna was needing me to start and not wanting to seem less enthusiastic then I am. I hadn't seen Jo's response until now and having felt so much guilt writing the resignation email, I feel hesitant to read it.

Dear Sophia,

This is incredibly disappointing news, I had hoped after investing in your development here, you would stay with us for longer.
However, as you will be going to a competitor, please assume today was your final day with us and take the next two weeks as gardening leave.

I wish you the best,
Jo

Well, it wasn't as bad as I thought it would be and the idea of two weeks off feels very appealing right now. I have a pang of guilt for letting Jo down after she had put so much faith in me, but also the idea of never walking into those studios and seeing the crew again fills me with sadness. However, the idea of dealing with Miles' petulance outweighs all of that right now and I also have to put my future first and I'm pretty sure an opportunity like the one at Freedom, does not crop up that often. Anna will hopefully be thrilled I can start the date she requested and now I have time to sort my sorry excuse for a private life out. This feels like impeccable timing as I haven't spoken to my big sister Charly since Christmas. She lives in Knutsford and having finished her training as a GP, she's settled and lives there with Harry in a pretty fancy house, living her best Cheshire life. Harry is a surgeon from an affluent family in the area, so those two never seem short of anything and also have more than enough space for me to take a retreat for a few days. Something Charly has always offered, but I have never had the chance to accept, until now.

'Congrats little sis. That's fab news and in equal measures, shitty news. You really know how to pick'em don't you?'

'looks like it, but I really need to start this job feeling fresh and hanging around here is not going to do me any favours, I feel so trapped and can't face Miles right now.'

'Well pack yourself up and get on the next train, text me your arrival and I will be waiting. Go to Crewe and then the connection to Knutsford. I know the perfect lunch spot to cheer you up, my treat.'

'Thanks Charly, you really are the best sister. Just don't tell Margo that,' I tease. We hang up and I jump in the shower and pack as many clothes, shoes, cosmetics that will fit into my weekender bag. I'm rushing to ensure I can leave a casual note on the breakfast bar, updating Miles on my departure and not actually having to face him anytime soon.

After a mad dash and one Uber down, I make it onto the train in time. With the third coffee of the day in hand and my favourite magazine, this is perfect. Headphones in and gazing out the window as we start to pull away from Euston and I feel like I am escaping the madness and overriding relief hits me. My phone buzzes and I see a few messages from Miles stacking up. Very quick, angry-looking rants.

So that's it, you just go? You went last night, you vanish today?

Do you even CARE where I was?

Maybe you should find somewhere else to live.

So, last night was indeed a ploy to get my attention by the sounds of Miles' message. It seems he is desperate for me to react and to be insecure, begging for answers from him and I'm sure he imagined missed calls from me and angry texts. He probably envisaged walking into the apartment today and I would be there sobbing, begging for forgiveness. I know all this because these are the mistakes I made before when my ex also tried to control me. It lasted two years too long with Richard, but now I have learnt my lesson and I will never, ever be manipulated or mistreated like that again. I message him back,

Simon said you were fine when I was worried and called him. He said you had been with your bestie Emily, so I assumed you were in good hands. Yes, I totally agree, I will find somewhere else to live as soon as I am back.

Chapter Eight

'Seriously, Charly, since when have you driven a Range Rover?' I throw my bag onto the backseat of Charly's plush car as she picks me up from the train station.

'Harry bought it for me for Christmas.' I look out of the corner of my eyes at her, 'WHAT? I know, I know, it's over the top, but I was the only one in their family who didn't have one.'

'You do realise that doesn't make it sound any better, right?' We giggle and I silently envy her.

Charly has always been the smartest one out of the Williams sisters. I personally think the prettiest one too, but she will deny that until the cows come home, which makes her even more bloody perfect. I have always known I could call her and she would do whatever it took to make me feel better and the four years age difference means she has always mothered and looked out for me. As annoying as it has been on occasions, it's times like these that make me remember how lost I would be without her. I fill Charly in with the events of the past few days, the good, the bad and the ugly.

'I will find you an eligible bachelor. Harry must have a phone full of successful, educated men, who would be very happy to take you out for a drink.'

'Honestly, Miles and I are clearly not made for each other, but I'm not interested in meeting any more men in the near future. Well, unless it's Ryan Reynolds?'

'Pah, you know Harry is not that cool to have him in his phone book.' Charly laughs as she manoeuvres around the second Ferrari in two minutes.

'Seriously, how rich are people around here? Jeez. Anyway, I'm after nothing more than a chilled time with my sister and preparing for my new job.'

'How very grown-up of you Soph, I'm proud to hear it. I have some fab news actually to help you with all that. I have secured you two months in one of Harry's family apartments in Hampstead. It's an investment rental and they are keeping it free for you. Meaning you can get out of where you are and also giving you time to find somewhere more affordable. They want nothing for it, but I have bought a bottle of Champagne on your behalf as a thank you, so please don't drink it.'

'WOW, that's incredible, thanks so much Charly. That really gets me out of a crappy situation.'

'There is, however, one stipulation. You dump that guy for good. Take my word for it, he is no good for you and if the alarm bells are ringing already, you need to listen to the warning signs. This is your escape Soph, take it and move forward and try not to move in with any more men before I give them the thumbs up. Please?' It's a harsh ultimatum, but I know she is right. Charly isn't controlling, she is caring and wants the best for me, she's heard enough over the past couple of months to know I need to get off the Miles rollercoaster. I look at my phone as it buzzes, another text message to add to the voicemails I am yet to listen to, all from

Miles. I switch my phone off and give my brain the space it needs to make a rational decision.

After a very fancy lunch at apparently one of the more "low key" establishments in Knutsford, Charly drives me back to her double fronted detached house down a beautiful, leafy street. Here's me, barely able to keep a roof over my head for a month at a time and my sister, who appears to have so much accomplished in life already. We pull onto the large gravel driveway and before Charly stops the engine, Harry has already opened the front door and is running over to us.

'Sophia, darling,' he wraps me in his arms with the loving embrace of a brother-in-law.

Since meeting Charly at Uni, Harry has done his utmost to fill the void I have of an older brother. Growing up as the tomboy of the three sisters, while they were playing dress up and dolls, I would dream of having a big brother to help me climb the Oak tree in our garden and go on adventures a la the film, Stand by Me, sans dead body, preferably.

Harry must be around 5'11, dark short and tidy hair and looks every bit the surgeon he is. I would trust him with my life as many others do on a daily basis. He's aura exerts kindness and although extremely privileged, (if you look past the matching Range Rovers, Hunters wellies lined in the hallway and a coat rack of Barbour jackets,) he is one of the most personable and caring humans you would be lucky to meet.

'You look in need of a good fill little sis,' he says, scanning my limbs and lifting my arm, obviously assessing my BMI.

'Well, apparently that is not on her agenda at the moment,' Charly cackles, teasingly.

We eat homemade vegetable soup and fresh bread, both delicious and both cooked by my sister. 'Charly, how come you got all the good genes. A Doctor who can cook, if you weren't my sister, I would hate you.' Charly doesn't even look up from her food, there is something wrong and I'm pretty sure I have put my foot right in it. Harry puts his hand on hers and it confirms my fears.

'The thing is Soph,' Harry's tone totally changes, 'We have had a bit of bad news regarding our ability to conceive naturally and it looks as though it could be a long slog ahead if we are to have the family we are dreaming of.' I have a sudden urge to cry. Their world seems so picture perfect and you would assume they had everything. 'BUT, we must not despair as thankfully, due to your incredibly smart sister, she has done all her research and we have many options ahead of us.' Harry smiles reassuringly at Charly.

'I'm smart but I can't do the one thing I was put on this earth to do.' She finally whispers and gives in to her tears. I quickly go to the other side of their large oak dining table and hold her.

'You guys are so blessed with this lovely life, I know it will work out and before you know it, there will be at least three mini yous, outwitting me at every turn.' I attempt to lighten the mood, but I fail. Charly looks up with reddened eyes,

'I sit in my office and at least two times a week, over the past three years I have women and couples coming in, hearing the news that they won't be conceiving without medical help. I have sat there, feeling awful for them and weighing up their chances in my head. Now that's me, something I had never imagined. It's all my fault.' I look at Harry and he gives me a knowing stare. What I assume Charly is referring to, it the time she had to face an abortion at 19. She was just starting out and with a totally unreliable boyfriend, she felt it was her only option. For the golden child, this was the first time in her life that Charly had faced a negative response from our parents and had felt like she let them down.

'The great thing is, you have been pregnant, so we know that's possible. There were no complications so that surely cannot have affected your fertility?' There is silence and I realise, unless I can miraculously magic a baby inside Charly's womb, there is absolutely nothing I can say to make any of this better. 'Right, let me clean up and you guys go to relax. I can't be here, scrounging off you both and not be pulling my weight,' they don't move and just look, surprised at each other, 'go, for goodness sake, before I change my mind.' They head off into the snug and I clear the table and realise that I have come up here to get away from my inane problems and within minutes my sister has solved my short-term housing situation and makes my life at least a billion times easier. All the time, knowing she has her fertility worries weighing on her mind. If anyone in this world would make the perfect mother, it is her.

I pop my head around the door where they are sitting, wrapped up in each other's arms and staring into the open fire, 'Good night guys, love you both.' I whisper in their direction.

'Sleep well Sophia, we love you too.' they whisper back in unison.

I throw myself onto the huge bed in my sister's guest room and find myself staring at the ceiling, with the information I had just received, running through my head. Our Nana always said to my sister's and me, that she would say a little prayer for us all each night before bed. I have never had a religious faith in particular but if I did, now feels like it would be a good time to say a little prayer for Charly. Instead, I put it out to the Universe that they will have the baby they so desperately long for. I cosy into the, god knows how many counts of Egyptian Cotton, bedsheets and grab my phone. The past few hours have confirmed that the irate messages from Miles need to be deleted and forgotten. Hearing his rage is not going to fix anything between us and quite honestly, it all feels irrelevant to me now.

Hi Miles, I hope you have calmed down. I have somewhere new to live, so I will collect my things when I return and leave your keys on the side if you are not in. Thanks for helping me out, no matter what has happened between us, I will always be grateful, thank you x

Two weeks of relaxation in the compounds of my sister's home and I feel like a new woman, a new woman who has possibly outstayed her welcome. I have barely ventured out apart from the odd meal and coffee with Charly. There has been a scattering of snow, which was just the excuse I needed to hibernate and find solace in front of an open fire and researching a few more shows for my new job starting tomorrow. I must have sat through at least six catch-up episodes of "Cooking with Dominic", one where they are filming in Sorrento and another in Rome and all over Italy. It suddenly feels real, that I will actually be part of that team and possibly on one of these amazing trips. As I take the last slice of Charly's homemade carrot cake, I realise I have probably eaten at least half of it to myself and glance down at my curves finally reappearing. One meal a day, with excessive city walking is a diet I intend to never do again.

'Right, Sophia, are you ready to go in about thirty minutes?'

'Yes, I will be ready, my bags are by the door,' as I ingest the last bite of home baking I will have for a while.

Charly scurries around and we have pretty much avoided the baby conversation since the first evening of my arrival. Harry mentioned that until they have a few more tests, there is little more to discuss and she seems more adamant to focus her attention on me and fixing my life. As much as it gets a little overbearing, if it helps distract her from her worries, I will take it, and let's face it, I need it.

'Did you ever get a response from that Miles?' Charly asks, not even looking up from searching for whatever she has lost in her bag.

'Actually, that's a point, no. Just hoping I can get into the apartment to get my things without any drama.'

'Mmm, well, any issues and let us know. I'm sure a couple of Harry's London friends would help you out. Anyway Sophia, here are the keys and address to the apartment. There is an alarm system which is written here. Please do not keep the code with the keys,' Charly looks at me like I'm a totally incompetent child, I feel like being sarcastic, but she is saving my skin after all, so I bite my lip and nod my head instead. 'It's important Soph, I need a yes from you.' Jeez she really is pushing my buttons now.

'YES Charly, totally get it. Like I understand about the red wine and handmade silk rug.' I love London for all its diversity, but going from sharing a tiny single bedroom with bed bugs to now being careful of a silk rug seems a crazy leap in lifestyles.

'You know what? I think you should roll the rug up and put it somewhere safe as soon as you arrive.' Charly says as though it's a suggestion, but I am well aware it's an order.

'Yes, I will do that, great idea.' I say, compliantly.

The train pulls into Knutsford and I turn to Charly, giving her an extra tight hug and whisper in her ear, 'If you need some ears, just call.'

'Thanks, I will, if I ever catch you in your busy city life,' she teases. 'Sorry Harry missed you, he had back to back surgery today.'

'I know, I know, he's busy saving lives, I wouldn't ever expect anything less.' One more hug and I jump on the train and quickly finding a window seat just in time to pull a stupid face to Charly as we pull away, she does her normal eye roll and fake despair and I know my little sister duties have been fulfilled for now.

I'm pretty sure I can't stand outside Miles' apartment all day as I stare up to the top floor from the street. All I need is a sign that he is not there. I ring the buzzer and thankfully there is no response, especially as I had no idea what I would say if he had answered. It's a freezing cold day, so I quickly swipe my way into the lobby door, into the lift and up to the apartment.

'Sophia is that you?' Fuckerty fuck, he's here and from the sounds of it, he is just out of the shower.

'YES, I will just be five minutes and I will be out of your hair.' I work as silently and quickly as possible as I gather all my clothes and belongings. I try to remember every item as I really do not have plans to return to this apartment anytime soon.

'So you have nothing to say?' Miles catches me as I carry the bundle of my belongings, hoping to have made it out of the front door without confrontation. He stands with a towel wrapped around his waist and sweeps his towel-dried hair back from his face. I'm pretty sure he knows exactly how sexy he looks right now, but I promise myself to not get distracted. Even if it's feeling near impossible. I mean, those abs. I take a deep breath, remembering Charly's advice. I must be strong and remember what a dick he has been.

'I really don't think there is anything more to say though Miles, you said it all not coming home that night,' I think back to the reason why I was so upset and I feel irked just remembering who he picked to spend the night with and I know I need to leave before I get upset or angry.

'Right, well yes, that was an arsehole move, I get it. I was totally in the wrong, but you have got to believe me, it was innocent. I just crashed on Emily's sofa.' I look at him and feel the anger bubbling inside and my cheeks heat.

'Innocently staying at Emily's place? The one who made me so unwelcome and sent your lunatic of an ex to make me feel an inch tall and humiliate me. Do you mean THAT Emily? Nothing innocent about it. That was the TWATYIST OF TWATTY MOVES.' I started to shout and take a breath. I need to walk out of here NOW.

'I know, I could tell the next morning she was lapping it up. She was asking how you would react. So, I guess she got what she wanted.' He looks downtrodden by his own stupidity.

'Yup and you handed it to her on a silver platter, well fucking done. I will take great pleasure in never having to see that vile human again. You did this Miles,' I pause as I see Miles' face looking even more hurt than I imagined. 'Look, you have been amazing to me and I will be forever grateful. You helped me when I was in desperate need and we have had a fun time, but we both know this is not the right relationship for either of us.' I don't want to waste another moment being angry. I just want to leave with my head high, knowing I have been as gracious as possible, even if I could throw every swear word in Miles' direction right now.

'I knew this would happen. This is exactly why I never let people in, because it always turns out like this.'

'Well, where was this going anyway? You made it abundantly clear from the beginning that this relationship had no future and you could never love me. The fate was sealed then'.

'What if I said I love you now, would that change anything?' He looks at me and has a glint of hope in his eyes and starts to move closer.

'Sorry Miles, it's just too late for that,' as I step closer to the exit. 'I don't want a relationship full of mind games, it's too much stress and although I will always be your friend, I cannot be in a relationship with you. Staying with Emily has dented my pride and hurt me more than you can obviously appreciate.' Not another word is said as I walk out the door for the final time, leaving my key behind.

I get into the cab and although I am surrounded by all my things in bags and boxes, the irony is that I feel a huge weight lifted from my shoulders.

'Thank you so much,' I shout back to the cabby, as I wave him goodbye, after passing my final box of belongings into my new temporary home.

One floor up and I have broken into quite a sweat. As I look at the carnage of rushed packing at my feet, I am wishing to myself that I had taken more belongings home at Christmas and lived a less clothes, shoes, bags and general clutter filled life. I swing the front door open and step into a vast hall area, which is perfectly decorated and the scent of Jo Malone hits me instantly. I only know because it's the same scent I buy my mum, at her request, each birthday and Christmas every single year. The walls are white and the furniture all feels very

French country chic. As I haul in my bags and boxes through from the landing, I feel like a total intruder.

I take my tour around the two-bed, exquisitely decorated rooms and before I move any of the dusty boxes through, I quickly roll up the silk rug and position it in a place of safety, behind the dark blue velvet sofa. 'Definitely only white wine to be consumed within these walls,' I mutter to myself, as I assess the enormity of the damage I could actually do here. I make my plan for the evening to unpack, eat and sleep. My first day at Freedom is tomorrow and I need to be on my best form. This is the start of a new era and hopefully the making of my career, a concoction of nerves and excitement bubbles in my belly.

'Right guys, please meet Sophia, she is joining us as a new Assistant producer.' Harriet, the Senior Producer walks me around the production offices, introducing me, one desk of extremely cool-looking people at a time. I hear at least thirty names and vaguely recognise some faces from my little research/stalking session I did the evening previous, on the companies website.

'Sophia, this is where you will be seated,' Harriet holds out her hand to a desk with the fellow Assistant producers, they all look up with smiles and waves. 'If you set-up all your logins, Michael will talk you through some processes and the current production calendar. Any questions and you will find me over there,' Harriet gestures to the other side of a huge open plan office. 'Make Sophia feel welcome please team.'

'Hey, welcome to Freedom,' Michael holds out his hand. He has a huge sparkly smile and instantly I feel welcomed. 'Right, before anything else, we need to establish the priorities on this desk.'

'OK, right.' I say quickly grabbing the pen and pad which I assume have been left for me on my new desk.

'You won't be needing those quite yet,' he grins, 'whose for coffee?' Not a word is said, but hands all rise from behind laptop monitors. 'If you are going to fit at Freedom, you need to make sure you can work the coffee machine. Follow me and I'll show you.'

I follow Michael back from the kitchen, carrying four Freedom Production branded mugs and keep praying that I won't trip and make a complete tit of myself within the first ten minutes of being here.

'That's for Carly; that's for Josh, that's for Shauna, yours and mine. Well done Sophia, your first task is a success.'

'Well, I am pleased I am over my first hurdle,' I nervously laugh.

We have a chat over our drinks and the team are asking me, what feels like a hundred and one questions, some about my previous work experience, some about my love life but then, to my relief we are being rushed into a first production meeting and away from the inquisition.

'This is a biggy Sophia, quite a lot for your first day, but there is a new series of "Cooking with Dominic". This time it's South America, so further afield than our normal European shoots.' Michael fills me in with as much detail as possible as we follow the entire office into the boardroom. Feeling very aware of being the new girl and unimportant, I squeeze in and hide towards the back of the room.

Five minutes after a quick rundown of the ratings for the recent shows and general news from Anna the same, supercool Anna who hired me, the room then goes silent as the famous Dominic walks in.

Dominic is as good looking in person as he is on TV, a little shorter than I had imagined, but pretty much the same. 'Hey guys, great to see you all,' as he high fives a few of the team as he walks to the head of the table. 'We have some great news. I'm sure you may have heard by now, but we have a new series commissioned for our normal slot and I am positive, with this team and our plans so far, this is going to be the best series yet.' He is bubbling with enthusiasm and it flows through the room with whoops, cheers and a round of applause. 'So, for those of you who haven't yet heard, we are off to South America and all of you are going to be on this fab journey with us.' More applause and excitement as I try to take in the news, attempting not to get too excited. Being my first day, surely this does not include me?

'Are you excited Sophia?' Michael turns and asks as we are dismissed and head back to our posts. 'It's a lot for the first day, isn't it?'

'It is exciting, but I'm not sure how I will be involved seeing as it's my first day.'

'Oh no, you will definitely be coming with us. All the AP's go, we have so much support work to do for the Producers, we are all needed. No use resting on our laurels here,' he shrugs and I laugh.

'Resting on our laurels, I haven't heard that for years!' I tease.

'Here she is guys,' Michael exclaims with waving hands, as we arrive back at our desks, 'first day and already taking the piss. I reckon you might just fit in here Sophia.'

I head home and as much as the excitement of the first day at Freedom is on repeat through my brain, I need to get back and call Charly. Today was test result day and I'm feeling a little sick to the stomach. I have managed to put it to the back of my head all day, but now my full focus is on making sure my big sister is OK. I throw my jacket and bag onto the plush hall chaise longue and dial Charly.

'Hey, I have been thinking about you, how was your first day at the new job?'

'It went so well thanks, but that's not the reason I am calling. What's the verdict, all OK?'

'So,' Charly pauses in the style of an X-Factor host and the suspense is like torture. 'It's not ideal Soph, but there are a few things we are going to try. First is Tubal Flushing.'

'Jesus, what the hell is that?' Charly laughs at my reaction, which is a relief as it could have come across as incredibly insensitive.

'It's quite common and I had already assumed this would be where we begin with this process. Sometimes this is all it takes to clear out the womb and leave a fresh path for the eggs to travel.' I suddenly get choked up and can't bring myself to say anything. 'Sophia, you are still there? Don't worry, I know it sounds full-on, but this is, even if a little invasive, well worth it.' I take a huge gulp and try to rein in the sore lump in my throat.

'As long as you will be OK Charly. I just want it to all work out for you both, so badly.'

'I know you do. I'm so lucky to have you on my team. ANYWAY, less about wombs, how was your first day?'

'Well, it looks like I'm off to South America for three weeks!'

Chapter Nine

The first week is under my belt in my new job and it's been amazing, but I'm absolutely shattered. It's Friday after work and I'm joining a few of the team for dinner, which is a relief, as I have been eating alone for the past few nights and I've got really lazy, pretty sure I haven't hit my five-a-day for at least four days. We are heading to a restaurant called "Made in Brazil" in Camden Town as supposed research for the new show, but it seems more like a ploy and excuse to have a few drinks.

It has transpired over the week that we would be travelling to four different locations in South America, starting in Brazil, then to Argentina, Chile and then finishing in Peru. Excited is an understatement, overwhelmed is another! So far my passport has been handed over to Freedom, so all my travel permits, flights etc are planned. I have spent the week alongside the team of researchers, planning and confirming all shooting locations and starting in Rio, I have managed to confirm a stunning filming location, which has views of the Sugar Loaf mountain and Christo Redentor. I received pats on the back all round and it gave me the boost in confidence I needed to confirm that I am in fact capable of doing this job, even though my self-doubt had crept in on more than one occasion throughout the past week.

As I walk into the restaurant, I realise this isn't just the small team of AP's getting together, it pretty much looks like the entire production company has taken over the restaurant and I even spot Dominic in the corner. I stick with Carly; Shauna, Josh, Michael as a pack and we find a table capable of fitting us around. 'Wow, I thought it was just us guys.' I say with genuine shock, looking around at all the faces I am beginning to recognise.

'Oh yes. Sorry, I just assumed you knew that it was more of a company outing.' Michael said as he passed me the cocktail menu. Shauna looks over her menu at me,

'The best thing about these evenings Sophia, is that it's always on Dominic, as a thank you. His wife will be here shortly and a few of his friends who always end up out with us.'

We start with a round of the traditional Brazilian Caipiroska cocktails and I promise myself to take it slow, the last thing I need to do is make a drunk fool of myself in front of a restaurant full of new colleagues.

After getting our starters and totally absorbed in the excited conversations of the places we will see and the adventures that lay ahead, I look up to see a group huddling around Dominic. His wife, Arabella is there, who is just as gorgeous in real life as she is in the books and the shows she has appeared on. You really would expect nothing less from the wife of Dominic the world-renowned chef and if Carlsberg made couples, they would totally fit into that idea of perfection. I feel a pang of jealousy, not directed at them, just that I envy their lives and the way they just seem to have it all so sorted. Partway through my envious thoughts, I get distracted by a tall, dark wavy-haired guy who is looking straight at me. We make eye contact and I instantly feel embarrassed when it occurs to me that I have just been sitting and staring in his direction, while my thoughts had been whirring around my head. I quickly look away and grab a sip of my drink, feeling my cheeks blush. How totally uncool, I must have looked like a total fangirl. I roll my eyes at myself as I continue to drink my embarrassment away.

'Hi, sorry, I just wanted to say hello, my name is Seb, well, Sebastian, but Seb is just fine.' Jeez, he is beautiful, he must be gay or in a relationship, I think to myself. He's too perfect to be hetrosexual and single. Or he's a total player and arrogant with it. I irrationally conclude, with the haze of alcohol hitting me.

'Hi Seb, so nice to see you again,' thankfully Michael steps in to save me. 'This is Sophia, she has just joined the AP team.' Michael gives me a subtle jab to my arm.

'Oh yes, hi, sorry,' I hold out my hand in Seb's direction and he shakes it, 'Sorry, I'm just a little distracted by all our work plans and was on a different planet for a second.' I'm doing my very best to drag this back from looking like a total moron that I feel.

'It's so exciting, isn't it? I can't wait. I've never been to South America before,' Dominic shouts for Seb from the other side of the restaurant as their food has arrived, 'OK, well I have been summoned, but it was a pleasure to meet you Sophia and looking forward to travelling with you all.' he scans around the table and does a salute goodbye as he walks back to what is definitely the cool kids table.

'Oh wow he totally likes you Soph.' Michael teases.

'Erm, I think he's more on your team than mine Michael!'

'Pah, I wish, but no. As much as I would love him to be Soph, he is as straight as they come. The rumours are that he has just broken up with his girlfriend, which is a relief because she was a total bitch.'

'Total bitch.' Shauna and Carly confirm with an echo.

'She was fit though.' Josh throws in his two pennies worth, which I kind of wish he hadn't.

'Well anyway, he doesn't even know me to like me. I think he was just being polite.'

'Nope, you will definitely end up fucking in Brazil.' Michael says far too loudly.

'For god's sake Michael!' I look at him wide-eyed, totally shocked, then scan around to make sure nobody outside of the table had heard. Thankfully it seemed everybody is as equally absorbed in their own chats to notice Michael's profanities.

'I won't lie Michael, worse things could happen in Brazil, but so far my reputation remains intact at Freedom and I would very much like it to stay that way.'

'Not even just a little fuck?' Michaels laughs as I glare back in despair. 'Sorry, Sorry. You are absolutely right my dear. Getting involved with a colleague probably wouldn't be the smartest move to make.'

'Everyone, if I can get your attention please.' Dominic stands on a chair at the other side of the restaurant, clinking two bottles of beer together. 'I just want to say, I am so excited to have such a fab team behind me on this new show. It's going to be a lot of work, a lot of long days, but I can promise that we will fill it with fun too. Here is to the next month of adventures and getting to know each other even better. Cheers.' There is a roar of cheers that fills the restaurant and as I take a cheeky glance over in Seb's direction, he is also looking straight over at me. Although, I am pretty sure he must be looking over my shoulder and against my better judgement, I look over to check and there is nobody there. I turn back to Seb as he continues to look, but this time grinning with a slight tilt to his head. I realise his eyes are in fact, on me and the cocktails I have consumed take over as I lift my glass to him. Seb responds to the air cheers with a raised beer bottle and a huge smile and I instantly feel a little twinge of excitement in my stomach.

I walk home linking arms with Shauna and Carly, who flatshare a few streets down from my temporary digs. Michael, Josh and a whole host of others carried on to a bar, but with funds low and my sensible work head-on, I knew it was the right time to call it a night. Listening to the girls run through the evening's events, I find myself feeling a little giddy at the prospect of spending a vast amount of time in the presence of Seb in a foreign country. There is something about him that makes me feel drawn to him, it's like instant chemistry that has already started to bubble.

'She's totally daydreaming about Sebastian.' I get a nudge to the arm and realise what Shauna and Carly are discussing, as I have been daydreaming.

'Erm, no,' I protest unconvincingly, 'pretty sure after Josh's comments about his stunning ex, he won't really be interested in me anyway. EVEN if there was a tiny little bit of me that was thinking about him.'

'SHUT UP, are you kidding?' Carly stands in the middle of the pavement dramatically waving her hands from my head to my toes, 'You are bloody gorgeous and you know what makes you even more gorgeous Sophia?'

'You don't even know it,' Shauna adds as they both high five each other. I blush, even on the cool February evening I feel the heat rise to my cheeks. I really need to learn how to accept a compliment graciously.

'Thanks ladies, that's very sweet of you to say, but I'm not so sure. Anyway, Seb is like some kind of Greek God.' They both continue to protest as they hug me goodbye and drop me at my front door and head in the direction of their own home.

As it's only 10 pm I cosy down into my pyjamas and make a hot chocolate, planning to catch up on some shows I have missed recently with all my late nights held up in the office. As I settle on a drama series, my phone starts to ping and I see I have numerous Instagram notifications popping up on my screen. I click through to see and it's him, Seb has managed to track me down on social media and is now following me. He has liked at least five posts and it looks like I have a DM from him. Wow, he does not mess about.

Hey Sophia, so pleased to meet you tonight. After our brief meeting, I had to do a bit of Social Media stalking... sorry if it's a bit weird, please don't hold it against me. Looking forward to our holiday... do not tell Dom I referred to it as a holiday, he will kill me, haha!

Esssh I have read it, Seb will see I have read it. If I don't reply it will be even more awkward. I really shouldn't encourage this. I really need to avoid work relationships at all costs. 'Remember Miles, remember Lucas,' I whisper to myself. I can't get a new job every time I get myself in a difficult relationship situation. It all rushes through my head at a hundred miles an hour and I come to the conclusion I just have to be nice and friendly, but not too friendly.

Hey Seb, really lovely to meet you earlier. It was a fun evening and pleased you found me! I definitely won't give the secret away and risk your life :)

Send. OK, I am happy with that, what is the worst that can happen with a little flirtation? A month of awkwardness in faraway lands on a work trip and getting overly involved with what is essentially your bosses best mate? Shit... And breath. That is pretty bad actually.

'Darling, can you just please check they have kidnap insurance? These things happen all the time in South America, especially Brazil and I just don't think we have the funds to pay a ransom and get you out of trouble.'

'Thanks, mum, that fills me with so much excitement, I can't wait to fear for my life throughout this trip.'

'Sorry Sophia, but Dad and I were watching a documentary on how people, just like you, get taken and made to walk through the rainforest for days and months upon end, so they cannot be found, just for the hostage money and Dad and I just don't have that kind of money lying around.'

'Give me the phone please,' I hear Dad say and there sounds like a scuffle, 'Sorry Soph, Dad here. Excuse your mum, as you know, she always means well. I just recommend you don't go out alone or walk through any Favelas and stick in a large group.' I know they are right and I can't imagine the feeling of seeing your once young child, go off so far into the world and I appreciate their love and concern. However, their fears are only adding to my long list of worries already stacking up about this trip.

'Yes, you are right, but there will be plenty of crew who are taking care of each other and there will also be security.' I say, assuming this will be the case, bearing in mind we will have a world-famous celebrity in our presence.

'Can you just make sure you email us once a day? We know calling will be a lot to ask, but the easiest way just so we know you are not lost in deepest, darkest Peru.' My mum has taken back hold of the phone.

'I'm not Paddington Bear, Mother!'

'Oh, I had wondered where I had heard that before,' we giggle and I am hoping that distraction will be the end of my parents' lecture. Thankfully they move on quickly and I get a few updates on Margo's failure to fly the nest, much to my parents continuing annoyance, also Charly's progress with her treatment and the hurdles they seem to be facing daily. I make my promises to email and call when I can and we send all our love and hugs. I hang up the phone and stare at the empty suitcase and pile of what was once, reasonably well ironed clothes. It's time to pack and stop procrastinating.

Halfway through my packing and I notice an unread DM, it's Seb.

Hey, fancy a coffee? I'm all packed and could do with a distraction from the mess in my apartment, I could grab a coffee at that vegan cafe round the corner from yours?

Wait what, he knows where I live? Not sure whether to be flattered or totally creeped out.

Just mid-packing, how do you know where I live?

Oh, shit, sorry, Michael mentioned it. Well, I asked him actually. I have freaked you out, haven't I? Sorry :(

I have just realised that I don't actually know anything about this guy, what he does for a living, how old he is, his surname, I know absolutely nothing!

Erm, a little freaked I'll be honest. Although I could do with a break, coffee sounds like a plan.

It's daylight, I know where he works at least and he is as hot as hell, I would be crazy to turn down the opportunity to get to know him a little better.

Great, be there in ten :)

'TEN! Jeez,' as I gasp and quickly give myself the once over in my mirror. I look like a bag lady. Having been trying on clothes to see what to take, I am totally mismatched and look like a mess. I grab skinny blue jeans, an oversized grey jumper, trainers. My hair is in a top knot and I'm not looking in the slightest bit glam, I add a little lip gloss and feel as ready as I'll ever be with ten minutes notice. I step out on a cold February Saturday and there are still signs of frost on all the windows of the beautiful three-story houses and cars down the street and I head to the only Vegan cafe I know in the hope it's the correct one.

'Hey Seb,' he's standing in the doorway of the cafe looking down at his phone,

'Oh good, I was just checking you hadn't cancelled or changed your mind.'

'I only said yes 11 minutes ago!' I roll my eyes jokingly and walk into the cafe. Considering I just had a huge pang of nerves shoot through my stomach as I looked into his large blue eyes, his loose dark brown curls of hair casually lying in a natural quiff, I managed to outwardly keep my cool, even if inwardly I am melting.

'Here OK?' I say, pointing towards a nice snug table in a corner.

'Perfect, what would you like?'

'A Cappuccino would be great. Thank you,' as I sit and watch Seb getting our drinks. I see the looks he gets from the Barista, the hair flick and coy smiles, I then also see her look at me as he walks over. I'm pretty sure I saw daggers shoot from her eyes and straight towards me.

'Here you go Soph, do you mind if I sit here?' He chooses to squeeze onto the cushioned bench next to me, without even waiting for my answer.

'Can I give you a little kiss on the cheek please?'

'I know you have bought me a coffee, but that's a little forward, don't you think?' I try to tease, actually attempting to disguise my shyness.

'Well, actually, it's because that Barista asked for my number and to not offend her, I said you are my girlfriend.'

'Ahhhh, now I understand the dirty look she just gave me.' I have no idea what part of my brain just took over, but I put my hands on Sebs cheeks and kiss him gently on the lips.

'Do you think that will do the job?' Suddenly feeling less shy.

'No, actually I don't,' as Seb leans in for a much longer kiss. We both sit back and without saying a word, we pick up our drinks and take a sip in symmetry.

'I realised early, when it turned out you have been stalking me,' I shoot Seb a playful grin, 'that I actually know zero about you!'

'I thought the same about you, as I was sitting outside your house and watching you eat ice cream out of the tub with your bare fingers in your granny nighty.'

'Oh dear, I think you must have been watching the wrong house. Well, that's embarrassing for you. I always use a spoon, so I know it can't have been me,' as I give him a dig to the ribs. 'In all seriousness, what do you do? Where do you live? How do you know Dominic? Do you always go away with him and how old are you?'

'Right, quite a few questions there! So, I am a short filmmaker. I have had a couple of films nominated at the Cannes Film Festival, haven't won as yet, but hopefully one day I will make it! Dom and I grew up in the same village in Dorset and played Rugby together from when we were kids. He has always been my best mate and he gets me to go away with him because firstly we have a laugh and also his wife Arabella isn't a huge fan of all the filming trips. This trip is a little different as I am filming a "behind the scenes" for him. Oh, I live in Hampstead too and I'm 28. Is that everything covered?'

'OK, well that all seems nice and normal, I don't regret kissing you now,' Seb laughs and I feel uncharacteristically at ease with this virtual stranger.

'Fantastic, that is a relief to hear! So now tell me about yourself please Sophia?'

'I'm 25, soon to be 26. I am only temporarily living in Hampstead in my brother-in-law's family apartment. I haven't had so much luck with living arrangements in London so far, but work has been improving dramatically, thankfully. I grew up in the Cotswolds in a small village, went to Uni in Brighton and I'm aiming to be a TV Producer in the next few years. That's about it really.'

'When is your Birthday?'

'It's actually when we are away, so hopefully, I can squeeze a few drinks to celebrate. I have promised to call my parents on the day and not get kidnapped.' Seb nearly spits out his coffee.

'Kidnapped? Wow, that hadn't even crossed my mind. I will be keeping an eye on you. Well, I always am, aren't I?' He laughs and in a city full of people taking themselves far too seriously, it's refreshing to be in the company of someone who has self-deprecating humour and the ability to laugh at themselves.

'Well, as unnerving as that sounds Sebastian, if you are willing to save me from any kidnap or hostage scenarios, then I guess I should be grateful?'

Chapter Ten

For at least the tenth time, I check my bag and yes, my passport is still there. Which shouldn't be unsurprising as I have not moved from the chaise longue in the hallway of my apartment for at least ten minutes, where I await my cab to Heathrow with my luggage for the next three weeks. I have managed to keep it to one large bag and one carry on, which is a miracle as the weather seems so unpredictable in South America over the next few weeks, if any of the five weather Apps I have checked are to be believed. The doorbell rings and thank goodness my taxi arrives on time. Which is the first hurdle out of the way, but until I'm sitting on the plane with a drink in my hand, my fear of missing the plane and work trip, especially as I'm still in my probation period, is causing all kinds of anxiety in my mind.

I watch the chilly London streets pass by from the taxi window and they are perfectly quiet as it's 5 am and the only people who can be found on the streets are the milk deliveries, people heading to early shifts and the ones stumbling home after a heavy night out.

'So madam, where are you off to? Anywhere nice?' The cab driver breaks the silence.

'Well, I am off with work, have you heard of the show, Cooking with Dominic? I'm going on location to film that.' That's the first time in a few days I have said that out loud and to a stranger, I suddenly feel pangs of excitement at the reality of it. Spending the last few days letting the anxious thoughts get to me, I realise how bloody cool this actually is.

'WOW, I LOVE that guy, he is probably the only guy I would trade my wife in for, I mean seriously, that guy can cook!'

Bags are checked in and I have been directed to the lounge. I walk in and I can hear the production team before I see them as they are all buzzing, the excitement is palpable and extremely loud. I look over to see Dominic and Seb, they are both sitting and looking at the back of a paper, chatting among themselves. As much as I want to go over and say hi to Seb, I have promised myself to keep work and pleasure as separate as humanly possible. I wave over to Michael and the rest of the gang, who are all perched around a table with what looks like extra-large coffees in hand and with it not even being 6 am, I head to the bar and order myself a double shot Cappuccino as all the caffeine is definitely needed right now.

'Hey you,' Seb walks up and puts his hand on the lower part of my back, 'This is Sophia I mentioned Dom.' Dominic walks over and I realise this is actually the first time we have met.

'Oh hi, yes I recognise you from the office. It's nice to finally meet you,' he kisses my cheek.

'Nice to meet you too,' I say a little taken aback from how personable he is being. I try to not look, but I am feeling cautious that this interaction is not going unnoticed by the rest of the crew.

'Right, I need to call the wife. See you in a minute.' Dominic walks back to his table and Seb kisses me on the cheek and whispers in my ear.

'If he gets to kiss you, I do too' and flashes me a grin. Shit, I probably should have had the conversation about keeping it professional with Seb before the trip started. Before I even get to respond, we are summoned.

'Right guys, think we need to start boarding,' shouts out Harriet, the Senior Producer.

'I will see you on the plane Soph, pretty sure Dom has got me sitting next to him.'

'OK great, see you then,' as I walk off to join my team as inconspicuously as possible, although this feels impossible as Michael does not miss a beat.

'Erm, what was that my dear? None of us got a kiss from the two hunks of the pack.'

'Oh, right, yeah,' even the air conditioning can't stop my red cheeks, 'I might have a few things I need to tell you.' Michael's eyes light up and having come to know Michael pretty well already, I am sure I can trust him with this bit of intel.

Thankfully my seat is adjacent to Michaels but has lots of privacy which is handy as this is, theoretically my first sleepover with Seb, even if it is on a jumbo jet with hundreds of others. The last thing I want is him to see me potentially drooling when I sleep. I settle in and take a glass of bubbles offered to me and kick back, lapping up this luxury I suddenly find myself in. What a difference a few months make.

Spending my last pounds on a bug exterminator in my tiny bedroom, to now sitting in Business Class and about to have the experience of a lifetime. I think back to some of the decisions I have had to make and thank my lucky stars I took the risks and the leaps, not hanging around in failing relationships. Miles crosses my mind. I had received a couple of clearly intoxicated messages since we broke up and part of me did miss the fun we had, but as I sit here now, I know he would never have been happy with me going away for so long. All his insecurities would have been pushed onto me, potentially ruining this trip and the entire experience. I sit staring out the window and turn to see Seb standing a few rows down, trying to force a case into the overhead locker. His T-Shirt is riding up enough to see his Brad Pitt, Circa "Fight Club" abdomen and all potential regrets of past loves are instantly forgotten.

'Hey Soph,' I wake up and the cabin of the plane is dark, Seb is slightly peering into my business pod and I quickly fix my hair and check my face in the reflection of the TV screen. I scan around the plane and the only noise is the air conditioning and everyone is lying back in their little zones and seemingly asleep.

'Don't worry. I waited until nobody would see us, I understand we should keep this professional,' he whispers, 'but I just came over to check if you are OK and if I could steal a little kiss?' The image of his torso flashes back into my head and I lean in and kiss him. He slides his body into my little booth and the kiss intensifies and I'm not sure if the bubbles are still in my system or the cabin pressure has gone to my head. Suddenly Seb retracts out from my seat and an air stewardess walks past,

'Shit, sorry Soph, I just got carried away.'

'Me too, you better go back to your seat. I'm sure you could get away with anything being the boss's best mate. Me, on the other hand, might not.'

'You will be alright with me kid, don't worry,' as he kisses my head and returns to his seat. I feel pretty sure I am safe in his hands, but if the past few months have taught me anything, it's not to become too reliant on anyone I have met in London.

I swing open my balcony doors and breath in the sea air. This is bliss. The past three hours of plane and airport faff means we have been given three hours to settle into the hotel rooms that are ours for the next few days, refresh and then head to our first production meeting of the trip. I stand and take in everything for a few moments, the room, the view and how kissing Seb on the plane had given me the worst case of butterflies I have felt for ages, possibly ever.

Most of the team have had to share rooms, but due to an odd number of the production crew and me being the newest of the bunch, somehow I have managed to wangle my own seafront room with a view of the entire beach. It's nearly lunchtime in Rio and from the fourth floor, I can make out the people sitting, eating their food and playing volleyball on the sand. Considering the warning we were given on the coach drive from the airport by our local fixer, it seems hard to believe how potentially dangerous this city could be as I look over what looks like heaven. 'Esssh' as I sniff my hair I can smell the lingering scent of the plane on me and as much as I would love to take a siesta, it's obvious my time would be more wisely used having a shower.

'How's your room Soph?' Michael looks up as I walk into the lobby where he and the guys are all perched around a laptop, reading the running order for the following day's shoot.

'A.MAZ.ING! How about you guys?'

'OMGOSH, just the best,' exclaims Michael with his standard dramatic jazz hands.

'Great, apart from the small issue of sharing with him.' Josh casually points to Michael and gets feigned shock in response.

'Anyway, Soph, let's grab you a drink before the meeting,' Michael stands and starts to walk across the fancy marble floors of the hotel's lobby.

'It's really OK Michael, I can go alone.' I say, slightly surprised he feels the need to escort me to the bar.

'I know you can Soph, but it's the first time I have got you alone and away from those bunch of reprobates,' he jokes, gesturing over to the table of our team. 'Look, I have to be honest with you, I saw your sneaky inflight snog with the hunk that is Sebastian Simpson, I can't say I wasn't a little bit jealous,' he cheekily winks at me.

'Oh crap, busted.' I sigh, this is exactly what I don't need.

'At first, I was shocked as I hadn't realised you two even know each other that well. Then I got worried. Look, I wouldn't be a friend if I didn't warn you of how totally tits up this could go for you.' Michael whispers and looks around, cautiously of anyone in earshot.

'I know, I know and I really appreciate your concern. It's all crossed my mind, but...' we both look over in Seb's direction as he stands, both hands in his cargo pants pockets as his biceps bulge out of his tight-fitting white t-shirt, laughing with Dominic.

'He's bloody perfection personified. I get it Soph, I totally do. Just please don't fuck this job up as it's too good of an opportunity for you. No matter how good the body looks that's attached to the penis.'

'A Cappuccino obrigada,' I attempted my best Brazilian Portuguese to the guy behind the bar, hoping he hadn't clocked on to Michael's use of the word penis or understood it for that matter. 'You are totally right, we have both agreed to keep it professional and I know I am the one with more to lose.'

'Good, I'm relieved to hear. Anyway, we better crack on, rapido, rapido we have a show to produce.'

'Right, all the kit is with security and Harriet has a few things to confirm with tomorrow's shoot, but so far, all looking good.' We had been back at the table for five minutes and although I have tried to give Michael my full attention, I have also been distracted with his words of warning, which could be deemed as ironic, considering my focus on work is already wavering.

'We have a lot to film and are weather reliant, with Rio being tropical and renowned for downpours, we have to expect at least a few hurdles along the way. Is everyone good with what we have discussed?' We all nod in agreement, even though I am pretty sure I only picked up on thirty per cent of the meeting.

'LOOK IT IS HIM, I TOLD YOU.' A group of American girls are pointing over in Dominic's direction and near screeching. I'm more than aware of his international fame, but over the past few weeks and seeing him act just like the regular guy he is, for some reason, I am taken aback by these California looking, glossy and glam girls fawning over him and Seb. They seem to be taking an interest in both of them and why wouldn't they? Although Dominic is obviously the rich and famous one, Seb is actually much, much better looking. Michael looks at me and I am sure he is gauging my reaction and I shrug, pretending it's nothing and try to find my inner coolness and fight the urge to go and drag Seb away. After five minutes, which felt like an hour, the over-excited girls leave the lobby with their mitts full of autographs and I am pretty sure one of them had her boobs signed. I sit and act ignorant and as if I haven't witnessed any of it, staring right through the laptop screen which is now perched on my lap.

'Right guys,' suddenly Dominic appears at the coffee table which is packed full of the team, 'I think we need to head into the conference room and get this meeting out the way, then it's time for my famous first-night meal. You haven't experienced that yet have you Sophia? I promise it will be lots of fun.' Dominic smiles and ushers us into a private meeting room. Seb walks in behind me, subtly putting his hand on my bum as he walks past me, giving me a smile as he then walks over to sit next to Dominic at the head of the table.

'It took him two bloody years to remember my name,' Josh loudly whispers as I find a seat next to him, 'I'm pretty sure Dom has a crush on you.' I laugh louder than I should have, considering the room was only at a low murmur, but thankfully no one seems to bat an eyelid.

'I can promise you, Josh, that is absolutely not the case at all.'

The first night party is apparently a ritual of Dominic's, with the idea that it sets the tone for the show and his theory is, happy creatives equals the best filming outcome and due to every one of his shows being a hit, there must be something in it. This evening we are eating on the roof terrace and trying out some of the recipes Dominic will be cooking for the show, so we get a good insight to what we are filming. We have also been given a two-drink maximum and a 10 pm curfew, which seems sensible, if not a little boring.

I have worn a simple black T-Shirt dress and gladiator sandals, it's a humid 29 degrees and I am still fighting the beads of sweat as I glance around to find my team. They are standing near a long table with incredible panoramic views across Rio. It's possibly the most beautiful view I have ever seen. I clock Dominic at the head of the table with Seb sitting with his back to me and we are quickly herded to some seats and I take a spot in between Carly and one of the camera guys.

The drinks and courses are dished out and the evening's discussions revolve around the current and beautiful setting, also, how we need to enjoy this calm before the filming storm begins tomorrow. I sit back and take a deep breath, I appreciate how far I have come with my career so far and I can't bring myself to look in Seb's direction, as Michael's warnings are continually ringing in my ears. As much as I feel the urge to go and enjoy this experience closer to him, I know I can't be so obvious in front of the crew because anything I currently feel is purely based on lust and risking my reputation and position in the team, really doesn't feel worth it right now.

Thankfully, the evening is being wrapped up, I feel totally shattered as it's been the longest of days travelling. Even with the sleep on the plane, I just want to put on my pj's, wash my face and get into a fully horizontal bed with zero turbulence. The feeling seems mutual around the table and we all start to gather our belongings and head down to our rooms. I take one last look across the twinkling Rio skies and feel the excitement tingling in my very full and satisfied belly.

'5 am alarms ladies, hope you get some decent sleep,' as I blow a kiss to Shauna and Carly, who is in the room next to me.

'You too Soph. If you need us, just bang on the wall,' Carly says as she vanishes into her room. I go to close my room door, but before I get to fully shut it, there is a hand against it. I feel an instant pang of fear until I hear a whisper,

'Hey it's me.' I release my weight from the door and Seb is standing there,

'for fuck's sake, you scared the crap out of me!' I put my hand on my chest and felt it racing.

'Oh, I'm so sorry, hadn't meant to scare you,' I walk over and collapse on the bed,

'It's just, after all the warnings about safety today, feeling the force of a hand stopping me from closing the door was pretty unnerving.' Seb closes the door behind him and walks over, sitting on the bed next to me.

'I hadn't even thought of that, I just wanted to surprise you. The whole meal I could hear you laughing and chatting and I felt like I was missing out,' I look at his puppy eyes as he learns his elbows back and lies onto the bed, I knock his arm from under him playfully and it makes him fall flat on the bed.

'You little git,' he starts laughing as I quickly get up and run to the balcony doors before he could retaliate.

'Come here and Look at this, it really is possibly the most beautiful view I've ever seen.' Seb walks over and as I open the doors and look out, he grabs my hips and pulls me back into him and kisses my neck. He stops and we both stand for a few moments, looking at the most incredible horizon across the South Atlantic Ocean and I can't help myself, I turn and kiss him. I feel like a film siren from the 1920's Rio De Janeiro, being wooed by one of the most handsome men I have ever met.

'Right you,' we stop kissing and our noses gently touch, 'we have an early start and your mate, also known as my boss, is relying on us to do our jobs and I am shattered.'

'Yes, you are right and as much as I want to stay, we do have a big day tomorrow and I don't fancy being on the wrong side of Dom, he can be a total grouch. See you in the morning, but this will be continued,' as he kisses me one last time and sneaks out of my hotel room.

After waking to the alarm ringing in my ear at 5 am and mild panic as to what is actually suitable to wear for the predicted thirty-degree heat in Rio, I ended up rushing down to the lobby to grab a coffee and a slice of toast on my way out. Which was a close call, as the final load of the filming kit was being loaded onto the coach just as I boarded, more flustered and panicked than I had hoped. I edge into a free seat and take a sigh of relief that I made it on time and try to calm my heated and slightly sweaty cheeks.

The first shoot location is a very extravagant penthouse apartment and has the most amazing views of the Christo Redentor and Rio. Well, that's what the booking website promised and I am just hoping it lives up to expectations because if not, the team and I won't be getting off to the best start with our location scouting.

The last to climb on the coach is, of course, the star of the show, Dominic with Seb in tow as he films every move of the superstar for his "behind the scenes" footage. I watch in awe as Seb does his job and try not to look too obvious as I give him the once over. I am totally distracted by his t-shirt clinging to his biceps and flattering board shorts which fit perfectly around his bum, I suddenly realise I have been shovelling the remains of my breakfast rather inelegantly into my mouth.

'OK Soph, I think you are going to need an intervention for this one.' I nearly spit my coffee out as I see Michael has been watching me from the gap of the seat in front.

'Jesus, Michael. How long have you been watching me? You weirdo.'

'Long enough my darling to know you are smitten,' as he rolls his eyes and shakes his head, 'don't complain to me that I hadn't warmed you Hunny.' He turns back in his seat and I sigh deeply. It could all go so wrong, but what if it goes so right too? Maybe I shouldn't be so cautious, so much time wasted on men who were never right, maybe for once, Seb could just be the one for me.

We arrive, driving through huge gates and guards onto the complex. It's more stunning in reality that all the photos the team and I had been sifting through. I step off the coach and head over to a balcony overlooking the city and I watch the sunrise over the ocean, taking it all in for a moment.

'It's amazing, isn't Soph?' Seb stands next to me, also with his eyes transfixed on the pink and orange glow of the sky.

'Come on you guys, there is an even better view up here,' Dominic shouts to us and grabbing a few bags of kit we follow the crew up into the lift and up to the penthouse suite.

'Drop that stuff and come over here you two. Seriously, whoever found this spot needs a pay rise.'

'Oh good news for you then Soph,' as Seb jokingly digs an elbow into my side.

'You found this location?' Dominic turns to me and I suddenly feel slightly coy.

'Erm, Yeah I did, but in fairness, the whole team had a part to play.'

'Actually,' Michael is suddenly appearing and standing next to me, 'it was down to Soph. I in fact, was unsure to start with. Take the credit when you can Soph, you might not hear much more from Dom as he's a tough one to please.'

'Hey you, I'm not that bad,' Dominic protests as Michael has already walked off laughing. 'I'm not that bad, am I mate?' Dominic turns to Seb for reassurance.

'I'm not getting involved in this one.' he shrugs and looks at me, nodding in jest.

'Whatever let's get on with this shoot,' Dominic grunts as he skulks off.

'He is hard to please, but you did an ace job. Proud of your Soph.' Seb rests his hand on my shoulder and before anyone can witness this moment I spot the team gathering in a huddle and head over to join them, 'Thanks Seb, it is a great spot,' I say loudly and casually as I walk off. It's slightly cold and abrupt, but we did promise to act professionally.

The shoot is going to plan and everyone is beaming ear to ear. Even though it's summer here in the south of the Equator, the sun sets early at around 7.30 pm, so we only have until 5 pm with good enough natural light to shoot in. As it's already 4 pm, the entire team is scurrying around and setting up for the final scene. This will be a slow pan across the table of guests eating the food Dominic has, along with his co-chefs, prepared. It's the most important shot of the day as it's the classic pan of the meal that supports Dominic's brand and image of "Food with Friends", which is the reason he got so famous in the first place.

'Sophia,' after avoiding even eye contact most of the day, Seb sees his opportunity to grab a quiet chat as everyone over analyzes the position of some candlestick holders as they crowd around the camera with the director. 'We should be back to the hotel by 6 pm. Do you fancy a little stroll along the beach, before it gets too dark? I have a feeling that people are free to eat in the hotel or rooms this evening, so we could spend it together and away from the glare of that lot,' as he points subtly to the team, who are still debating a candlestick. 'That's unless you have made plans of course?'

'Well, I was going to meet up with a hunky Brazilian guy in particularly small and clingy Speedos, but thinking about it, you are more my type.'

'Jeez, I actually started to believe you for a second then Soph. Well, I can't promise Speedos, but if you like a guy in boardshorts, then I am your man,' Seb says, perching his hands on his hips and raising his jawline, jokingly showing off his physique and probably not realising how damn fine he actually looks.

'It sounds like an ace plan to me. I do, however, have to email my parents and reassure them that I am alive, but after that, I am free.'

'Amazing, I will catch you at the hotel.' I feel a shiver of excitement down my spine as Seb walks off to wrap up his shooting and I head to join the fellow AP's in the hope they are finally over the candle saga.

Chapter Eleven

Hi Sophia darling,

Dad and I are so pleased it's all going well and thank you for the photos of your room and view, it's lovely to see you are enjoying it so much.

All is fine here, your sisters send their love and Charly thanks you for your good wishes message. The treatment seemed to go well and we will find out soon if it has helped in any way when the results come back in a few days, we will keep you in the loop, don't worry.

Dad is sitting next to me and keeps butting in, but before I launch the laptop at his head, he has been on that bloody YouTube again and keeps watching videos about Brazil. He wants to remind you to not wear anything expensive-looking and try to blend in.

Next time, could you please just go to Spain or something? That would really save us a lot of worries!

Keep up with the emails and photos,

We love you and stay safe,

Mum & Dad xxxxxx

I can imagine them bickering, sitting together at their office desk and it brings a smile to my face. I feel bad for being away for so long and leaving them so concerned, but also, they have forever encouraged my sisters and me to take on these challenges and adventures. Our motto growing up was, "be brave, be happy and always be kind". They missed out on the, "don't go to developing countries and out of our comfort zone" part, so their bad.

The door knocks, it's 6.30 pm on the dot, so I know exactly who to expect. 'Hey, are you ready?' Seb stands, khaki shorts hanging low, with a relatively fitted white T-shirt and shades, propping up a few curls on his head.

'Yes, I don't need too much, do I? I've hidden some cash in my bra as apparently carrying a bag here screams wealth and makes me more likely to be mugged. According to my slightly overbearing parents, that is,' I roll my eyes and Seb laughs.

'In fairness, your folks are right. As much as I would love to take my camera and take some amazing shots of that sunset, I'm pretty nervous about showing off a piece of kit like that. Let's start with a walk and see how brave we feel after that!'

Walking down the famous patterned pavement of Ipanema Beach, one of the most renowned promenades in the world, I link Sebs arm, not just because I want to be close to him, but because being close to him makes me feel incredibly safe. Although, as we walk and talk, watching everyone having fun in the last of the evening sun, there feels very little to be worried about in Rio. Numerous Volleyball matches and at least a dozen football games being played along the beach and it's exactly how I had hoped it would be. I see a store selling the famous, Brazil flagged Havaiana flip flops, 'Do you mind if we look in there, if there is anything we need to take home with us, it's a pair of those!'

'Wowzaas, that's like £4 or something?' Seb says shocked holding a pair.

'I know, crazy right? What colour do you like and what size?' He grabs a blue pair in a gigantic size and holds them against his feet,

'These will do.'

'Jesus, are you sure they are big enough? Glad I know what I am working with.' I say cheekily and instantly hoping that Seb doesn't catch on to my filthy mind.

'Well, maybe you just have to find out for sure,' as he leans in and kisses me softly on the lips and it confirms he did indeed understand my "rated 18" thoughts.

'Buy?' The shop assistant sets us both back with a startle.

'Dios,' Seb waves both pairs and I hand over the money, 'No I will get those,' Seb tries to protest.

'Seriously, on me. You got us coffee in London, I can stretch to a pair of flip flops in Brazil. Hashtag relationship goals.' I mock as Seb takes the bag the flip flops and holds my hand as we head back onto the infamous mosaic path.

'Well thank you, I will treasure them forever. I also like that you referred to this as a relationship.' Seb wraps his arm around my waist and pulls me in a little closer.

'Well don't get too excited, there are lots of versions of relationships. I have a relationship with my grandparents, parents and dog!'

'Seriously, you aren't comparing me to your dog, are you?'

'Erm, kinda. It's just that there are many, many versions of the word relationship. I am just managing your expectations,' I flash a grin at Seb. As controlled as I want to be around this man, there is something about him that just makes me want to lose all my guards.

'Anyway,' he changes the subject as we walk slowly in the pink and orange light of the sunset, 'Dominic has to have a meeting this evening with the Exec Producers, so I was wondering if you fancied dinner in our suite, it's the penthouse, I'm not sure if I mentioned that bit,' he says in a joking and bragging manner.

'I did wonder where you are staying. I'll be honest, the idea of crossing paths with Dominic feels like a professional line could blurred very quickly. I, however, have a beautiful room all to myself and a balcony which would be a perfect setting for dinner, if you would like to do that?'

'That, my gorgeous Sophia, sounds like the best plan yet.'

We continue to walk along the beach for a few more minutes, but as the sun dips out of sight, we walk back to the hotel slowly. 'I really feel very lucky right now,' I say to Seb. 'It's been a bit of a strange time so far in London, a few housing issues and I put my trust in people, that didn't quite work out. Being here now though, this life experience really makes all that stress worthwhile and obviously meeting you has been pretty cool too.' I get a gentle kiss on the head from Seb.

'Sorry to hear that you had a shitty time, I can totally relate. I could have easily written off the end of last year, but had I not been through the dramas with my ex, I wouldn't be here now. It's times like these, you realise how wrong situations and relationships were. I don't want to sound like a total cheese ball, but I have honestly never met anyone like you Soph. All my relationships failed before as I just couldn't see it lasting and my focus of work always annoyed my ex. Today, I loved working alongside you and us both just doing our own thing, it was actually really sexy watching you so invested in your work. I also love that you totally turned down spending anytime in Dominic's company and the penthouse. The number of exes who were so desperate to be near him and his fame got so frustrating.'

'Scientists, surgeons, nurses, those kinds of people I bow down to. No disrespect to Dominic at all, but I'm just not fussed. The way I see people stare at him and pamper to his needs, it's all a bit cringe if I am going to be totally honest. Although, please don't tell him that, I can't risk damaging his ego as he does pay my salary.'

'Don't you worry, I would never risk denting that fragile ego of his,' Seb laughs, 'I totally agree. I've known Dom forever and to me, he will always be that geeky teen, barely able to find a girl who would kiss him. It's amazing what a good haircut and some fame can do for a guy.'

'I'm sure you have never had that problem hey, have you Seb, with those perfect curly locks?' I tease.

'Well,' as he straightens his T-Shirt, 'I have a queue a ladies lined up, as you can see,' he turns around and ironically there are a group of women in bikini tops and the smallest cut-off jean shorts, walking a few feet behind us, he looks back at me sheepishly and shrugs.

'I expect nothing less. In fact, Seb, if you weren't so in demand, quite honestly I wouldn't be interested.'

We arrive back at the hotel and have managed to get from the lobby and to my room with no one witnessing us together. 'Right, here's the menu, what do you fancy?' I hand Seb the room service list and open the balcony doors, pulling a small tea and coffee table and two chairs in front, creating an idyllic eating position. The warm breeze flows through and the remains of the sunset light the room.

'Right, I have decided what I want, what do you fancy?' He puts his arm around me and his hand caresses my bum. I instantly drop the menu and without even an effort, he pulls my legs up around his waist and lies me down onto the bed. We kiss as I pull his T-shirt over his taut torso and strong shoulders. Pulling back, he undoes the button on my jean shorts, slipping them over my hips, my feet and then gently throwing them on the floor. Running his hands back down my thighs to my hips, I sit up so he can pull the T-shirt over my head and we fall back slowly together as he kisses my neck and his hands are exploring and caressing me all over. I feel tingles every inch he touches and I start to undo the belt on his shorts, managing to slide them over his hips and he kicks them off in one easy move. I sit up and twist my legs over the top of Seb's lap as we kiss and I can't argue with the fact that I'm prepared to risk it all right now.

We lie with the warm breeze flowing over our naked bodies, half covered in the crisp white bed sheets. I had imagined what it would have been like with Seb, on more than one occasion and in my current state of delirium, I have zero regrets. He strokes my arm as I lie with my back into him, both of us looking out to the beach. 'The chemistry I have with you is something else Sophia. I don't know what it is, but just smelling your skin makes me want to do all kinds of things to you.' I roll over and kiss him on the lips,

'Same here Seb. I'm really, really hungry, shall we order?'

'Morning Sophia,' Seb kisses my neck and cheek, 'I will head back to my room and get ready, it's 5.15, so we have 30 mins before meeting downstairs,' I stretch out feeling relaxed.

' SHIT. 30 mins.' I jump out of bed and run towards the bathroom, 'see you downstairs.' I dash in and out of the shower and the only good thing about this constant humidity is that drying hair is not an issue. Hair thrown up in a top knot, a simple navy T-shirt dress and a pair of the Havaianas I purchased are perfect for today's shoot.

Today was going to be the more challenging ones, as the location and theme is more traditional Brazil, so we are heading a little further into the less cosmopolitan side of town. We have been warned traffic is an issue and that could potentially eat into the day significantly, so the call time is particularly early this morning. It's a local 85-year-old woman who Dominic will be cooking with and she speaks very little to zero English, so with the translator and all the hurdles that will bring it may just be one of the more interesting days and not necessarily in a good way.

We all load onto the coach and there is silence for the majority of the hours drive. I am sitting next to Michael and he has already gone back to sleep on my shoulder, which saves any awkward questions of how I had spent my evening. So, although the weight of his head is slightly uncomfortable, it's also a blessing.

As warned, we start to hit traffic as the rush hours approach and there are cars back to back everywhere, with a lot of them at standstill. There must be hundreds of mopeds buzzing in and out of the hoards of vehicles and with the beeping horns and revving of engines from every angle, I have the overwhelming feeling of claustrophobia and being stifled. Even from the comfort of the air conditioned coach. Seb, who is sitting four rows in front of me has been asked to put his camera away and out of sight. I assume this must be due to security reasons and trying to not look so obvious that we have a celebrity on board. This is the first time I have seen the security stand and look the most "on-guard" since leaving the Rio airport. My anxiety is rising minute by minute. There is something very daunting about our current situation and I hear a few other murmurings from my colleagues who confirm my fears. Seb turns to look at me and subtly mouths 'are you OK?' I shrug back. I can't lie, my face clearly says it all. I just want to get to our destination safely and then return back to the hotel without another drive like this.

Finally, we arrive and the moment we offload straight into the local restaurant where we will be filming, all my anxiety seems to calm and I feel ridiculous that I let that coach drive get the better of me. I look around the restaurant and it is full of local charm and the co-star, Marcia, is sitting patiently surrounded by all her local ingredients with a huge welcoming smile and the setting could not be more perfect.

‘Right guys, we haven’t got long to set up. Let’s crack on and get this one in the bag,’ Dominic calls from his Director's chair, as he has his hair coiffed and face powdered.

A few hectic hours later, we break for lunch. Which is handy, because there is a whole array of traditional Brazilian cuisine which has just been freshly cooked as part of the show. The smell has been filling the restaurant and making my stomach groan for the past hour and after a rushed slice of toast at barely the crack of dawn, I am ready to eat a feast. We all sit down and tuck into plates piled high and catch up after an evening away from each other. 'So what did you get up to last night Sophia? We did knock on your door before dinner, but obviously you weren't in,' Carly asks from across the table with a raised brow. I had anticipated these questions so had considered my lie in advance,

'Oh I fell asleep and had about an hour nap, then ordered room service. It was a very chilled one. What about you guys?' Quickly I deflected.

'Well, the four of us just went to the hotel bar and pretty much stayed there all night.' Michael says, looking at me with a questioning look over his glass as he takes a sip of his drink.

'It's frustrating we can't investigate the city more. I hope we get a chance to at some point before we leave.' Shauna gripes. Before any of us had time to respond, our attention has been drawn to some kind of kerfuffle at the restaurant entrance. The security guards are both standing together with what looks like a group of other men outside of the door. It's caught the entire room's attention instantly and everyone's heads are turned to assess what is going on. I look to see where Seb is and we lock eyes as he looks back at me from the other side of the room. I catch in my peripheral view, Dominic being moved to the furthest point away from whatever is happening, by one of the security team. Jesus, it suddenly crosses my mind, he is known to be worth millions of pounds and here we are, miles away from the hotel and with a security team of two. The fear that we have greatly overestimated their ability to protect us hits me as I grab our file of contacts and the numbers for emergency services. Scouring through and trying to refrain from panicking, I find the Federal Police number and write 194 on my hand. 'Guys, who has their mobiles?'

I whisper to the table as everyone remains transfixed on the commotion, 'I have stored everything in my room safe and don't have mine with me.' I continue, urging someone to respond.

'I have mine,' Michael taps me under the table with it. He's obviously on the same page as me and I flash him the number on my hand as he types it into his phone. 'He leans over and whispers into my ear, 'it's saved under BP, for Brazil Police if you need to find it. My password is 1999.'

A few heart-racing moments later, one of the security guards has walked back in and it seems the men causing the problem have dispersed. He heads to speak with the Director and Exec team and within seconds there is an announcement. 'Right guys, Ben, Dom's personal security has recommended we pack up all the kit up, in the quickest, but calmest fashion we can. The coach will be here in a minute, so start to gather everything we own and get it packed and board the coach, ASAP. Absolutely, and I mean ABSOLUTELY NO HANGING AROUND.'

Seb walks over to me as I start to gather every item we own in my surrounding area, 'right, I have to go with Dominic in a car that has just turned up for him. Apparently, he is not safe and a few of the less desirable locals have recognised him. The plan is to get him out of here to diffuse the situation. I don't want to leave here without you Sophia, I am so sorry I have to do this.' He looks at me with concerned eyes and it pains me that we are surrounded by colleagues and I can't just grab him.

'It's fine, that sounds like a sensible plan. You better go quickly, they are all heading for the door,' he rubs the top of my right arm.

'You stay safe,' he says walking away.

It's incredible how long it can take to set-up a location shoot, but yet a few panicked minutes later, the entire production team is packed onto the coach and the restaurant is empty of our belongings. Thankfully, we still have one of the security guarding the front of the coach and at least five people have been selected to keep the emergency police number dialled in their phone, just in case.

We have been driving back to the safety of the hotel for what feels like an hour, but in fact is only ten minutes as I look out of the tinted coach windows, down to the dusty and winding suburban Rio streets, still packed full of cars, vans and scooters. I look around the coach and Michael, who is sitting next to me, is happily chatting away to colleagues across the aisle and the feeling of tension has been slowly lifting.

'How are you feeling?' Asks Michael, as he turns to face me.

'My anxiety levels went pretty high for a moment, but feel like my heart rate is calming. Maybe there was nothing in it anyway. We could have just overreacted? It may well have been a misunderstanding. There is the language barrier after all.' I try to convince myself.

'I know right? It did feel A LOT at the time, but actually, I'm sure it was nothing. Always better to be safe than sorry I guess. Security seemed pretty adamant to get Dom out of there, so what can we do? Without him, we haven't got a show anyway!' He barely finishes his sentence when the coach comes to a grinding halt.

'EVERYONE DOWN, GET TO THE GROUND NOW,' the security guard is shouting at us. Michael and I scurry into the footwell of our seats and we can't see a thing. I can't hear exactly what is being said, but I am pretty sure the security guard is no longer on the coach. A large bang and by the shake of the coach, it sounds like the luggage compartment is being opened. I'm physically shaking and suddenly feel the urge to throw-up as I look over and watch Michael scramble for his phone and he dials the police number we saved earlier. The only other sounds inside the coach are what I assume are the other colleagues making the same call to the police and the sound of heavy, panicked breathing. I am pretty sure it's Carly who I can hear, having her sobs stifled by Shauna, who is seemingly trying to quiet and calm her. Suddenly a Brazilian voice starts shouting in broken English, 'UP, UP, UP NOW. UP, WATCHES, JEWELS, PHONES, HERE NOW.' I cautiously stand to see a scruffy-looking guy with what I can only guess is a semi-automatic gun in his hand and is waving it above his head. He has a sports looking bag in the other hand, which my colleagues are starting to throw their items at. I can see people in tears, removing wedding rings; engagement rings, earrings, everything valuable they have on them. I take my earrings out, I only have two sets of small gold studs in each ear and fumble to keep them in my shaking hands and do everything I can, to not be sick as the robber approaches us. His cold eyes glare at me, up and down, as he checks I am free of all my belongings and suddenly, from nowhere, Michael gets hit on the side of his head with either part of the gun or hand, 'PHONE NOW,', Michael throws his phone in relunctly and the thief continues up the aisle.

'Oh my gosh, are you OK?' I whisper as I put my arm around Michael's shoulder and look to see a bloody graze on the temple of his head.

'I feel a little dizzy, but don't make a fuss. He's coming back.' I peer out the window, desperate to see help, but there is not a siren to be heard and all I can see are at least five other guys, emptying the contents of the coach onto the back of an old rusty pickup truck. Of course, there is no number plate, it's just a white, filthy truck. The gun-wielding guy runs off the coach and there is silence as we all watch them jump onto the back of the pickup as it drives off.

'SHIT, WHERE IS MATTY?' One of the camera guys shouts out, I realise Matty must be the security guard who was looking after us. The coach driver jumps off with a couple of the team and I can hear a few shouts and suddenly they all climb back on with Matty slumped over their shoulders.

'HE'S OK, IT LOOKS LIKE A KNOCK TO THE HEAD, BUT HE'S ALIVE.' Which are words I hadn't anticipated hearing today. There are sobs throughout the coach and suddenly the coach driver closes the door and starts to pull away.

'SHOULDN'T WE WAIT FOR THE POLICE AND AMBULANCE?' Harriet shouts.

'LADY, I AM NOT HANGING AROUND HERE FOR A MOMENT LONGER. WE NEED TO GET THIS GUY SOME HELP,' the coach driver shouts back and starts to drive at speed. Michael is staring and shaking so I put my arm around him and do my best to comfort him.

'It's OK, we are all alive and we are going to be back at the hotel really soon.' I don't really know what to say, that's all I can manage and I barely believe it myself. One of the PA's is administering first aid to Matty and the Coach driver is speaking on his walky-talky, I understand nothing of what he is saying, but I hear polícia being repeated at volume a few times over.

As we pull up to the hotel, there are four police cars lined up outside and one ambulance. Dominic and Seb are standing there with the security guard who left with them and he is the first to run on to the coach and help carry Matty off to the ambulance. Everybody starts to clamber off, row by row and the police are taking a few people aside at a time. I help Michael get off the coach and pass him to one of the paramedic women, 'he got a knock to the head with a gun and I am pretty sure he is in shock,' the woman nods, assessing the graze and then walks him over in the direction of the ambulance. I stand and evaluate the current situation I find myself in, in total disbelief. My colleagues are holding and comforting each other, a couple of the team look like they are vomiting behind the coach, but before I get to feel any kind of emotion other than shock, Seb grabs me and pulls me into his chest.

'For fuck's sake I am so angry for leaving you. I am so, so, so sorry. There were us thinking Dom was in danger, but actually it was the coach that was the target.' I can't find any words as he wraps his arms around me, but within a second of being in the safety of his hug, every second of fear comes flushing back and I start to sob into his chest.

'Seb, take Sophia to the penthouse, everyone is going up there and we will all stay there for a while. It feels like the safest place right now,' Dominic is ushering everyone into the hotel and I see Shauna, Carly and Josh all huddling through together,

'Do you know where Michael is?' I ask them.

'He's having what seems like a panic attack, so they are just keeping a close eye on him right now. They asked us to leave him, so they could manage the situation,' Carly whispers. Seb has his arms around me and no one flinches or questions it because everybody is holding and caring for everybody right now and I don't even care, I just need to feel safe.

We get to the Penthouse suite and everybody is being offered a hot drink and are being seated, 'Sophia, come here for a second,' Seb directs me from a large lounge area down a corridor and into a bedroom, 'Use this phone and call your parents now. It will be all over the news very quickly that Dom's coach has been robbed. They need to know you are OK,' as he hands me his mobile. I dial the home number and try to compose myself.

'Mum, Dad can you hear me?' I swallow down the lump in my throat.

'Hi darling, it's Dad, terrible line. We weren't expecting a call. Is everything OK?'

'Is mum there?'

'Yes I'm here, you are on loudspeaker Sophia.'

'Great. Well I don't want you to panic, but we had to leave a filming location as we were under threat of some locals and then as we left, the coach was robbed,' I pause, because I know I have to be honest, it's only a matter of time before they see the news, '... It was robbed at gunpoint.'

'Sophia,' Mum starts sobbing.

'Please get on the first plane home. I don't care what it costs, we will pay,' Dad says and I can hear his voice cracking.

'It's OK. I'm fine, I'm shaken up and feeling a little sick, but I just handed over my earrings and that was it. Some of the team had to give their sentimental jewellery and the security guard is currently getting medical attention. It was so scary, but honestly, I am fine.' I start crying. I'm not fine. I am way out of my depth and being back in the Cotswolds in the family bubble sounds perfect right now.

'Hi Mr and Mrs Williams, my name is Sebastian and I am on the trip. Unfortunately, I wasn't with your daughter, as we had assumed it was Dominic that was the problem, so we left. I can only promise that I will not leave Sophia out of my sight again and will get her home safely to you.'

'Hi, erm Sebastian was it?' my mum suddenly stops crying, 'Sophia, could you take me off loudspeaker please?' I take the phone and hold it to my ear. I know what is coming.

'Who is that? He sounds handsome.' Typical mother, how can anybody "sound" handsome.

'Yes, well, he is and hopefully you will get to meet him one day soon.' I look at Seb and he smiles, which is the first one I have seen for at least an hour. 'Mum, I have to go, this is Seb's phone and I need to get back to the team.'

'OK darling, well we both love you more than you will ever know and thanking our lucky stars our baby is safe. You take care of her please Sebastian.'

'He can't hear you mum, but I will pass on the message. Love you both and I will email later.' I hang up and hand the phone back to Seb. 'You have to take care of me, mum says.' Seb walks over and grabs me and plants kiss after kiss on my head and then a gentle kiss on the lips.

'I want you to be my girlfriend,' he looks me directly in the eyes with his hands gently on my shoulders, 'what happened today confirms to me that I couldn't imagine you not in my life. I want to take care of you and I was so scared and angry when I wasn't able to protect you.' I kiss him on the lips, 'is that a yes?'

'Absolutely,' I smile and Seb grabs my waist, lifting and spinning me around his excessively huge hotel room and it's brought to a halt with a knock at the door.

'One second,' Seb calls out whilst putting me down and heads to see who is there. It's Dominic.

'Hi you two, are you OK Sophia? I am so sorry we left you like that earlier, I feel so devastated this has happened to the team,' he walks into the room.

'I'm OK. How is everyone else? Any updates on Matty or Michael?'

'Yes, concussion for Matty, he was hit by the grip of the gun. He just needs to rest as he refused to go to the hospital. Michael is in shock and is in the other room. Do you both mind coming out to the lounge, we need to make some announcements?'

'Of course,' we say in unison. We follow Dominic to the large open plan lounge, where everybody is either sitting or standing around with a low volume of nervous chatter that fills the room.

'Right guys, firstly, can I just say how awful I feel for leaving you like that. We were under the impression I was the issue, so security thought it was safer to get me out of the situation. Obviously we totally cocked that up and they were after the kit etc. Anything you have had stolen, I will get replaced and anything that is irreplaceable, I will do whatever I can do to put it right. I have spoken to the Police and they believe there was a tip-off. I doubt very much that it was Marcia, but one of her family or restaurant-goers could have got wind that we would be there. We hadn't realised what sitting ducks we were. So, I have made the decision to cancel this trip and I want you all to be reunited with your loved ones immediately. We are in the process of changing the flights, but I just need to confirm with a couple of you what you would like to do. For the next two weeks, you will all be on enforced holiday which is paid and won't affect your allocated days. I want my team to be happy and safe. Unfortunately, with all it's beauty that Brazil brings, it is not for us and we were not prepared enough. We will get back to the drawing board and probably revisit somewhere in Europe as an alternative. For now, stay here, go to your rooms, do whatever makes you happy and feel safe and by the end of today, we will have everything set for getting the hell out of here and back home.'

Chapter Twelve

Everyone has left the penthouse and I find myself stretched out and lying back on a lounger, on the enormous decked terrace overlooking miles of Rio through the glass balcony panels. 'Here you go,' Seb passes me a glass of chilled white wine and perches next to me.

'Hey you two, just off the phone from Arabella and she is livid. Blaming everything and everyone, forgetting we were the only ones who were actually unscathed,' Dom points between him and Seb. 'She's flying to LA tonight and I am going to meet her there, hopefully, tomorrow evening. It's amazing that Arabella will never go anywhere with me, but of course, LA is never a problem for her,' he rolls his eyes mocking and gives a very different impression of the relationship that is photographed in all the magazines. 'What are your guy's plans? I was kind of hoping you would come with me?'

'Well actually Dom, I would rather get Sophia home safely, I also promised her parents I would.'

'No, you tit,' he slaps Seb's knee, 'Not just you, both of you. I would love Arabella to meet you, Sophia. She will be so happy to meet the woman who has cheered this miserable shit up.' I look at Seb and he glances back, shrugging. A trip to LA feels like a difficult offer to turn down and I don't feel desperate to get back to the UK, just eager to leave Brazil right now.

'Look, neither of you is in work for a couple of weeks and we have the Condo there waiting for us. It's my treat for you both. I need to make it up to this one, for making him leave you earlier Sophia. He was worried sick, I have never seen him so wound up. He asked to go back to the coach, but no one was willing to take him,' Seb shrugs in response to Dominic's version of events.

'It's true, but in fairness Dom, we were all nervous for your safety. Having my girlfriend on there though, was pretty intense.' I look at him, with all the sudden decisions taking place and changes, I had bypassed the fact I had agreed to be his girlfriend.

'ERM, girlfriend? In which case, you definitely MUST join us for a couple of weeks vacay,' Dom clasps his hands in a mock pleading manner and Seb looks to me for my reaction and I shrug casually.

'I'll be honest and say that my head is a little all over the place. Today has really wiped my brain of any clear thinking, so I am actually happy for you to decide Seb. The idea of a break in LA is not sounding totally horrendous right now.' I lay back and soak up a little more sun and enjoy a moment of calm.

'In that case, I will keep taking advantage of your current state of mind and say yes Dom, we would love to join you and Arabella in LALA land.'

As the coach fills, flights home have been confirmed for the majority of the team and they have managed to be accommodated for this evening's departure. The remaining few of us have one more evening in the hotel, but the plan is that all of us will have departed Brazil by lunchtime tomorrow. It's only been a few hours since the coach robbery, but the PA's have been working non-stop to fulfil Dominic's wishes to get everyone home as quickly as possible.

'Sophia, are you sure you are OK here? It doesn't feel right leaving you. No AP should be left behind!' Michael stands next to me with a bandage covering his head wound.

'I will be fine. I appreciate your concern though Michael, I really do. How do you feel?'

'I'm OK, I just want to be home and with my mum. God, I sound like a child, but that's all I really want.' I hug him tightly one last time.

'I don't blame you, get home safe and I will see you soon. Email if you can, when you land, so I know you are back safe.'

'Of course,' Michael promises as he heads towards the coach door. Josh, Shauna and Carly are all leaning against the windows and waving maniacally from the coach and I wave back, blowing them kisses. Having only worked for the company for a few weeks, it's amazing how close an encounter such as the one we just experienced, can bring you instantly closer together. I feel a pang of sadness to see them drive away and leave in such unexpected and scary circumstances. The few of us remaining, Dominic; Seb, two camera people, one of Dominic's PAs, Matty and Ben will be either flying back to the UK first thing in the morning or in the opposite direction to Los Angeles. We all stand a little dumbstruck as we watch a police escort direct the coach out of sight.

'Right guys, let's grab some dinner in the penthouse and then get some sleep, early doors in the morning and I'm sure, like me, you are all in need of a strong drink.' Dominic sets the plan for the evening as we head back into the hotel.

'Sophia, if it's OK with you, I would like to grab all your belongings and take them to my room? I just do not like the idea of you being alone in the hotel and as you know, there is more than enough space with me.' Seb puts his arm around my shoulder and pulls me closer as we walk through the hotel lobby and to the lift.

'That sounds perfect.'

'I've ordered a whole range of food from the restaurant and they will be up in about thirty mins, so if you want to grab showers etc, this is the time to do it.' Dominic seems to have it all covered, the guilt for leaving the team is clearly weighing heavily on his mind.

'I wouldn't mind a shower and freshening up if that's OK with you Seb?'

'Of course, I will go and get us a drink ready for dinner and I could do with chatting to Dom about our trip. There are a few things I have always wanted to do in California and never really had the chance, it's always been Malibu and shopping malls. Would you mind if I planned a few things?'

'Definitely not, I'm totally up for an adventure. If you fancy a little trip up the Big Sur, that is supposed to be A.MAZ.ING and also I have always wanted to visit Carmel.'

'NO WAY!! That was on my list, I love that Clint Eastwood was the Mayor there!'

'I KNOW, RIGHT?! I also have another request though, if we go, please can we stay at Doris Day's Inn?'

'Your wish, dear Sophia, is my command,' as Seb grabs my hand and spins me around. 'I know it's been the worst day and abrupt ending to the trip, but we will make the next couple of weeks so much fun and I promise today will be a distant memory.'

'Yes please, that would be amazing. Everything seems so surreal right now and what with the robbery and now this intense excitement of a sudden trip to LA, it all feels a bit like a weird rollercoaster. Part of me thinks I might wake up in a second and it's all been a dream.' Seb walks over and wraps his arms around me, kissing my forehead.

'I think the best thing for you right now is to get into that shower, freshen up and then feel free to use the hotel phone to call your folks. They probably need a little more reassuring you are safe, especially as the news has apparently already hit Twitter. Maybe let them know the plan for the next couple of weeks if you are definitely, definitely sure you don't want to go home?'

'I'm sure I just want to stay with you right now. The fact we will be in California is a massive bonus.'

'Well that is music to my ears. I promise we will have loads of fun. Come out whenever you are ready and I will have a glass of whatever you would like waiting.'

'A cold glass of white wine would be amazing please. Also, thank you for everything Seb,' I peck him on the lips and he heads out of the room. I walk over and perch myself on the edge of the bed, looking out across the miles of ocean as the evening draws in and prepare in my head, what I am going to tell my parents. The fact that I won't be returning home, but will be going to stay with a world-famous chef, his wife and my new boyfriend in LA. If I wasn't living it, I wouldn't believe it.

I walk out to what appears to be a banquet laid out in the lounge and dining area. People are chatting, eating and laughing. Something, whether it's Dominic's hospitality or the flowing wine, has definitely helped improve the spirits of the remaining workforce.

'Hey,' Seb spots me and breaks his conversation to walk over, 'everything OK?'

'All good, probably the best shower I have had in ages. Oh, and yeah, you probably are referring to my parents and are they OK with me not going home? I'm not sure if it was the bit about me staying with an A-lister and his wife, or the bit about my new boyfriend, but they were surprisingly excited about the whole situation. I'm sure my mum is organising a friend get together as we speak, purely for the purposes of gloating about her daughter's new acquaintances,' I laugh, but actually there is more truth in that than I would honestly want to admit.

'Well, whatever the reason, I am just happy to get to keep you to myself for a bit longer.' We both turn to the chime of a glass being tapped and our attention is caught.

'Hi all. If I could have your attention for a minute please. So, the guys are all on the plane and heading home. They will arrive on schedule in the morning and cars will meet them and drive them to their homes,' Cat, the PA announces to the room. Cat must be about twenty-eight, she seems sweet with big brown eyes, light blonde hair and is petite. She is never seen without her phone glued to her hand and Dominic is clearly, extremely reliant on her.

'Well done you absolute star. You never fail me, do you?' Dominic pats her on the shoulder and walks a few feet to join Seb and me. I continue to watch Cat's reaction and she seems to look longingly after him which instantly feels odd.

Suddenly, she clocks me watching her and we have a moment of awkward eye contact, so I think fast,

'Cat, come and join us if you are free?' I try to cover over the fact I was staring directly at her.

'Oh no, I won't. I must go and arrange our transport for LA tomorrow, but thank you Sophia.' I am instantly taken aback for a second that she knows my name, I'm not sure why, but I feel so new, little and irrelevant in the grand scheme of this company, that it always surprises me when people know who I am.

'Cat is coming to LA?' I say aloud, without even thinking. Both Seb and Dominic turn to acknowledge me and Dominic's expression is little caught off-guard.

'Cat comes EVERYWHERE with us,' Seb laughs it off, 'Dom cannot live without her. I'm pretty sure she even wipes his arse.'

'Fuck you mate,' Dominic says to him playfully, 'anyway, we need your help Soph with important choices to be made. How many nights in Vegas shall we book in for?'

Sophia, doll, I can't believe what I read. I hope you are OK?! I have good news though, I am moving to London sooner than I thought, so we can finally be flatmates! Give me a call when you are back, I am moving up in about 3 weeks time, take care darling xxx

It's Poppy and she has stayed true to her word, but thankfully moving up to the city even sooner. Which solves my housing crisis for my return to London. Only having a few weeks left in my current, lent residence, Poppy's timing could not be more perfect.

AMAZING NEWS, yes please, I will be back in two weeks and will fill you in with all the details then. All fine, very strange day, but safe now xxx

I breathe out a huge sigh of relief as I send my response to Poppy and throw my phone on the chair next to me. Looking at the screen is starting to give me a headache. It's that or I just need to get to bed and sleep off the stress of the day and maybe the three glasses of wine that slid down my throat quicker than planned have also not helped.

'All OK Soph? That was a very big sigh,' Seb sits down next to me on the sofa.

'All good thanks. My friend Poppy was asking after me and will be moving to London soon, so I have a new flatmate. Which solves a huge problem that I had. Also, my head hurts, if you don't mind, I might head to bed to try and sleep it off.'

'Of course,' Seb hugs me into his chest and pecks me on the lips, 'Get some rest. I have lost track of the time today,' he checks his watch. '8 pm, right, I won't be far behind you. We will be up at 5 am to catch our flight, so I will set an alarm for us.' I kiss him one last time on the lips.

'Goodnight everyone. I hope you sleep well,' as I wave and head out of the lounge. There are murmurs of goodnight and sleep well which follow me down the corridor as I close the bedroom door and feel a flood of relief that today is nearly over.

Eesh, my head hurts. I wake up and it's pitch black in the hotel room. Seb is in bed next to me and I realise it must be late, or early as the case is, when I check my phone

151

and it's 3 am. I forgot to take a bottle of water to bed with me and as the glasses of wine were consumed too quickly the evening before, I am feeling considerably dehydrated. I quietly get up and tiptoe silently to the lounge and bar area where I remember there being a fridge full of anything you could possibly desire. I head over and grab a chilled bottle of water, crouching down as I close the fridge and I jump a little when I hear a noise. It sounds like someone else is also sneaking around too. My heart races as the memories of the day previously flood back. I look slowly around the bar table and I nearly breathe a sigh of relief when I see it's Cat. Although, the relief quickly turns into confusion as I establish that she has just, in fact, walked out of Dominic's room. She is dressed in an oversized T-shirt and walking barefoot, carrying what looks like her clothes and it's obvious that they haven't been discussing work. I decide to keep quiet and thankfully she had been oblivious to my presence. The thought of spending the next few days with Arabella, Dominic's wife, makes me feel instantly uneasy and as soon as Cat has left the hotel room, I quickly rush back to bed, trying not to disturb Seb.

I lie wide awake, peering over to a very deep sleeping Seb and wonder if he is aware of any affairs and if he is, would he condone his best friend messing about with his PA? My instant is no, but then, they have been friends for so long, how can I really know the pacts and secrets they keep? It's such a bloody cliché, a boss shagging his PA and even though I haven't even met Arabella yet, my blood boils for her. The nerve of Cat. So that was the cause of the lingering looks at Dominic and pampering to his every need, she has been shagging him for who knows how long.

I wake with the sound of Seb knocking his phone to the floor as he tries to silence the alarm ringing out. It's another 5 am start and I really can't wait to stay in bed past 7 am one day soon. We don't have much time to drag our feet, so I can't dwell on my overwhelming exhaustion for too long and we both get ready, barely exchanging words.

As we drag our bags from the room and into the hotel room lounge, the first person I set eyes on is Dominic and what I witnessed in the early hours all floods back to me.

'Good morning love birds,' he says under his shades and sipping a takeaway coffee.

'Morning mate,' Seb shakes his hand.

'Morning Dominic.' I can barely make eye contact with him.

'Soph, you can call me Dom. My Mum calls me Dominic and it always makes me feel like I am in

trouble.' He laughs, unaware of how much of that is actually true.

'OK, I will bear that in mind,' trying not to sound sarcastic or arsey, but obviously struggling to hide my

true feelings when Seb glances at me with a puzzled look.

'Are you OK?' He whispers as we drag our bags down the corridors to the lift, 'have you changed your mind, we can go back to the UK if you are not sure?'

'I'm OK, just let's speak when we are alone, nothing to do with us, don't worry.' I try to reassure him.

We arrive safely at the airport and get ushered from our car, straight on to a charter flight. It didn't even cross my mind that we would be flying like this and suddenly I feel overwhelmed by Dominic's wealth and generosity as I sit down in my seat. I look over and watch as Cat sits opposite Dominic, all smiles and giggles. Since leaving the hotel, I have watched on as he brushed her hand when she passed him a drink, the way she keeps laughing at everything he says and how he hangs back to wait for her.

It now feels so obvious, but maybe not to everybody else. I am pretty sure Seb is none the wiser, or maybe he is just used to it.

'Dom, what time is Arabella getting there?' Seb confirms he is definitely none the wiser, why would he inquire about Dominic's wife in front of his potential mistress?

'Erm, can't remember mate. She will just go to the condo anyway.' I can't see his face, as he has his back to us, but I can see from Cat's expression that she feels awkward.

'I can't wait to meet her. How long have you been married, Dominic?' I say, defending the woman I have never met out of respect for their marriage, which is clearly more than her husband is doing. Dominic turns around to talk.

'Please call me Dom. We have been married two years now, but together since we were 16. A long time.'

'Wow, that is true love. I love the idea of childhood sweethearts, saves kissing too many frogs,' I watch Cat as she squirms a little in her seat.

'Hopefully, I'm not one of those frogs though Sophia?' Seb looks at me with a daft face, which I can only presume his interpretation of a frog, but he manages to distract me from getting even more internally wound up at the obvious lines being crossed, right in front of our noses.

After what felt like a Michelin Starred meal aboard the plane, I recline back and cuddle into Seb, feeling so tired I could probably sleep for a week if given the chance. This is the first time in 24 hours I feel safe, which is ironic as I am thousands of feet up in the sky. I catch Cat and Dominic sharing some kind of joke, but before I find the energy to take an interest and listen in, I must have fallen asleep.

'Sophia, we are landing,' I wake up and look out to see what I guess is the bird's eye view of LA and it's coastline,

'How long was I asleep?'

'I reckon we must have had at least eight hours,' Seb says, not breaking his gaze at the land below. I look over to see the continuing flirtation and giggles from Cat, who seems to be getting less subtle by the hour.

'Earth to Sophia,' Seb mock waves his hand in front of my gaze.

'Oh shit, sorry, I was just thinking about stuff.'

'Not bad stuff I hope. You aren't regretting coming with me, are you?'

'No, no, not at all. Sorry, something else, but will speak to you in private. Please don't worry about me and being here. I'm really excited, honestly,' I try to ease his mind, but I definitely can't keep this to myself for much longer.

We finally land after circling LA for what seems like hours, I grab my bag and we all head straight off the plane, into a large fancy blacked-out people carrier and we are all driven straight off the airport grounds and apparently towards Malibu. Cat is sitting opposite Seb and I. 'Cat, where are you staying and how long are you here for?' I'm intrigued that she even has the nerve to come this far with us, knowing at any point in the next hour she will be in the presence of Dominic's wife.

'Oh I am staying with you guys,' she looks over at Dominic smiling, 'I always stay in Dom's Condo. There is enough room for us all.' What actual planet is this woman on? My blood boils a little and I just can't stop myself,

'Oh wow, that's so generous of you to let us all stay Dominic. I can't wait to meet Arabella, she always looks so beautiful in the magazine shoots and seems like such a genuine and lovely person. Don't you think Cat?' I shoot a glance at her, waiting for her reaction.

'Erm, yeah. She's nice.'

'Oh, I think she must be more than nice to let us all stay in her home,' I give Cat a smile and she forces a smile back to me.

'I guess so', she smirks.

'Heeeeeey guys. Oh my gosh, I have been so excited to meet you Sophia,' Arabella runs over and throws her arms around me. By the way Dominic has described her, I hadn't anticipated such a warm welcome. I also hadn't expected to see her with a baby bump.

'So lovely to meet you too and wow, a baby, that's amazing. Congratulations.'

'That's lovely to hear Dom has been spreading the good news,' she rolls her eyes dramatically but in a playful way and then hugs Seb, 'so, Dom didn't tell you either I am guessing?'

'Hello gorgeous. Massive congrats and no, your dickhead hubby decided to keep it from me. Otherwise, you would have heard from me by now.' Seb turns and playfully punches Dom.

'Sorry mate, just thought it would be fun for you to see for yourself. Arabella and I have tried to keep it quiet until three months passed, her bump has only just started to show the past week or two,' Dominic walks over to Arabella and holds her bump grinning ear to ear and I can't help but look to see Cat's face and she looks as surprised at the news as the rest of us.

'Right, Sophia and Seb, you make your way into Condo and freshen up. Seb, your normal room is all ready for you both. Dom, can we have a word, please? You can leave us for a minute.' Arabella points to Cat, but doesn't look at her and dismisses her in such a manner that suggests Arabella is no fool and has clocked on to whatever it is, between her husband and his PA.

'Follow me Soph, I suggest we get out of the way ASAP,' as Seb grabs my bag from my hand and leads the way through the giant doors and into the palatial Condo.

I am overwhelmed by the floor to ceiling windows that have direct, uninterrupted views of Malibu beach and out to the Pacific Ocean. I turn back as I hear raised voices coming from Arabella and Dominic. Arabella is now in tears and Dominic seems to be pleading with her,

'Seb, should you check if they are OK?' He turns and looks back and pauses for a second.

'It's probably best we leave them to it for now. Cat, maybe you should stay out of the way too.' It's clear Seb has no idea what is going on as he heads down a long corridor. I hold back a few moments. I can't let this girl stand here, knowing what I know and not intervene.

'Actually Cat, I don't think you should stay here at all,' I can't stop myself. Nothing angers me more than the audacity of her, standing in this home after what she has been up to.

'Why would I leave Sophia? I am Dom's PA and he needs me,' she tilts her head, looking for my reaction.

'On the basis that I saw you leaving Dominic's room last night at 3 am. I'm not even sure how anyone would have the nerve to step foot into another woman's house after that. I'm hoping at the very least, you were also none the wiser to their pregnancy news?'

'What is going on?' Seb startles me.

'Sorry Seb, I wanted to tell you when we were alone. I woke up at around 3 this morning and needed a drink. I was getting one from the bar, when I heard a sound and it was Cat leaving Dominic's room, barely dressed.'

'No, no, no, fuck. NO. Surely he wouldn't do that.'

'That's what I saw Seb. Ask her,' as I point to Cat, she now looks a little less smug and is rummaging through her bag.

'What were you doing in Dom's room then Cat?' Seb is looking more pissed off by the second and Cat doesn't respond, she just shrugs petulantly. Before any more can be said, Arabella and Dominic enter the Condo, 'Dom, chat now please,' Seb directs Dom back outside and closes the front door behind him.

'Arabella, do you mind if I put the kettle on?' I say, with the intention of getting Arabella away from Cat as quickly as possible.

'Of course not, I will make you a drink. This way.' We walk through the large open plan space and over to a gorgeous white marble-topped kitchen area, leaving Cat where she was. 'It's not the first time,' she has her back to me as she gets some cups out of the cupboard and turns around and looks directly in my eyes, 'he's done it before, with another one, but I thought now.' Suddenly Arabella bursts into tears, 'I just thought that now we have the baby we have always wanted,' she waves her hands in despair, I drop my bag and scurry around the kitchen island to hug her.

'You go and sit down, I will make the drinks. What would you like?'

'Just a glass of water would be great, thank you.' I quickly pour us both a glass of water and join her on the dark blue velvet sofa. I have managed to take in a little of the decor and it's all beautifully chic and nautical, although now doesn't seem the appropriate time to compliment her decor choices.

'Did you know?' Arabella asks, looking up from her glass, clearly nervous of my answer.

'I saw her leave his room last night, I had no idea before that though. I'm so sorry. I couldn't believe it when she had the nerve to step foot in here,' I get distracted by the front door being opened and I watch Cat skulk out.

'Was that her?' I nod, 'well at least she got the hint to leave. I'm not risking this baby by losing my cool with her. I won't give her the satisfaction. She's just another silly little girl who has fallen for the famous boss. It's so pathetic and so am I, for thinking he would ever change.' She slams down her glass and throws her head into the hands.'

'Hey, no, you are not pathetic. You trusted him and assumed he would do the right thing for you and your unborn child. That doesn't make you pathetic, that makes him a terrible human for letting you down.'

'Thank you Sophia. I'm so grateful you and Seb are here. I couldn't imagine if those two had just turned up.' We sit in silence for a few moments and I am lost for what more I can say. I have only just met Arabella and literally nothing I have to say can fix this for her. No advice in this world can take away the hurt she must be feeling. Thankfully Seb appears through the front door and heads straight for us.

'How's the baby and mummy doing?' He gently puts his arm around her and hugs her close to him.

'I've been better Seb. I could tell something was going on, the same signs as last time and the time before.'

'He's a complete prat Arabella, I don't know what else to say. I was oblivious. Obviously I would never have allowed her into your home had I known.'

'I know and I appreciate it,' she rubs her bump, 'but this time, I know we deserve better, I am not living like this anymore Seb. Waiting for him to let us down, fuck him, this is my baby and I will do what I can to protect it.' I feel a lump in my throat and my eyes start to sting, I feel so sorry for this woman. You see these people on TV and in magazines, assuming their lives are perfect, but really, they are no different to anyone, especially if it turns out you married a dickhead.

'I will do whatever you need me to, I have known you as long as that idiot and you are my best friend. I promise to look out for you and the baby,' Seb gently puts his hand on the baby bump.

'I know my sweet friend, I know. Sophia, you have a really good one here, a real diamond in the dust,' before I get to respond, Dominic comes bounding through the front door and over to us.

'Don't worry, you will all be pleased to know she has gone.' I look for Seb's reaction and he is looking in shock at Arabella, who remains focused on her bump.

'Go with her Dom, you aren't needed or wanted here anymore. Do the baby and me a favour and fuck off with that dizzy cow. My Solicitor will send you my terms of the separation and don't even argue it unless you want your fake public persona destroyed.' Dom looks over at us, dumbstruck.

'Arabella, darling,' he runs over and kneels by her side, 'you know she is absolutely nothing to me and you and this baby are the only people I care about.'

'No Dom, you care about yourself and your dick. That is literally all you care about. Sorry, correction, you care about your shitty cooking show too. Now go, I can't even stand to be around you.'

'Fine, I will give you time to calm down. I need ten minutes to grab some more things, so you still have a chance to change your mind,' Arabella smiles and shakes her head.

'Dom, I will never. EVER. Change my mind. Let that be very clear.' Dominic looks like he has just been slapped around the face and begrudgingly leaves to pack his things. Seb sits and comforts Arabella and I suddenly have the overwhelming urge to check whether Cat has left the premises,

'I will be back in a second,' as I walk towards the front door and see at the top of the long drive, Cat is standing on her phone.

'Naaa he won't stay with her, he's said how done they are, even with the baby it won't save them now.' Jeez, this girl is more ballsy and heartless than I thought possible. My blood has finally boiled and all I can see is red.

'Cat, put the phone down and have some common fucking decency,' she jumps out of her skin and hangs up instantly, glaring at me with a face full of attitude. 'Why are you still lurking here, surely you should have gone by now?'

'I'm waiting to see if Dom sees sense and leaves with me,' she grins and it's really going to take all my willpower to keep my calm.

'If he leaves with you, it's because he has no other option. Not because you mean anything to him other than an easy shag and an ego boost.' Her smarmy grin quickly fades, 'you are surely aware that you aren't the first girl to drop her knickers so easily for him?' I'm on a roll, but before I get too carried away I hear the wheels of a suitcase being dragged up the drive and the raised voices of Dominic and Seb.

'Mate, you fucked up and you are going to have to do what Arabella asks. If not for her, for the sake of your baby. She can't be under this much stress right now.'

'Alright. For fuck's sake, I GET IT. That is my house, my wife and my baby though and I'm not going to give it up that easily.' I look at Cat's reaction to hearing it from the horse's mouth and she looks at me, obviously embarrassed that Dominic has no interest in her presence.

'See. I told you,' throwing her the same grin she had the nerve to give me a couple of moments earlier. 'Cat is under the impression you are leaving with her Dominic.'

'Seriously, it's DOM and not a chance. Get yourself an Uber Cat and remember the NDA you signed. Go home and forget about any of this.' He climbs into the people carrier and is driven off without another word exchanged.

Chapter Thirteen

I wake up to views directly of the Pacific ocean and for the first time in a few days, I feel calmer and a little less anxious. One of the first things to dawn on me as I fully wake and adjust to my surroundings, is that it wasn't all a bizarre dream triggered by too much time reading gossip magazines. I did in fact witness the breakdown of my famous boss's marriage and I now find myself waking in his house, where he is in fact, not welcome. Seb is not lying next to me and as I throw my legs out the side of the bed to stand up. 'Get back in there,' Seb comes barging into the room with a tray in his hands and plonks it on the bed. 'Arabella picked up more than a few things living with a chef and she has kindly made us breakfast fit for kings and queens.'

'Oh I feel bad, she should be relaxing and being looked after, not doing all this for us.'

The previous evening, the three of us had ordered some posh Malibu sushi and sat, eating, talking and watching the waves roll onto the shore until late into the evening. Maybe it was the soothing sound of the ocean or the copious wine, but I ended up feeling very comfortable in the presence of Arabella and we instantly hit it off, despite the dramatics surrounding our introduction. I heard it all, including the previous infidelities and the ones she was sure happened, but could never prove. I was in shock at what I was hearing, he definitely didn't give off the vibe of a cheating husband and the fact he had not been splashed all over the press with all these sordid love affairs is a huge success on the part of his PR team. Obviously a little help from numerous NDA's and an entire legal team on payroll can work wonders to keep the truth suppressed.

'I'm just surprised a woman as tough and confident as Arabella, stood for Dominic's crap for as long as she did,' I mumble to Seb, shovelling in another mouthful of the maple syrup coated pancakes.

'Well, they have been together since they were both kids and have such a long history. Arabella has always found it difficult to walk away from the grips of Dom, even with his bullshit. She has seen his struggles of self-doubt and loathing at the beginning of his fame and as much of an arsehole he has been, it's nearly impossible to cut him out because we have all been through so much. This baby though, it has given Arabella the strength to do what she has needed to do for a long time and break free. As sad as it will be for a baby to be born into an already fractured home, it will want for nothing. Arabella will absolutely make sure of that.' I put my hand on his knee and feel such pride and also relief that he is such a sensitive, smart and kind soul, the inner me is reeling in smugness that I have somehow landed him as a boyfriend.

'You are the greatest Seb, have I mentioned that?'

'Not enough,' he laughs and kisses me with sticky Maple syrup lips.

'Well, you are. I feel very lucky, but don't get a big head, we don't need another Dominic on our hands. Speaking of which, have you heard from him?'

'Yup, he asked if I could speak to you about keeping this quiet, in fact, he is sending over a confidentiality agreement for you to sign.'

'Is that the same NDA he mentioned to Cat?' Seb shrugs, 'I'm assuming it probably is.'

'I'm not signing it, so please don't ask me to.' Seb smiles at me and carries on eating.

'I was never in any doubt that you would sign it Soph. He has already been working out other ways to buy your loyalty.'

'What does it matter now anyway, surely people will find out? They will be divorcing and figure it out in the end.'

'The problem is, his whole brand is based on the good-guy image. So, there will be as much damage control as possible. He would lose contracts and a large fan base if this type of news got out. He even suggested a position as a Producer, a quick promotion to sweeten you.'

'Wow, and I thought you had to sleep your way to the top, not find out that other people have been sleeping around! No, I will climb the career ladder my own way and not based on bribery. I won't say anything anyway, It's not my business to share his gossip. It's not just him who will be hurt anyway, it's Arabella and the baby. They are the ones who we should be concerned about. Definitely not his brand and image.'

'I could not agree with you more Soph.'

'So my darling Sophia, California is our oyster. Where would you like to start?' We sit on the driveway in Dominic's fancy Mustang, which Arabella has kindly let us borrow for our LA adventures.

'Well, Santa Monica Pier, Hollywood and the sign. Rodeo Drive, although I can't afford a thing, but I do owe it to my Pretty-Woman-loving-self. I wouldn't mind seeing Venice beach too.'

'Right madam, your wish is my command. Let's start in Hollywood and work our way back to the coast.'

'Oh I am so excited,' I get butterflies of excitement as we pull out of the electronic security gate, 'you realise this is our first proper full day together, just the two of us?'

'That thought had crossed my mind too. So let's make it an amazing one shall we?' Seb grins and his perfectly white teeth glisten in the sun, with his shades on, signature white t-shirt and a hint of tan he has caught over the past few days, he is looking every bit the Californian beach sex god.

'Next stop, Rodeo Drive!' After visiting all of the Hollywood hot spots and ticking the necessary tourist boxes, we walk around Beverly Hills and towards the famous street. You can feel the wealth seep out of every passerby and the shops are luxury brand after luxury brand, it's exactly what I had expected. 'Let's look in here,' as Seb directs me into a jewellery shop, which seems far too out of our league. Before I even get to question why, one of the suited and booted sales staff is welcoming us in.

'Afternoon, how can I help you?'

'Hi, it's my girlfriend's Birthday and she recently had her earrings stolen, so I would like to replace them.'

'Sorry to hear that ma'am, please follow me, we have a fabulous collection over here.' Firstly, I had barely remembered it was my Birthday myself, it was only due to waking up to a message from my Mum and Dad that had even reminded me of the date, little more was I aware Seb knew. I had decided to keep it to myself after everything that had happened the previous day, I didn't want people to feel obliged to celebrate or make an effort for me. Seemed a pretty selfish move after seeing Arabella's marriage fall apart right in front of us. Now I find myself in a jewellers with Seb and he is wanting to replace my stolen earrings, which is quite probably the sweetest thing anyone has ever done for me.

'This is so lovely of you, but it's a little much,' I whisper, not wanting anyone to hear and risk embarrassing Seb.

'It's really not, I have been thinking about replacing your stolen earrings since it happened and thankfully your mum messaged me to let me know. I can't believe you kept it to yourself, I remember you said it was your birthday coming up, but didn't recall a date being mentioned. Also, one set is from me and your mum has instructed me that the other set is from them.'

'I can't believe you guys have been in touch, must mean you really are my bonafide boyfriend then?'

'Yup, pretty sure it's fully confirmed now.' Seb grins gleefully.

We are ushered over to a large jewellery display unit with all the sparkly earrings a girl could wish for. Seb is chatting with the salesman out of my earshot, but before I know it, I have two large velvet trays full of earrings in front of me. 'Soph, please pick a pair from me and then also another from your parents, you can take your time obviously. There is no rush.'

'I can't see any prices and that makes me nervous,' I whisper to him.

'It's OK,' Seb smiles and plants a big kiss on my cheek, 'these are all in your parents and my budget.'

Half a glass of champagne down and I have picked two cute pairs of earrings, 'are you really sure? This feels very extravagant and I'm not really sure what I have done to deserve it.'

'Yes, for the tenth time. I promise you I would like to treat you for your birthday. Anyhow, let's go and you might want to video call your folks. I kinda promised your mum that you would and it's getting late in the UK.'

'Hey Sophia. Happy birthday to our girl.'

'Mum you are too close. I can literally just see your forehead!' Every single time we attempt a video call, this is how it starts! When I finally get to see both of my parent's faces, I introduce them to Seb.

'Wow, he is handsome, isn't he? You have good taste Soph, just like your mother.'

'Mum, he can still hear you.' I glance at a rosy cheeked Seb.

'Oh, that's OK. Please don't be embarrassed Sebastian. You will get to our age and be grateful for any compliments you get, make the most of them now,' Seb looks at me and smiles, but it's the first time I have ever witnessed him look genuinely uncomfortable.

'We will try to remember that mum. I rang to thank you for the gorgeous earrings. Look, I have them in already. You really shouldn't have though. Far too generous.'

'Our pleasure. Just so pleased you are OK darling. Mum and I were extremely worried when we saw the news reports and knew our little girl had been involved in that bloody robbery.' Mum grabs the phone and her forehand is the centre of attention again,

'You two get on with your fun day anyway and enjoy yourselves, don't go dwelling on what happened. We know you are in safe hands now Sophia. Please take care of each other,' and before we even say our goodbyes, mum had unsubtly hung up.

'OK, well I think they like me anyway, so I class that as a good call?'

'Yes, you can be reassured in the knowledge that you definitely have the thumbs up from my parents. Mum can just be, well, mum. You will get used to her, I'm sure.'

'I'm sure I will. Anyway, let's head to our final destination of the day and continue the celebrations. There is plenty more fun ahead.'

We park up on Santa Monica Boulevard, with the ocean in view. It's magic hour and the sun is turning the sky every shade of pink, orange and yellow that Farrow & Ball could dream of. As we walk to the Pier, it feels too perfect and like a film set. The Ferris wheel is spinning around slowly and everyone around us seems relaxed, happy and laughing. 'Can you imagine being born here and having this as your life?' I think out loud.

'It's just amazing isn't it, I would probably move here in a heartbeat if I could get a job,' Seb hugs me into his side as we carry on walking the length of the pier and absorb the sunset and watch the surfers float on the waves.

'Fancy a ride on the Ferris wheel?'

'Why the hell not,' I say with excitement but also a little trepidation when I realise how high it actually is.

Within minutes, we are climbing into our seats on the Pacific Wheel and it slowly starts to spin around and I rest my head onto Seb's shoulder. The sun has just about set and the lights on each side of the pier illuminate the coastline and it's beautiful.

'Thank you for having faith in me and coming along on this trip. It would never have been like this without you. I really hope you have had the best birthday possible.' Seb wraps his arm around my shoulder.

'It's seriously been the best birthday ever, thank you again for my gorgeous earrings. It really means a lot that you had spoken to my parents and surprised me like this. Nobody has done anything like that for me before.'

'Your folks are brilliant and hilarious and you Miss William's are very, very special to me. You have no idea of the anger and worry I felt, knowing you were on that bus and what was going on. I realised then, with you being in that much danger and there was nothing I could do,' Seb pauses and stares out to the Ocean as we sit still at the top of the wheel, 'I realised that I must really be falling for you.' He looks me in the eyes, 'I don't want to scare you as I know it's early days, but we have been through so much in such a short amount of time and I actually feel like we have known each other for so much longer,' I kiss him on the lips to ease his obvious nerves.

'I feel the same Sebastian Simpson. You make me feel so safe and protected. I know I am falling for you too.'

'Are you sure I can't get you to stay, just a few days longer?' Arabella looks at us with a little plea in her eyes.

'You know we would love to, Arabella, but I have a few things up my sleeve for this lady of mine and we will run out of time if we don't leave today. I promise everything will work out OK for you and I am only at the end of the phone if you need me,' Seb goes in for a long bear hug and holds Arabella tight and reassuringly. I can see her eyes welling up. It must be so daunting, watching Dominic leave and then knowing there is a rough road ahead as potentially a single parent.

'Thank you Sophia, for all you said and have done. I'm sorry you had to be part of this. The point of you guys visiting us was to try and forget the Brazil nightmare, now you have been embroiled in more dramas.'

'Honestly, I'm fine and thank you so much for letting us stay, you have been so generous. Good luck with the bump and hopefully see you again very soon. It feels like such a stupid question, but are you going to be OK?' As I lean in for a hug.

'I think so. It's the first time I have been alone in my adult life, so that's a little overwhelming, but really, as long as the baby is OK, I will be OK. My sister and mum are flying out at the weekend, so I will have them mollycoddling me in no time. Now you guys go, you have a fair few miles to get through today.'

We pack our final bags into the white, VW convertible Beetle that Seb randomly picked as our "perfect road trip car" and say our last goodbyes to Arabella as Seb pulls onto the freeway and we start to head north, up the Californian coast. I look back at the stunning Condo and feel an odd, anxious mix of happy and sad.

'Don't worry. Arabella will be fine and I'm sure she will be back in London once the separation news is out and the tabloids are bored of it all. She is in the best place to relax and focus on the bump. As for us, we need to have our own adventures now and put the dramas of the past week behind us,' Seb flashes me his best reassuring smile.

'How did you get so wise Sebastian?' I say teasingly, but also genuinely intrigued how he always seems to stay calm and have the answers.

'Well. I wouldn't say I'm wise, but there is a lot you don't know about me yet. Over time you will know it all,' He has a cheeky glint in his eye.

'Hmmm, is that a threat or a promise?'

'Well, Sophia, I guess you will just have to wait and see!'

We have been driving for hours, taking in all the beauty of the Big Sur. I knew it would be gorgeous, but I had no idea quite how amazing it actually is. We had stopped off for some lunch at an old looking ranch-style restaurant perched on a cliff and overlooking the Pacific. We ate Clam Chowder and sat in the March sun and felt the cool ocean breeze on my face. It felt like the perfect holiday that had been in planning for months. The reality is very different, as for the first time in days, there wasn't a feeling of anxiety in the pit of my stomach. I would be lying if I said the robbery hadn't been played through my head on a number of occasions and the "what ifs" hadn't been considered daily since it happened. Although It had been slightly dwarfed with the outing of Dominic's affair, the memories still lurk like a shadow in my mind. Entwined with all this drama, I also have had some of the highest highs. Just being with Seb was making my life significantly happier and possibly having the greatest birthday in my adult life, it feels like a huge and never-ending rollercoaster I am currently strapped onto.

'What are you thinking? You have been gazing out of the window for ages,' Seb breaks my thoughts.

'Sorry. I was off in my own little world. Just playing through the last few days,' before I get to divulge my thoughts any further I see the sign for the town, Carmel-by-the-sea. 'Oh my gosh, I can't believe we are here. You remembered!"

'Of course I remembered and we are staying at the Cypress Inn as promised,' Seb looks incredibly proud of himself.

'Eeeeeeeek,' I screech with sheer joy. This town has been on my radar since I used to cuddle up with my Nan on the sofa as a child and watch Doris Day films back to back. 'This has literally made my decade, you have no idea how much I have wanted to visit this place. Thank you so, so much Seb.'

'Well, I have always fancied a visit myself and actually couldn't think of a better time or person to come here with. Time to switch off the stress of the past few days and just enjoy it Soph.'

I fall onto the bed, spread out like a star, 'Please tell me we can just live our lives like this forever Seb. Don't make me go home.'

'If only Sophia, I would do it in a second. Hang on, I just need to take this,' Seb walks out onto a small balcony attached to the room and closes the door behind him. I start to unpack my bag and hang up the extremely creased clothes I have. The further north of California we get, the more the temperature seems to be dropping and the clothes I had packed for a Summer in Brazil are not quite fulfilling the needs of the Californian Spring. The couple of jumpers and jeans I packed as a back-up, are now turning into my wardrobe staples.

'Right.' Seb is off the phone and his expression has significantly changed as he re-enters the hotel room. 'I don't want you to stress about this. Everything is under control I promise, but before I tell you, please confirm you trust me that this will all be fine?' Jesus, my heart instantly sinks.

'Please just tell me. I suddenly feel sick.'

'Ok. So, I'm not really sure how to say this.'

'Seb for God's sake, this is not helping.'

'Shit, OK, so the thing is, the story of Dominic's affair has somehow got to the UK press. They have no idea how, as there were only a few of us who know about it. It wasn't us, obviously it wasn't Arabella or Dom so that only really leaves Cat.'

'Oh no, poor Arabella, this is not good at all. I can't believe Cat has most likely cashed in for her fifteen minutes of fame.'

'That's the bit we don't understand Soph. It's not her that has been accused of being the mistress. I don't really know how to put this.'

'Put what?'

'Well. Jesus, it's ridiculous, but it's you who is being accused.' I just stand for second and consider what Seb has just said, surely this is just some weird joke or I have heard it wrong.

'Sorry, I'm confused. Me? What do you mean, ME?'

'I know, it's totally fucked up. Dom's theory is that Cat is covering her own back and you were an easy target. The problem is, they have a photo of you two in Brazil, which has conveniently cut me and some others out. So this is seen as proof to the tabloids, that you were at least in his presence to make this story viable. Also, Cat knows you won't fight back and name her as the actual person, as that will confirm Dom has had an affair. She's a total fucking lunatic bitch.'

174

'Can you do me a favour and call my folks and explain it, please? I need to warn them and make sure they know the truth. I don't think I can do it without crying right now.'

'Of course Sophia, I will do it out there and give you a minute,' he walks out onto the, what now seems like the "balcony of bad news" and I grab my phone and put it on. It's been switched off for the entire day and I'm dreading the messages I am about to face. Within a second of it getting signal, there is ping after ping. My parents; my sisters, Michael, Poppy, friends I hadn't spoken to in months. I check my emails and there are at least thirty emails in my inbox. More messages from friends. Parents again. What looks like email addresses belonging to tabloid journalists.

'For fuck's sake,' I sigh. I'm not sure how much more of this I can take. Never in my wildest dreams had I ever imagined being branded a mistress and homewrecker, how dare that bitch drag my name through the papers like this.

'Soph, they want to speak to you,' Seb walks in and passes me his mobile.

'It's not true,' I say in defence before my parents can say a word.

'We know darling, we know. Seb just told us the whole nasty story and what a madam that girl is. We didn't believe it anyway. We know you aren't capable of doing something like that. We have both been shocked how quickly the news seems to have spread,' my mum sounds tired and I feel even more guilty.

'Well, I guess he is one of the most famous chefs in the country and the press loves a villain,' Dad chirps in, sounding less fazed by the news.

'I just don't know how she could do that to someone. It's not enough to rip a marriage apart, but to then try and tarnish my name to top it off. Even knowing what we went through in Brazil,' my eyes burn with tears and the lump in my throat is sore.

'Darling, some people are just nasty to the core. We have chatted to Seb and we all agree that you should stay out there and enjoy as much of your trip as possible. The moment you step foot back here, you may get more attention than you bargained for. You can't come home to get away from it either, we have already had a few reporters knocking on our door.'

'Oh no, I am so sorry,' this time I cry. 'This has all been one huge drama and the moment I think I am nearly in the clear, something else comes to fuck it up. Sorry for swearing,' I can hear both my parents chuckle.

'That's alright, you deserve a good swear right now.' Dad says, making me smile.

'Look, Sophia, darling. This will all get fixed. Seb has promised us that it is in Dominic's best interests to correct this issue and at the end of the day, you are dating his best friend! So everyone will soon see what a load of old rubbish it is soon enough.'

'I hope you are right and thank you for being understanding. Anyway, more importantly, how are Margo and Charly, any updates on the baby progress?' There is a little shuffle on the phone and I can't make out what they are saying, 'Hello, are you still there?'

'Oh hi, sorry about that, all fine, Dad just interrupted me. Can you email us when you get a chance and send us some more photos please, we are desperate to see some of Seb's Big Sur photos. You both get a good night's sleep and I promise the past few days will be a distant memory soon enough.'

Chapter Fourteen

'Well, that was a perfect meal to end an interesting day.' We walk hand in hand through the quaint evening streets of Carmel. Seb and I had made a pact to enjoy our evening with phones off and not another word about the day's revelations.

'It was,' I agree, even though I still have pangs of nerves about my name being slandered across the British press. I can tell Seb has tried his best to distract me from the reality of my situation, which I feel incredibly grateful for. Although, it's very difficult to fully immerse myself in the fun we should be having, when I am continually wondering when it will be safe to go home, see my parents and return to my job. If I will ever be able to return to it after all this debacle.

'Do you fancy a drink here?' Seb, gestures to what looks like a really cool and chic little spot, set back off the main road.

'Not really Seb. Sorry for being a Debbie downer, but I actually just want to go to bed and forget about today. Sorry. You made all of this so special and now I just feel like something amazing has been overshadowed, yet again.'

'That's fine, you really don't have to apologise. Let's head back to the hotel and get some sleep.' We turn to walk back to the hotel and catch a photographer a little further down the street with a huge camera and lens aimed in our direction. Before it even occurs to me what is going on, Seb has let go of my hand and is chasing them, with the guy fleeing into a car and seemingly disappearing. I jog to catch up with him and he is already on his phone, 'Mate, who the fuck found out we are here? There is no way anyone recognised us. So, who the FUCK was that pap?' This is the first time I have heard Seb shout. He is raging and I have already guessed who he is talking to. 'You could have at least given us a heads up or allowed us one fucking evening to enjoy. Do you realise the shit you have put Soph through the past few days? She's not a fucking pawn in your life to help cover up the shit you create.' He hangs up and puts his head in his hand and I give him a moment to calm. 'It was a ploy Soph. He tipped off the pap and the plan is to release a story tomorrow, proving you are the girlfriend of his best mate and nothing to do with the "scandal". He said he had tried to call, but obviously our phones were off. He still could have waited until we knew.' I'm not sure if I should be annoyed at Dominic by yet another intrusion or relieved he is helping to find a solution.

'But that's good though. Right? If all goes to plan, the tabloids will see the obvious error and lies that have been published and at least my name will be cleared?' I feel optimistic that the end is in sight and I will be able to go home without my name tarnished. Seb turns around and wraps his arms around me.

'Yes, you are absolutely right Soph. I'm just annoyed at the whole situation and this was all supposed to be so different. It's all down to Dom and keeping his precious reputation intact. It's a shame he can't just be a more decent fucking husband, for all our sakes.'

'Right, I have changed my mind. Let's go to that bar for a drink, I feel like celebrating my name being cleared and I think you could do with a large drink too.'

Stepping out of the shower with a brand new day ahead, which includes plans to explore Carmel, I feel a spring in my step. Seb and I had stayed out late, enjoyed a few drinks and chatted with some locals. It ended up being an amazing evening and for the first time in days, it was just about us, laughing, flirting and being carefree. The slight throb in my head thanks to the cocktails, pulsates, but it's nothing that some water and the Californian sea air won't fix. I walk out to Seb sitting on the edge of the bed and engrossed in his phone. 'Oh my gosh, that is such a good shower!' There is no response from Seb, 'Hello, earth to Sebastian. What are you reading that's so interesting?'

'You might want to have a look at this. Turns out the photos of us together aren't as interesting as your ex.'

'What? What are you talking about? My ex?' I feel totally confused, what have any of my ex-boyfriends got to do with anything? I grab the phone and read -

Sophia STOLE my man too.

Was the headline, with a really tacky lingerie photo of Mile's ex-girlfriend. 'Wow, I thought Cat was a bitch. Who knew there were so many money-grabbing and attention-seeking women out there.' I'm in shock and I read the article which is filled with lie after lie. The only truth in it is my name and the fact I did date Miles. 'So is there anything, anywhere about us being together and me actually being the girlfriend of Dominic's best mate?'

'On one of the websites there is a short article, but it really doesn't matter now, as this girl has a more interesting story to tell apparently.' Seb doesn't even look up in my direction, he is still sitting with his back to me and I suddenly feel very alone and isolated.

'You know It's all lies, right? I did date him for a couple of months and he was decent enough to help me out when I needed it. I would have been homeless or god knows where. It just wasn't right with us and that's it, nothing more than that. He had been broken up with her for months when we got together. I didn't even know she existed until she randomly turned up at his apartment one evening and totally humiliated me. Obviously she enjoys making people feel like shit.' Seb still does not turn around. 'Seb, I REALLY need to know what you are thinking right now. Please talk to me, or even just look in my direction. That would be nice.' I feel the frustration rising and my already short patience is really being tested.

'Well. It's just not nice reading about your girlfriend's ex,' he finally turns around and faces me.

'ARE YOU FUCKING JOKING?' That's it, after days of being worn down, I have finally lost it. 'SHALL I FUCKING TELL YOU WHAT'S NOT FUCKING NICE SEB? BEING FUCKING ROBBED AT GUNPOINT, BEING ACCUSED OF HAVING AN AFFAIR WITH YOUR MARRIED BOSS AND NOW BEING SLANDERED BY SOME ATTENTION SEEKING BITCH. FUCK THIS, I AM DONE.' I grab my clothes and put them on as fast as physically possible, drag my wet hair into a top knot, trainers on and grab my purse.

'Calm down Soph. Where are you going?' He stands up and starts to walk over, I need space and I need it now.

'Don't you fucking DARE tell me to calm down. I should have gone home when I could, before getting wrapped up in this weird fucking world of Dominic and his bullshit lies. LEAVE.ME.ALONE.' I walk out of the hotel room, I barely check what I have, all I know is I need to get out of here, away from Seb and find a place to calm and work out what the hell I am now going to do with my life.

Before I know it, in a whirlwind of thoughts and fast walking, I have grabbed a coffee and breakfast muffin and find myself on the beautiful white sand beaches of Carmel. Finding a rock, I perch and gaze out to the Ocean and try to clear my head. My heart is slowing down and even with the stimulation of the caffeine, the power of being so close to the vast calming sea, seems to be working. So many thoughts have whirred through my head, I'm still struggling to think clearly. Even the consideration of selling my very own story. I might not even have a job anymore, so maybe I should cash in and make my life easier off the back of this nightmare. I could go travelling alone, see the world and get some perspective. Then I remember Arabella and also the fact I'm not that kind of person. I wish I was, because that seems like the easiest plan right now. Take some money and run, start fresh.

'Sophia,' I jump as my train of thought is broken and I turn to see Seb standing behind me. 'I've been looking all over for you. I have managed to book our flights home from San Francisco, but it will mean leaving in an hour if we are going to make it in time.' His delivery is cold and to the point and I feel sad and sick to my stomach. One of my only allies has dropped me so quickly because he didn't like hearing lies about an ex. How fragile we must really have been, for Seb to be able to forget what we had so quickly.

'OK, I will come and pack in a few minutes.' I have already turned my back on him and feel the tears burning my eyes, but I am not going to let him see. How dare he believe that lying bitch over me. I can hear him finally walking away and the tears flow, every ounce of self-pity is flooding out. I know I don't deserve this, I never asked for any of it. I sit and my emotions switch between anger and sadness until I finally pull myself together, dry my eyes and make a plan. I will pack my bags, go home to my parent's house and hide out there until this has all blown over. This will all be a distant memory to the tabloids soon and I will return to being irrelevant to the gossip columns in no time, which will suit me perfectly. I pop my phone on and await the signal to kick in and the barrage of notification pings that I am sure are awaiting me. I have already disabled all my social media accounts to cut out that avenue of potential abuse and trolling. I scroll through the messages of friends and relatives wishing me well and the confirmation that people know it's lies. A wave of relief flows over me. There is an email from Miles, apologising on behalf of his ex and offering any help he can, with a press release his manager has typed up also attached. I quickly message him back and accept the offer, anything to dispute these lies can only work in my favour. Even if it is only Seb who reads it and understands the extent of the rubbish that has been written, that will be enough for me right now. An email from my parents suddenly pings up.

Sophia,

We got the news of your return from Seb, we will be at the airport as requested to pick you up. Don't worry, we will get you home and you will be safe here until this whole rubbish has passed by. I promise it will darling, we hope you are OK and cannot wait to have our girl back home and safe with us. I will have your favourite dinner ready and we can binge watch all our favourite films, I will also get some ice cream in for us and we can slob out for as long as it takes.

We love you so much, have a safe flight, Mum & Dad xxxxxxxx

Deep breath. I knew I could rely on my parents, I knew they would be on my side. I'm going to ignore the fact that Seb has clearly arranged to be rid of me at the first possible opportunity. To go to the trouble to organise my parents to take me off his hands, what a burden I must now be to him. I grab my things, taking one last look at the sea and turn to head back to the hotel, feeling so sad that a place I have always dreamed of visiting has been so horribly tarnished with all this craziness.

I look out of the plane window, watching the lights of London getting closer and illuminating the UK's night sky. The long car drive from Carmel to the airport in San Francisco had been painfully silent and barely a word had been exchanged between Seb and I, since leaving the hotel. The moment we checked in our bags, we went our separate ways as it had transpired that our flight seats had been purposely sat apart. I couldn't bear to even look at Seb for a moment longer. He had uttered, 'I assumed that would make you happier,' as I found out I would be taking the long flight alone and I couldn't even find the words to respond. The realisation that it must really be over has haunted me the entire flight home and knowing Seb is sitting only a few rows behind me on the flight feels like torture. There have been moments I just wanted to get up, go over to him and cry into his arms. Then the reality of how he had been so cold since reading the article hits me and my blood boils. How can he switch off his emotions for me so quickly? After knowing the turmoil I have been in since all this rubbish was written in the press, I feel so hurt and heartbroken.

After what felt like a riot trying to disembark the plane, I barely caught a glimpse of Seb, apart from the back of his head as he stepped off the plane and out of view. I managed to make my way off and after negotiating hoards of people in the terminal chaos who were rushing in every direction, I hit the passport control queue. Somehow, Seb is near the front already and the hopes I had of catching up with him seem to be getting slimmer. Not knowing when I will, or even IF, I will ever see Seb again has left me feeling physically sick. Surely we can get over our first fight? Not that it was even a fight per se, I try to rationalise with myself. I know I shouted and lost my cool, but who wouldn't under the stress of being publicly humiliated and judged? He can't really believe the article, he already knows me so much better than that. The last thing I wanted to do was end up pushing him away. Lost in my thoughts, before I know it, I am at the front of the queue and I flash my passport. I rush to find the conveyor belt with our luggage in the hope our paths will cross and we can at least leave our trip with a little hope. Again, people everywhere, bags everywhere, if Seb was a needle in a haystack I might stand a greater chance of finding him. I zig-zag my way through the crowds and over to the furthest conveyor in the large hall, where I see my bag already circling in a very lonely state. It's typical, the times I have waited hours for a bag to be unloaded off a flight and the one time I could do with the delay, there it is, how annoyingly efficient of the airport. Of course there is no Seb in sight and I take a deep breath and hope it's only my parents at the arrivals hall. I have had, possibly irrational fears, but fears nonetheless, of walking out to a mass of paparazzi and hoards of booing Dominic fans on my arrival home. As I edge my way cautiously down the nothing to declare aisle, for the first time ever, I hope they pull me over to search my bags and buy me a little more time before I walk through the sliding doors of what feels like doom. As they glide open the only faces I see instantly in the arrivals hall are Mum, Dad and Margo's.

'Sophia. Thank goodness,' Mum runs over and hugs me, followed by Margo and then Dad.

'Sweetheart, we have been so worried,' Dad also wades in, giving me a huge and reassuring hug.

'Sis, so pleased you are back. Mum thinks she saw Seb rush out a few minutes ago. What's going on? Are you guys not together?' Margo's skill of jumping straight in at the deep end never ceases to amaze me.

'Can we get out of here before I get into any of that please Margo,' I plead.

'Yes, Margo. I did suggest you at least wait until we are in the car to interrogate Sophia,' Dad scolds her whilst grabbing my bag and we all head towards the exit. I feel eyes on me, I'm not sure if it's my paranoia or the recognition of my face from the tabloids, but I'm starting to wish I had invested in a baseball cap and wore my sunglasses at least to feel a little more incognito.

For the entire drive home, the car is silent. I catch glimpses of Margo pulling wide eyes and nudging her head towards me as unsubtle as she is and mum shaking her head and furrowing her brow in response. Part of me wants to put them out of their misery and explain what has happened, but the other part of me feels ready to burst into tears, even if I try to utter a word about Seb.

I must have fallen asleep, as the next thing I hear is the gravel of our drive as we arrive back to the family home and it feels like a sight for sore eyes. The chocolate box, Cotswold cottage surrounded by pristine Spring flower beds covered with daffodils and a rainbow of tulips. I can see Charly and Harry standing at the window, like a welcoming home committee. Charly has swung the front door open running towards us and before I can even unbuckle myself, she has her arms wrapped around me and is sobbing into my neck,

'For God's sake Soph, you are never going away AGAIN, do you understand me?' I climb out of the car and continue to cuddle Charly as we slowly edge our way into the house, Harry puts his arm around the other side me,

'So pleased you are safe Sis. Charly is a little more hormonal than usual, hence the floods of tears, but we can explain that to you over a coffee.' I feel pangs of guilt that I haven't even given Charly and Harry's baby treatment much thought over the past few days, but that will all change now I am home and I intend to make it up to them, I promise myself. Taking my coat and shoes off, I inhale the smell of home and the comforts I have been missing and needing so badly.

'Tea or coffee, Sophia?' Mum shouts from the kitchen and I walk in to find them all huddled around the kitchen table.

Before long, Charly and Harry have updated me on their week of hospital appointments and for the first time in a while, I forget all of my own woes. 'So, in a nutshell, I had too many eggs after the treatment, which is a positive thing, BUT, they will not continue the process until next month when hopefully I have fewer eggs present.'

'Why can't they continue now?' I say, with a mouth full of one of mum's homemade scones.

'Well, there is a huge risk of multiple pregnancies. Potentially six or seven at the moment.'

JESUS, so you would basically have a litter, like a dog or a cat?'

'Thank you for that comparison my darling sister,' Charly says laughing, 'yes, it would be far too dangerous and the potential of things going very wrong is too high.'

'This is all incredibly positive though.' Harry wraps a reassuring arm around Charly, 'soon enough I'm sure we will have some amazing news for us all to celebrate,' but before I get to respond with excitement of the prospect of being an aunt, Dad walks in with a furrowed brow,

'Sophia, please go and turn your phone off, or do something with it. It keeps bloody well bleeping and it's driving me around the bend, I can barely hear the golf and,'

.'...It's literally the only thing I watch,' Charly and I say in unison.

'We know Dad,' I roll my eyes at Charly.

'Very funny girls. Just please silence it, Sophia.'

I run upstairs and throw myself onto my bed, grabbing my phone,

Hey gorge, hope all is well? Back to the office next week and hoping you will be there too? Read the crap, obviously, we are all #teamSoph all the way. Where are you? Give me a call when you can.

Michael always manages to bring a smile to face, I make a mental reminder to call him when I have an actual answer for him.

SOPH! We need a catch-up. Still moving to London and actually a friend has hooked me up with a two bedder in Camden. It's nice, not the Ritz, but affordable and central. Let me know ASAPxx

Well, that is good news! One positive step towards returning back to London life,

Yes! sounds great, do you have any photos and how much? Need to check I still have a job first xx

Feels a little dramatic typing that out, but in reality, I probably should check I am still employed. Being accused of having an affair with your boss and then stories being sold which tarnish your name and reputation probably could give good grounds for being fired, even if it's based on a load of lies.

£800 and here are a few pics and floor plan, rooms are the same size, so we won't be scrapping over the bigger room! Sure you will have a job, if not I will be happy you use some of my law studies to look at unfair dismissal! xx

Hehe, appreciate the offer, but hopefully, it won't get to that. I will call the office now and let you know ASAP, thanks Poppy, I really, really appreciate you sorting all of this xx

No problem chica, you have had enough to deal with lately. Let me know and I will put the deposit down and you can just owe me, no arguments xx

I feel instant pangs of anxiety in the depths of my stomach as I dial Harriet, the Senior Producer at Freedom.

'Sophia, that is so funny, I was literally just about to send you an email. So pleased you rang, how are you doing?'

'Hi Harriet, I'm doing much better now, thank you. I'm home with my family and being pampered. How are you after Brazil?'

'Oh, I am so pleased. I am fine thank you. I'll be honest, the break after the incident was really needed, but feeling so happy to be back and busy at work. Cracking on with the fall out from losing so much of the filming time. That's why I was emailing as a lot of the team started back yesterday, but I would like to give you a little more time if you need it? Obviously that ridiculous story was sold and I totally understand your life has been a bit hectic.'

'Yep. Unfortunately, it didn't all vanish as quickly as I had hoped.'

'Well no, I did read the other desperado claiming her moment of fame, but what I can reassure you is that Cat has obviously been fired and the lawyers are dealing with her. So that is one person you will not have to face. The entire company knows the stories are lies and everybody and I mean, EVERYBODY, is totally on your side. So you won't have to return, worrying about the gossip, there is none. We are starting the prep for the alternative shoot for this season's shows and are obviously quite far behind production now. So, I would love you to come back as soon as you feel ready, but please take extra time if you need it.'

I sigh with relief and hold back the tears, 'Thank you so much, I have been really worried I would not be able to return to work. I'm just hoping the dramatics are over now and I can focus on my job.' Harriet laughs.

'Yes, well I can promise you, the past few weeks are certainly not the norm here and I will ensure your work life is much smoother from now on!'

'That Harriet, is exactly what I needed to hear, thank you. I will be back in the office on Monday if that suits you?'

'Perfect. I will let the team know, they will be ecstatic with the news. You take care and enjoy the next few days, see you soon.'

I fall back onto my childhood bed and gaze at the ceiling. Amazingly, in the past twenty minutes, I have solved two of my three current life issues. Do I still have a job? Yes. Will I have a home in London? Yes. So far, so good. Having not seen or heard from Seb since watching him walk out of passport control, I have pretty much come to terms with the fact that the, am I now single question, is a definite YES.

Chapter Fifteen

'Sophia. Sophia darling. Wake up,' I squint and find my mum learning over my bed.

'What time is it?' I shield my eyes from the dramatic curtain opening and the sun beating in, courtesy of my mother.

'It's gone 9 am and you have a visitor. Tidy yourself up quickly and come down please.' Before I even got to question who, my mum had scarpered out the door and I can hear her running down the stairs, promising to whoever was there that I was on my way. I jump up and quickly brush my hair, throw some fresh clothes on and quickly brush my teeth. I look at my reflection and am a total mess, but who the hell turns up, unannounced on a Saturday morning? There should be laws against this kind of rude awakening and intrusion.

'Sophia, please hurry up, people don't have all day,' Mum shouts, really annoyingly from the bottom of the stairs.

'Well mother, maybe people shouldn't just turn up at our house like this then,' I shout back out of frustration, probably a little louder than intended.

'Sophia, we all heard that.' My mum scorns and I bite my tongue and refrain from responding, it's just too early to pick a fight.

Running down the stairs I see a dark shadow at the front door, which is odd, I'm not sure why they would leave someone outside.

'Mum, Dad, there is someone out...,' before I get to finish, it all becomes clear. Dominic is here. I walk into the lounge and see him being catered for by every single person in my family, even Harry hasn't managed to keep his cool which is surprising and equally disappointing to me.

'Dominic, what are you doing here?' I'm abrupt and I intended to be.

'Sophia, for goodness sake, please be more welcoming,' mum says, blushing with a strange grin frozen on her face.

'It's OK mum, last week I was plastered all over the papers at his mistress and a homewrecker. Pretty sure I'm in a good position to question him turning up at my family home!' Dominic laughs

'Yes, it's absolutely fine, I expected you to be a bit surprised Soph. Apologies that I didn't pre-warn you. Do you mind if we have a chat?'

'No problem,' as I gaze around at everyone in the room staring at Dominic, they clearly have no intention of leaving, 'would you like to come into the conservatory.' It was more of an instruction than a question as I walk out of the room and with the assumption, Dominic would take the initiative to follow. I find a seat and a few moments later, Dominic appears, closing the door behind himself.

'Sophia, can I just firstly apologise for the crap you were drawn into. Obviously I messed up and there are no excuses.'

'It wasn't brilliant. I'll be honest, but you don't have to explain anything more to me.' He shuffles in his seat and I realise I am being slightly harsh, but I also don't feel any empathy for him.

'OK, well I am here as I just want to clear the air before you return to the office and make sure there is no tension. I am pleased you are returning and it would be great if we could start a clean slate. If, of course, you feel that is possible?'

'Yes, I think that would be a good idea for everybody involved.' Dominic smiles and gets up to hug me, I respond in kind, even though the image of a pregnant, broken-hearted Arabella runs through my mind and I remind myself that I have just agreed to a clean slate seconds ago.

'One thing though Soph,' Dominic sits back down, 'Seb. He is a mess and I have never, in my life, seen him so devastated. He has no idea I have visited you and wouldn't want me to "burden" you with this, as he refers to it, but pretty sure you have a right to know how much this has all affected him. I had to beg him to forgive me for my part in all of this and I promised to stay out of it. Obviously I have to let you know, just in case you think there is any chance things can be resolved?'

'I'm surprised he is even fussed. He couldn't wait to get on a flight, sit well away from me and he couldn't even bring himself to say goodbye at the airport. From where I am sitting, he didn't act like he was devastated.' I sit back in my chair and when I run over the last day with Seb out loud, it starts to infuriate me. If he still cared so much then none of that pain and upset was necessary.

Dominic runs both hands through his hair and looks frustrated, 'It's all my fault. I know it's all down to some shitty decisions I have made, I realise that and I promise I'm doing what I can to fix it. The last thing now is to make sure my best mate doesn't lose the love of his life because I will feel shit forever. I'm not sure how much you guys have discussed his past, but I promise you this Sophia, he does NOT fall for people easily. He has struggled his whole life, I'm not going into it anymore, as it's not for me to tell you. Please give him a chance and hear him out.'

I was silenced by being referred to as the "love of his life".

'You need to call him sis.' Charly ruffles my hair in a true annoying older sister fashion, as we all stand and bid farewell to Dominic and his entourage. It's a small village that we grew up in, so it hasn't taken long for the word to spread that the internationally acclaimed chef has made a visit, even though he had only been in the house for forty minutes at the very most! I wouldn't be surprised if mum had sent out a group message to spread the word and I am pretty sure I haven't seen this many residents mingling around the lane since a herd of cows had escaped the local farm and everybody gathered to try and keep them from eating their prize magnolias and roses bushes.

Heading back into the house alone, my family continue to mingle in the front garden. They are muttering excitedly and I have left Mum and Dad telling and retelling, what feels like the story of a Royal visit, the way everyone has totally lost their heads over it. Thankfully this means I can escape the madness and find solace in my room, where I intend to call Seb. The fear of rejection hits me, but as I call, I remember Dominic's words, why would he say all those things if Seb wanted to end everything we have.

'Hey Soph, so pleased you rang,' Seb answers after one ring and takes me by surprise as I was half expecting to be sent to answerphone.

'Hey, you. Erm, how are you?' I really should have thought this through first.

'I'm a bit shit actually. I feel crap about how things were left with us. How are you?'

'Not the greatest I have been. I am so sorry for shouting at you. It just felt like everything caught up with me and I assumed you believed the article as you seemed so cold.'

'Not at all, I knew that girl was selling lies. I have seen these things being closed down by Dom's PR team a hundred times before. I know what these people are capable of. I just realised that moment, that, well, literally none of it would have happened if we had just come home in the first place. I just thought a trip to California would put Brazil behind us, instead, it made things a billion times worse. I didn't mean to be cold Sophia, I just feel responsible for this mess.' I sigh a huge breath of relief, thanking my lucky stars I may not have lost Seb for good.

'You would never have guessed this was going to happen, so please stop blaming yourself. I wanted to go with you. Neither of us could have predicted this.'

'Well the one person we can blame is Dom. If it wasn't for him being shit, literally none of this would have happened. I can't even answer his calls at the moment, I messaged him to give me space to cool down.'

'Well, speaking of Dominic. The reason I am calling is that he actually turned up at my parent's house earlier, totally unannounced.'

'Oh for fuck's sake, he has even met your parents before I had the chance. Typical fucking Dom, he can't just back-off and let people sort it for themselves.'

'Don't get me wrong Seb, I was very surprised and not exactly ecstatic when I saw him in my lounge, but then, he is the reason I called you. He said some sweet things about you and made me realise I may have got the situation totally wrong with us. So, please don't be too mad with him for coming here,' Seb pauses for a moment.

'Can I come and see you please? It will only take me a couple of hours if I leave now.'

'Yes please,' I didn't have to pause for thought, 'I would absolutely love that. Bring a bag with some clothes so you can stay here if you would like too?'

'Absolutely, if you are sure that's OK. See you ASAP.'

I walk downstairs to my family huddled in the lounge, watching one of Dad's many war films. 'Oh a lovely little Saturday afternoon light watching I see,' Dad blanks my sarcasm, but everyone else looks over to me with rolling eyes of despair and I am pretty sure Harry is secretly watching Rugby on his phone.

'Darling, sit here,' mum pats the sofa next to her, I go, throw myself down and hug into her.

'He's on his way over,' I smile to mum and she kisses my forehead,

'He really must love you Sophia' and I realise, maybe he does.

After, what feels like hours of watching the clock on the mantel, there is a knock on the door and I jump to my feet, 'That's Seb, I will get it.' Before the bedlam of my family descends on him, I really just need a moment alone. After all, the last time I saw him he was walking into the distance and I wasn't even sure if I would ever see him again.

'Hey,' I swing the door open and step out to the porch, pulling it closed behind me. 'I just need a second alone with you if you don't mind.' I look up to see Seb's smiling but slightly pensive face so I wrap my arms around his neck and give him the kiss I have been thinking about for the past hour.

'Phew. I was so nervous Soph, that was definitely the welcoming I was hoping for,' his shoulders drop and he looks instantly more at ease.

195

'I was so worried I wouldn't see you again, it was such a horrible feeling. I literally felt sick,' Seb hugs me into his chest and wraps his arms around me.

'I honestly thought you would have been happy with that. All I have done is brought drama into your life so far.'

'Erm, no Seb. Correction, Dominic has brought the drama. Not you,' suddenly the front door is swung open and there stands my mum and sisters.

'Darling, we have all been very patient in here, but your time is up, can you please introduce us to Sebastian?'

'Your family is amazing Soph, I feel so welcomed' as he puts his bag down onto my bedroom floor and looks around.

'Well you will be pleased to know that Dominic did not get quite the warm welcome and he certainly wasn't allowed into this room,' I grab his hand and pull him onto my bed.

'I've missed you so, so fucking much Soph. Even just being on the plane and not being next to you was horrible.'

'I know, same here. Can we just forget about all that now and focus on the good stuff. I'm just happy you are here.' We then kiss a little, then a little more kissing. If it wasn't for my entire family most likely sitting below my bedroom, it would have been far less PG-rated.

I pull away and remember the comments Dominic dropped on his visit, 'Seb, I need to ask you something. It's something Dominic said and it feels like, if we are going to have a fully honest relationship, I need to know what he was alluding to.' Seb lies back on the bed and fluffs up a pillow to lean his head back onto.

'I know what you are referring to, he mentioned it to me too. I'm annoyed that Dom decided it was time to tell you because that isn't his call to make and also, I don't really want to add to, well, you know, everything else right now. It's not even a big deal, but I guess you should know,' Seb sighs and I can see that he is reluctant.

'It's OK, just tell me when you are ready, there is no rush and no pressure.' I put my head on his chest and feel his heart pounding as he strokes my hair.

'So, here it goes. I was abandoned as a baby at birth and left at the door of a hospital. I have never known my biological parents and it was Dom's mum, who was a nurse at the hospital, that found me. The family I was placed with, who are now my parents and the ones who have loved me and raised me, are good friends and colleagues with Sue and Paul, Dom's mum and dad. So we are like family, the closest I have ever come to a real, genuine family.' I sit up, slightly stunned by this flood of information as Seb continues to open up. 'That's why Dom is concerned about us and came here. He hates seeing me potentially losing someone I care about so much, because he has seen my life and knows how it's impacted me. So, I hope you understand, he is not being malicious or overbearing. Even though he can be a total dick sometimes, he does genuinely care about me and that means you too now.' I swing my arms around his neck and climb on to him, holding him as close and as tight as I possibly can. All that runs through my head is how I shouted at him and pushed him away in Carmel and now I feel so much guilt.

'I'm so sorry for being so aggro at you and shouting. I feel terrible,' I bury my head in his shoulder and I start to cry, clinging on to him. All I want to do is protect him and never let him feel abandoned again.

'Hey, no, don't you dare feel bad. You have had the shittest time Soph and I am not telling you this so you feel sad and guilty. Please don't act any differently because of something that happened to me as a baby. I have been incredibly blessed and fortunate. My family is amazing. They have given me a life that I would never have had if the woman who gave birth to me had kept me. She did me a favour.' Seb pulls me in front of him so we are looking eye to eye, 'Yes, I do feel nervous about losing you but not because of my past, but because I love you Sophia.'

'I love you so much too,' I say with tears streaming down my cheeks.

'Phew, well that's a relief,' Seb says wiping my tears away with his thumb. 'I don't want to scare you Soph, but I have never even thought about marriage or kids, any of that until I met you. I'm not talking this year or next, but I really feel like you could be, you know, the one,' he says coyly, 'Sorry if that sounds totally cringe and cheesy.'

'Well, of all the things a guy could say to a girl, I'm pretty sure I can live with that declaration of love. You may well just be the one for me Mr Simpson.'

'Scooby, here boy.' Our family dog, the most adorable King Charles Spaniel bounds up to me with his ears flapping as he speeds down the hallway. 'We are taking Scoobs for a walk,' I shout back into the house as Seb and I step out and into the fresh Spring evening.

We had spent the past couple of hours eating and drinking with many laughs and a lot of them being at my expense. Although, witnessing how at ease Seb feels around my family and how well he fits in, made it worth the embarrassment of all my childhood stories being shared.

We wind down the country lane and through a gate onto a public walk across a field, surrounded by beautiful countryside in all directions, 'It must have been difficult to leave all this to go to Brighton. Your family is awesome and this countryside is my idea of perfect,' Seb says, not breaking his gaze into the distance.

'I know, it wasn't a struggle at first as I had always taken it for granted, but I would like to move back one day and give my kids the same childhood. There was so much freedom and innocence for a long time. As kids, we walked these fields and had so many adventures. We loved it, they were some of the best memories.' Seb hugs into me and we watch Scooby dart across the field.

'Well I'm totally up for that, you don't have to sell that idea to me. I can't imagine a better childhood than that.' I realise, although I know significantly more in the past few hours than I ever had about Seb, I actually haven't asked him much about his family and where he grew up.

'So, what was your childhood like?' Seb takes a second and I can see the thoughts whirring through his head.

'It was good. I wouldn't say it was as idyllic as this all is but I was lucky and never went without. My parents, Caroline and Martin are brilliant. I also have an older brother Mark, who is a medic in the military, so I don't see him much. We keep in touch though. My mum gave up work when I arrived to focus her time on me. I was a surprise that happened so suddenly and there were a lot of hurdles my parents went through before they could adopt me fully. My Dad is a Surgeon and mum's a Doctor too.'

'Have you ever wanted to find out more about your biological family?' As soon as I say it, I regret it, 'don't worry if you don't want to tell me, it's fine. Sorry, that's really insensitive of me.'

'No it's not, I love these questions. I haven't spoken about this for a long time, so it's nice to talk about it. Especially to you,' he kisses my forehead and we stand, watching into the distance. 'The story of my adoption was quite complicated in the end, more so, because it was made so public. It was a sad story that the tabloids had latched onto and when these Doctors took me in from the brink of death and gave me a home, the papers printed photos of me being carried out of the hospital with my parents and released their names. So it was public knowledge, which made the process of adoption and the legal side of keeping them anonymous totally impossible, but they didn't give up on me. I will always be grateful for that.'

'Wow. That must have been so full-on for your parents, they sound like amazing people.'

'Yeah, they really are. If we go back to your parents now and mention Caroline and Martin Simpson and the abandoned baby, I'm pretty sure they may have a recollection of the news reports. I have seen the newspaper cuttings. My parents sat me down when I was very young and explained it all to me. Just so one day, some journalist or stranger wouldn't feel the need to do it for them. I tend to keep my parents' names out of the conversation around certain generations of people, just because they may well know the story. The number of times I have been called "Baby Blue" throughout my life when people find out.

'Baby Blue?'

'Yeah, it's the name I was given by the nurses and then the press when I was found wrapped in a baby blue blanket. I am used to it now, but I still don't want to be judged by something I had no say in.' I squeeze him tightly and feel the need to protect Seb from feeling any kind of hurt, ever again.

'I totally get that. Why should people know anyway? It's private.'

'Well, the thing is, going back to your original question,' in all honesty, I can't even remember what that was, with this influx of information. 'You asked me if I ever wanted to know more about my biological parents Soph,' he laughs, clearly recognising that I had lost track of the conversation. 'Well, unfortunately, because my parent's names had been made public, a few years later, my biological mother managed to track them down. It was really odd because I must have only been about three or four and this young woman kept appearing in different locations and talking to me. I vaguely remember being in a shopping trolley and this woman, well, girl really, walked over and held my hand and whispered something in my ear. I have no idea what she said, but I remember her kissing my cheek and then my mum running over, throwing a handful of food on the supermarket floor and screaming at her to leave me alone. That's when I realised there was something wrong.'

'Oh my gosh, that must have been so scary, for you and your mum. Caroline mum, not the other one.'

'Yep, it was more difficult to stop these surprise encounters, because nobody knew who she was. There was some poor quality CCTV footage, but not enough to track her down at the time. It's continued over the years.' Seb stops in his tracks, 'do you fancy going to that pub and grabbing a drink, I would rather bore you with all this over a beer?'

Chapter Sixteen

'Sit boy,' I tie Scooby's lead around the bottom of a table, in the beer garden of our local village pub. We have found the most secluded spot and Seb walks towards me with a beer in one hand and white wine in the other. After the amount of information unfolding about Seb's past, I don't want to make it too obvious, but I do really need that wine right now.

'Cheers Soph. To you, me and a history of shit that might just make you want to run a mile,'

'I'm not cheersing to that! Here is to you, me, honesty and well. Love.'

'Well, I guess that is a better toast,' we clink glasses and I wait with patience for Seb to continue his tale.

'Right, I have waited long enough, chapter two of the life of Sebastian Simpson, please.'

'Excellent, you have already inspired my autobiography title, I knew I would be able to rely on you,' Seb smiles and pretends to cheers me again. 'OK, so where were we? Oh yes, this chapter is titled "the shit didn't end there". So because nobody knew who my biological mother was, I would still see her appearing from time to time. I started to recognise her by four or five and after my mum's reaction in the supermarket the first time around, I knew her presence was not a good thing. So, I would tell my parents by pointing and shouting at her, but for years it was as though she vanished into thin air. Which seemed to be a speciality of hers.'

'Do you remember what she looks like?'

'Well, years ago she had very long dark hair, she was pretty but always a little bit scruffy.

I remember her being very skinny. It's obvious to me now, looking back, that she was either homeless or lived in extreme poverty, there was something not right at all. At the time it just seemed a little scary as a child. She was always smiley and gentle towards me. I think her heart must have been in the right place.'

'Have you seen her since being a child? Do you know her name or anything?' Seb sits back and sighs, throwing his head back and looking up and the darkening blue sky.

'A couple of times I thought I had seen her, but of course, she has changed over the years, so I could never be 100%. Until,' he looks at me with a slight pensive expression, 'but, well, while we were in Carmel, I had a call from Dom. Apparently a slightly erratic woman had turned up at the Freedom offices and was asking for me. Obviously nobody is aware of the situation apart from Dom, who knows the full history and worked out who she was. She actually went to hit Dom and told him it was his fault I had been in danger. Before the police arrived she had run off. Dom thinks she must have seen the news reports of the robbery and tracked down the offices assuming I would be there.' It's all ticking very quickly through my brain and things that have happened are all starting to make sense.

'Is that why you left the airport in such a rush when we got home?'

'Yes Soph, I wanted to get back and speak to Dom, and in all honesty, I couldn't face meeting your parents the way we were. There was so much going on at once and I just had to get my head straight.'

'I get that. It's fine, I understand now. Do you think she is following you again?' I suddenly feel a little on edge and scour the pub garden. 'You don't think she is dangerous, do you?' Seb grabs my hand and squeezes it reassuringly.

'She's never given me any reason to think she is unsafe, well, until now, due to her presence at Freedom and the verbal and attempted attack on Dom. She is now being looked for by the Police. They managed to get a good image of her from Dom's security cameras, so it won't be too hard to find her hopefully.' I drag a saucer of water over for Scooby while I try to get my thoughts together. Seb had warned me there was going to be more information, but I hadn't for a second expected any of this.

'Did you see the image of her, from the CCTV?'

'I did.' He looked away and I can see the deep gulps and I am sure he is trying to hold back tears. He wiggles in his seat and recomposes himself. 'She looked so much older, still skinny and if someone told me she has a drink or drug problem, I would totally believe them. Dom was pretty convinced she was drunk when she turned up at the offices.'

'Oh gosh, I'm so sorry.'

'This is why though, I think we should be cautious. She has never done anything until now, but I don't know her, or her capabilities. If she's seen the news reports, then she's also seen you and me together. She seems to have a funny knack for finding me.' I feel the instant urge to be in the compounds and safety of my family home and not a sitting duck in a pub garden.

'Would you mind if we head back Seb? I'm feeling cold now and Scooby could do with his dinner,' which is all true, but the reality is, the potential of his unstable biological mum searching for him has left me feeling extremely unnerved.

We walk home in silence and I am taking a moment to digest all the information I have just learned. 'Soph, I've scared you, haven't I? I totally understand, it's a lot of information and it's all so crazy. I don't blame you, I told my mum and her reaction was to pack her and Dad a bag and to stay in a hotel for a few days, just in case she turns up at my family home. Do you think it would be better if you just stayed here for another week, just until it's sorted in London? There is every chance she will appear again, but hopefully, the police will catch up with her, especially with Dom on the case.'

'Sorry I'm so quiet. All is fine, but I just need a moment to process it all. What will they do with her when they do find her?'

'I guess it's possibly classed as harassment; trespassing, threatening a famous chef. Who knows? I probably need to talk to her at some point, to figure out what she wants from me and make it clear that I don't want her in my life.'

'Hey darlings, good walk?' My mum bounds out of the front door and down the gravel path towards us and scoops up Scooby, 'Right little doggy, Scooby snack time. Oh, and one of your phones has been going continually upstairs kids. It's been driving your father bonkers Sophia.' Seb looks at me and runs upstairs, I'm pretty sure we are both thinking the same thing and that it must be news about his mother. I run up to my bedroom after him and by the time I reach my door, he is already on the phone.

'Yes. No. I understand I'm just not sure what I should do in this situation. I have never met her before, now I am being asked to bail her out.' Seb stands and his expression intensifies, 'No, you need to listen to me please, Dom should NOT have given you my number, I don't know Lucinda, in fact, I only know of her name because you just told me. That is how ridiculous all this is. If you are her friend, you can surely look after her.' There is silence from Seb and I can tell he is taking on a lot of information, I see my phone flashing and grab it to answer, it's a mobile I don't recognise,

'Hello?'

'Hey Soph, it's Dom, I need to talk to you. Seb will be fuming with me, I am hoping you will be able to help me out and calm him.'

'It might be a bit late for that. He is on the phone with someone now.'

'Oh wow, they didn't waste any time. Soph, I don't know how much he has told you, but his mum turned up again.'

'I know pretty much the whole story now. Well, I think I do!' As I look over to Seb and his face has turned from the normal olive glow to a much deeper red and angry shade.

'Good. That helps. So she turned up about two hours ago and threw a brick through the office window. Thankfully, the Police managed to arrest her this time. I didn't know what to do Soph. The Police suggested, for all our safety I should press charges and after Brazil, well you know, I don't want to risk any of the staff's safety again!'

'Dominic, I think you did the right thing, but who did you give Seb's number to?'

'Well, yeah, this is the thing he will hate me for. Soph, it was so sad. His Mum is so broken and some guy was with her, no idea who he is, but he told me her side of the story and she is desperate Soph. Desperate to see Seb.'

'He's hanging up Dom, I have to go, I will get him to call you.' I hang up the phone and walk over to Seb, who is now perching on the side of the bed with his head in his hands and he doesn't even look up at me.

'Was that Dom on the phone?'

'Yes, it was. He wanted to warn you of someone calling, but I presume it was too late?' There is no answer from Seb and it doesn't feel like the time to pressure him for answers.

'I'm going to make a drink, would you like one?'

'Yes please. Thanks, I just need a minute to figure something out.'

'Hey, where's Seb?' Harry asks, looking over my shoulder as everyone is gathered in the kitchen, drinking and chatting.

'Erm, just upstairs, something really weird has happened and I can't explain it until I know the full story.'

'Weird, in what way Soph. Should we be worried?' Dad has a look of concern across his face and the room has gone from the constant murmurs of chatting and laughing, to silence with all eyes directed on me.

'I don't even know where to begin and I have only just found out myself in the past few hours. I need to check with Seb first if he is happy with me to share it.'

'It's fine Sophia, I don't mind,' I nearly jump out of my skin as he walks into the kitchen and I notice his bag over his shoulder.

'Sophia, darling, are you OK? You are on edge and I am starting to feel very concerned,' mum walks over to me and puts a reassuring arm around my waist. I look at Seb for some kind of answer to her question.

'I have to get back to London as soon as possible, so I'm going to leave now. Thanks so much for allowing me into your lovely home and for a great afternoon meeting you all. It's frustrating that I have to leave, but it seems that it's just one drama after the next at the moment and I hadn't quite expected today to go this way,' he looks between my parents a little uneasy. 'I'm so sorry to drag this mess into your home. Do you remember the news story about Baby Blue?' My parents look at each other,

'That rings a bell,' my Dad is deep in thought.

'The Simpson couple?' My mum basically shouts as though she has just remembered the winning answer on a quiz show. 'The baby left at the hospital Peter, you know, then the lovely doctors adopted him and it was all over the news for weeks, well, months if I remember correctly.'

'Ah yes, I do remember now, that was quite the story at the time. Why Sebastian?'

'Well, I'm Baby Blue and it seems my biological mother has just made an appearance, but she doesn't seem to do things by halves. Apparently, some things never change. So, I'm on my way to bail her out.' Without hesitation my mum runs over and gives Seb the biggest hug, wrapping her arms around him.

'Oh, dear Sebastian. I remember thinking about what a lovely family you ended up with. You did have a good life with them didn't you?'

'Oh yes, definitely, I totally landed on my feet with them. I could not have asked for a better childhood and parents, I have been so lucky. I'm sure Soph will let you know the details more, but I really must go and sort this out. Thanks again and I really hope I see you all again soon.' I walk out with Seb as he heads towards the front door with the echoes of 'goodbyes' and 'take cares' following us down the corridor from my family.

'Would you like me to come with you? I feel like this is too big of a deal to do alone!'

'No, please Soph. You stay here until I have this sorted. Can you do me one thing though, please?'

'Of course, what?'

'Can you please reassure your family that I am normal? These few weeks of continuous ups and downs are not the norm for me and I will be a good boyfriend if you still want me with all this baggage?'

'Of course silly. I will let them know and no more talk of your baggage Sebastian Simpson. I love you and I promise I am here for you if and when you need me.' Seb lifts me off my feet and kisses me one last time, he puts me down and heads to his car. 'Please message me when you are back in London so I know you got there OK,' he gives me the thumbs up and before I know it, he has left.

As I sit at the kitchen Island, Charly perches next to me and tops up a glass of red wine, that I have been sitting and staring at since rehashing Seb's life story to my gobsmacked family. Everyone's opinions had been in full flow, but I must have missed at least half of it, as I sit and stare at my mobile, waiting for an update. It's three hours since Seb left and nearly eleven in the evening, my eyes feel heavy and I'm emotionally drained, but the idea of sleeping seems impossible right now.

'Soph, we have to head to bed, Harry and I are back in Cheshire first thing for a doctor's appointment and I can't be turning up with tired bags under my eyes.'

'Oh gosh, I'm sorry Charly, with all this crap I totally forgot about tomorrow. Please let me know how you get on? Looks like I will be here for a few days, so you know where to find me if you need me.'

'Thanks and vice versa. Can we have an update on Seb's mum and let us know the outcome?'

'Yes definitely, I will give you a call tomorrow afternoon, sweet dreams love birds,' as they vanish upstairs.

'Well, I reckon between the four of us, we could manage one more bottle. What do you think girls?' Dad waves a bottle of wine in front of mum and Margo and without even saying a word, they hold their glasses up. They have both been engrossed in whatever Google could offer them on "Baby Blue" and after trawling through website upon website of baby clothes for at least two hours, they had made a few discoveries and are now in full investigating mode of Seb's history. Dad walks over to join me, 'Soph, you have barely said a word the past couple of hours. Do you need to chat with your old man?' He wraps his bear hug arms around me and I feel like I'm five again.

'Honestly Dad, I don't know what to think. I thought moving to the city would be all fun. Starting my career, socialising and living the Carrie Bradshaw dreams.'

'The Carrie who?'

'Just a TV show reference Dad,' he rolls his eyes as he tops up his glass. 'In reality, it's been one stress after another and there have been some amazing bits, but I'm really not sure how long I want to be on this rollercoaster.'

'Look, Sophia, what I have always told you? You have to take the rough with the smooth and as long as you learn from the rough, every experience will be positive and worthwhile.'

'Alright Dalai Lama,' Margo jumps onto the stool next to Dad and playfully messes his hair, teasing him.

'Well Margo, hopefully, one day you will listen to my years of experience and put it to good use when you finally leave home.'

'Pah, keep dreaming Dad. This little birdy will not be flying this comfy nest for a while.' Margo is the ultimate wind up, but a much-needed breath of fresh air right now.

'All I can suggest Soph, is give it a bit more time. If it's not for you, you know you can come home in a heartbeat and we will be here for you. Even Margo by the sounds of it,' Dad gives Margo a playful jab and hugs us both into his side.

'Thanks Dad, I appreciate it,' as he stands up and leaves to walk out of the kitchen, he turns around.

'For what it's worth darling, I think Sebastian is a really good guy.'

I wake up to the sound of my phone ringing. My eyes sting as I try to focus on the illuminated screen, 'Hey,' I manage to find my voice.

'Sorry Soph, did I wake you?' It's Seb and all the nervous feelings have instantly returned.

'Yes, but it's OK. I was hoping to hear from you. All OK?'

'Sorry, I didn't want to call too late last night. It had been quite a full-on evening.' I shuffle to a sitting position on my bed and see that it's seven o'clock in the morning and rub my aching, tired eyes.

'So, what happened?'

'Well, I got to the Police station where they were holding Lucinda. I spoke to Dom on the way back to London and he said he would happily drop the charges if I felt like she was stable and would leave the Freedom offices alone. Which is good of him, considering the damage she caused.' He sounds surprisingly upbeat and positive. 'You are not going to believe it Soph. NOT GOING TO BELIEVE IT!

So, the man who was with her and the guy Dom decided to share my number with, that Sophia, is my biological father and his name is George!'

'Oh my gosh. So hang on, have you met them both?' I start to feel excited and impatient for the news.

'Yes! I met George first, who I sat down with and he told me everything. Everything from them being

childhood sweethearts, to Lucinda's strict Italian Catholic father and her having no option but to have me in secret when they were both only sixteen. They desperately wanted to keep me, but both of my parents were scared of what their families would say and do. So, they thought the best thing to do was leave me in a safe place and let somebody find me. Obviously the hospital seemed like a perfect choice. They were happy when they saw I had been found, but both of them, especially Lucinda could never quite get over giving me away. Hence her following me and watching me over the years.' Seb sounds so happy and I imagine he must be feeling relieved.

'Seb, that is so sweet, I am so, so happy for you, getting reunited after all this time, it's just amazing.'

'I know right! I have considered how this would feel throughout my life, but

never thought it would really happen.'

'So tell me everything. I want to know all the details, every single second please.'

'Well actually Sophia, do you fancy coming back to London? I would much rather see you and tell you the whole story, maybe even meet them for yourself?

Chapter Seventeen

As I drag my bag through Paddington Station, even though the call with Seb was extremely positive, the cautious nerves are setting off butterflies in my stomach. Meeting your boyfriend's parents under any circumstances is intimidating, let alone meeting your man's parents when he has known them for less than twelve hours and he has just bailed one of them out. I send Poppy a quick message as I wait for Seb at the main entrance.

Hey lady, I'm back in London. It's all a bit mad and A LOT to explain, can you let me know the score with the apartment and when I am able to move it? Staying at my old apartment for the next couple of nights, so no stress xx

As I press send, I look up to see Seb bounding towards me with a huge smile across his face. 'Thank you so, so, so much Soph. This honestly means the world to me.' I hug him, relieved to see the stressed and worried Seb who had left my parents house the previous evening, now looked relaxed and happy.

'Of course. I said if you needed me I would be here. I will be totally honest though, this is really overwhelming.' Seb grabs my bag handle in one hand and my hand in the other.

'I know it is, so let me get you a coffee and I will fill you in with the rest of the details, so you are prepared. Trust me though, there is nothing to worry about.'

We find a secluded spot in the corner of a coffee shop. This is the first time I have been back into a crowded city since I made my unfortunate debut in the national tabloids. It only just occurs to me that people may well recognise my face and paranoia sets in. Although my name has been cleared of all possible affair wrongdoing, I find a pair of sunglasses from my handbag to hide behind.

'Here's your coffee, my diva girlfriend,' Seb jokes as he passes me a flat white.

'Very funny. It's not ideal knowing my face has been splashed across the papers, so I decided to hide.'

'Oh Soph, I'm sorry. I have been so wrapped up in my news, that hadn't crossed my mind. I'm sure nobody will remember you. I mean, not that you don't have a memorable face. Jeeez, I'm digging a hole.' I giggle at his awkwardness and it distracts me from my worries.

'It's OK, it still plays on my mind and I haven't even reactivated any of my social media for fear I will have some horrible messages waiting for me. You can always rely on at least one Troll not having anything better to do with their lives.'

'Right, I'll tell you what. I will reactivate them and make sure there is nothing sinister and will exterminate any existence of Trolls for you. I will also delete all photos and history of your exes at the same time.' He gives me a cheeky wink.

'I'm good with both. You will definitely be doing me a massive favour. Anyway, I want to know more about your biological parents, you left me on a cliffhanger.'

'Right, yes, sorry. Soooo, you know about their parents and the pregnancy being in secret. So once they knew I was safe, they continued their lives together and the family was none the wiser. They actually got married really young, they were only twenty and the secret of me apparently bonded them together. Lucinda openly admits to tracking down my family home and it turns out, she was around more than my parents or I ever realised. As creepy as it felt growing up, now I have spoken to her and she's explained herself, it feels like it all came from a good place. She was so devastated at giving me away. When they were married and it was acceptable in her family to have a baby, she became obsessed about getting me back.' I sit back and sip on my coffee, feeling sad for this woman. Seeing Charly struggle to get pregnant and being so desperate for a baby, I can imagine how heart-wrenching it would have felt to have a baby, but then feel so much pressure to give them away. 'So her and George tried for another baby, it was their way to move on with their lives. Sadly, things didn't turn out very well. Awful in fact. Lucinda miscarried a number of times and the last one was late into the pregnancy.'

'Oh dear God, poor woman, how sad for them both.' I grab a napkin and try to dab my tears as subtly as possible from underneath my shades.

'I know Soph, I know. It was downhill for them from there. Apparently, because of having me and not seeking treatment or care after my birth, something had happened to Lucinda, that meant carrying a baby full term would be near impossible.' Seb shuffles in his chair and we sit quietly for a moment, trying to digest this story. 'After the final attempt, when Lucinda was warned she would be unlikely to carry a child full-term, George said she was extremely depressed for a few years and stopped eating properly and was put on medication to help. Things improved for a long time, but a few months ago Lucinda had run out of her medication and decided she no longer needed it. Seeing the photo of Dom and me on the paper, after the coach robbery, she took a turn for the worse and hence her unravelling the past week.'

'Well, that all makes sense. I really feel for her. I cannot even imagine having to go through all that, it would be devastating.' I get up and sit across Seb's lap and cling onto him around his neck, doing my best Koala impression. I feel the need to protect him and make him feel safe. 'I will admit, I did feel very pensive about all of this last night, but now, I feel more excited about what the future holds for you guys. I'm really pleased it's working out for you,' Seb smiles ear to ear.

'Well, I am so pleased to hear that. My aim now is to give them the son they should have had and I really want you to be part of that. That doesn't scare you, does it?'

'Nope, not at all Seb. Coaches in Brazil scare me, but making things right for your biological parents does not.' We sit and are both lost in our thoughts. 'Seb, have you mentioned any of this to your adopted parents yet?' He shifts in his seat and I climb off and perch next to him on the coffee shop sofa.

'I just haven't had the chance. It's been playing on my mind, but it's not a conversation for the phone, I need to see them face to face. I was planning on going to see them once the dust has settled here, maybe tomorrow. Anyhow, we need to get you out of the glamorous Hampstead pad and back down to reality in Camden, with your friend. What's her name again?'

'Ah yes, Poppy. Actually the sooner I move in, the better, I really need to feel settled in this city for a while.' I check my phone, realising Poppy had responded to my text, but I had been too consumed with Seb to notice.

Hey Soph, no worries at all. I moved in yesterday and it's fab. Looking forward to having my BFF live with me, I will put the Prosecco on ice. I want to know everything that has been going on - in fact, I will put two bottles on ice ;) xx

'So I can move in anytime now. Poppy's already in. I just need to grab my things and head over.'

'Cars outside, let's drink up and head and get your things. I have promised to visit Lucinda and George again later. Obviously you are more than welcome to join if you would like?' Seb grins and I feel instantly guilty.

'Do you mind if we give it a few days? I think you need to get to know them first and without being too selfish, I really need to get settled with Poppy, get back to work and some normality. Then I promise I will be the best version of myself to meet them. You don't mind, do you?' I clasp his hands in between mine.

'Soph, I get it. It's a great plan. Drink up and let's go.'

I quickly message Poppy,

Will be there in a couple of hours, will you be in? Prosecco on ice, yes please- needed xx

We pull up at the Edwardian, four-story townhouse and it's picture-perfect. It's located down a pretty, tree-lined street and considering it's central London, the road is peaceful and calm.

'Sophia, yaaaay, you are here!' Poppy bounds out of the house and down the stone steps, grabbing me into a huge hug. 'So, so pleased to see you and thank goodness you are OK.' She releases me and looks at Seb as he is grabbing my bags out of the car. Looking between me and him, her mouth wide open and giving the very unsubtle impression that she approves of my man. 'Oh and you MUST be Seb, what a tall drink of water you are,' she puts out her hand to shake his and he laughs.

'Poppy, you are going to scare him away, I would like him to visit us here!'

'Oh I am sorry, I didn't mean to embarrass you.'

'It's fine, nice to meet you. Right, where are these to go?'

In a joint effort, we manage to get all my belongings over the threshold of my new apartment and I am relieved to find a clean and fresh two-bed, nicely decorated home which I can actually see myself living in for more than two months.

'Please tell me you like it Soph? I was so worried you would turn up and hate the place!'

'Oh no, don't be daft, it's fab. Honestly, you should have seen the first dump I moved into in London, it was awful. This, on the other hand, is perfect for us. I had expected nothing less from your standards Poppy.' I walk through, looking around the relatively modern kitchen, clean and sufficient shower room and my small double room with views onto the back garden. Seb follows me into my bedroom with the remainder of my bags.

'Well this is nice, I can imagine myself waking up here quite a lot,' Seb smiles with a little glint of cheek in his eye.

'Oh you do, do you? Well, obviously I would love that.' Poppy peers her head around the door.

'I'm ordering in sushi and I have that Prosecco perfectly chilled. Seb, are you staying for food? As I will order more if you are.'

'That would have been ace Poppy, but I have family to go and see. I will be back later tonight if that's OK?' The guilt of not going to meet Lucinda and Michael with him kicks in, after him just moving my belongings, unloading them and now I'm letting him go alone.

'If you would like me to come with you Seb, I can, if you need me?'

'That's sweet Soph, but you need to settle in and catch up with Poppy. Anyway, are you back at the office tomorrow?'

'Crap, I am, I had almost forgotten about that.'

'So, actually, I tell you what, I will head off now and see you at the office tomorrow, by the time I have seen Lucinda and George, taken them for some food and picked up clothes for work, it will be late and we both have early starts tomorrow. I spoke to Dom earlier and he mentioned a big production meeting, the first one with everyone back in the office and the plans for the shoot in Europe.' I feel butterflies in my stomach thinking about work and getting back to the job I had loved so much.

'I'm actually so, so excited to get back to work again, it feels so long since we were filming.'

'Yeah, so long and all the crazy stuff that has happened in-between.'

'Erm yes,' Poppy waves a bottle of bubbles at us, 'you and me, young lady, are due a bit of a catch up.'

'Right,' Seb laughs, 'that is definitely my cue to leave and let you ladies get on with your boozing.' He grabs me and kisses me softly, 'I will call you later.'

Poppy dramatically flings her head back and slams her palms down on the kitchen table, 'I cannot fucking believe that girl, WHAT A BITCH. Obviously I knew it was bullshit when I saw the headlines, but I can't believe some tramp would do that to anyone.' We are a bottle of Prosecco down and working through our sushi delivery as I fill Poppy in with the previous month's drama.

'I know. She surely must have had an inkling Arabella was pregnant too. So, to have an affair and then sell the story to the papers with that knowledge, trying to embarrass us all. Total bitch. Let's just hope I never see her face again.' Poppy twists the cork of the second bottle and tops up my glass.

'Well you better hope I don't see her, I will bring her down a peg or two' and I know, without a doubt, she would. Poppy's beauty is intimidating enough when you first meet her, let alone her sharp and smart tongue. I look in awe regularly and am grateful I have a friend like her on my side because you definitely don't want her as an enemy.

'You know, this really feels like a fresh start. I feel like writing off the first attempt of my London life. It was such an amalgamation of crap, with a few good bits squeezed in for good measure.'

'Honey,' Poppy jumps in, waving her chopsticks like a tipsy conductor, 'you know what I always say. If that hadn't happened, you wouldn't be here now. Seb is bloody gorgeous, you have an ace job and the boss totally owes you big time! You have a fab new apartment with an absolute dream of a flatmate and it's just going to be fun times ahead.'

'You are so right, Oracle of mine,' as I cheers to Poppy for probably the tenth time this evening. 'It's onwards and upwards from here. I just have to meet Seb's newfound and adopted parents and then hopefully our lives will be less about the drama and more about the fun.'

'That's my girl, cheers to that.'

'Anyway Poppy, enough about me, what has been going on with you?'

We sit and chat all evening until we both give in and head to bed. I have barely managed to unpack my bags, apart from my all-important outfit for my return to work in the morning. Although I have been reassured that I am not hot gossip in the offices, I still fall asleep with slight feelings of apprehension, almost like I'm the new girl all over again. I check my phone and there is no message from Seb, so I send him a quick goodnight message and relax into my new cosy bed.

Chapter Eighteen

It's a fifteen-minute walk to work from the new apartment and after waking to a freshly brewed coffee courtesy of Poppy and a short pep talk, she sets me on my way. It feels good to wake up with a familiar face and start my day with someone I know I can fully trust. She won't leave me in the lurch or homeless, I know I have a new home for the foreseeable future and although I feel pangs of anxiety in the pit of my stomach, it feels like the first time I have my "shit together" in London.

I skip across the road, towards the office and it's amazing what a sunny Spring walk can do for the soul. I am ready for business, I am a woman on a mission and I take a deep breath, 'I've got this,' I whisper to myself.

'Hey all,' walking towards my desk I see a huge bouquet of flowers sitting there and everyone turns with a chorus of 'hey,' 'welcome back,' and 'great to see you.'

'Wow, who are these for and from?' I inspect the flowers not wanting to presume they are for me. Michael stands to hug me.

'They are for you my darling, but no idea who they are from. Amazing to have you back, we have missed you.' I hug Michael and feel so happy to be reunited with the gang. Even though it's only been my workplace for a short period of time, the amount we have experienced already feels like we have bonded beyond just work pals.

I notice a card buried among the gigantic display of flowers and it is addressed to me,

Sophia, we have missed you and are so pleased you are back, Love the whole Freedom team x

'So, who are they from?' Michael inspects the card from over my shoulder.

'Well, apparently they are from you. All of you,' I laugh, thanks guys.

'It must be Dominic on a mission, trying to make amends for all his shit,' scoffed Shauna, 'but obviously we are so happy you are back. I just meant, he owes you a lot more than a pretty bunch of flowers in my opinion.'

'I appreciate the gesture, but yeah, it's been a bit of a shit time, not just me, for us all really.' Everyone looks down at their screens and I turn to see Dominic and a few of the managers walking through the office.

'Guys, meeting in five,' one of Dominic's cohorts announces with his hand up, reiterating five. Dominic gives me a very subtle nod and I politely smile back. Which reminds me that I really need to message Arabella and find out how the pregnancy is going and life without Dominic in the picture.

Five minutes later and nearly the entire production crew is squeezed into the board room. 'Right,' Dominic stands up from the head of the table, 'I'm pretty sure we have the whole team back in one room for the first time in a while.' He stands and scans the room for a second. 'I haven't missed anyone have I?' As he says it, Seb comes bounding through the door, 'of course Seb, sorry mate, nearly forgot you for a second.'

'Yeah, cheers,' Seb says laughing and full of sarcasm, I watch him squeeze to the front of the room near Dominic and take a moment to appreciate that the hot guy is all mine.

'Right, NOW we are all together. Can I start by saying that I appreciate every single one of you for coming back and still wanting to be part of Freedom. I realised we screwed up massively in Brazil and left ourselves vulnerable to what happened. It was naive and poorly planned. I and the security team take full responsibility. All I can promise is, we won't be back in Brazil filming.' The room explodes with cheers, claps and the sighs of relief, 'but obviously we do need to get the rest of this season shot ASAP. So, management has discussed our options and we will be keeping it simple and doing a tour around France. Which ironically we haven't actually done before. So it's nearby, easy to arrange a coach over with the kit and hopefully, this time it will be full of fun and productive. On a more serious note, Matty is on leave for the next month as he took quite a hit to the head and I personally would like him to enjoy a break and recover fully. He wanted to come straight back on tour, but it's in his best interests to take this time off and stay at home with his wife and kids to rest and recoup. So that takes me onto security and I will hand it over to Simon, who, as you may tell from his sizable arms and stature, is an ex-Marine and will now be overseeing all security for Freedom.'

'Hi guys, great to be a part of the team. Sorry to have heard what happened out there in Brazil. It can be an extremely volatile country and sadly for you guys, you saw the worst of it. From my point of view, we won't be sending anyone into an environment like that again and if we do, we will be prepared for all circumstances.' Everyone is looking at each other around the room subtly and gauging the reactions.

Seb is looking over and smiling giving me a thumbs up, then getting distracted by the click of a projector and a map of France beaming down at us.

'So, this is the route we are taking around the regions in France. I will now go into detail of the security which will be on hand for this trip. You guys may just think this is France, but we all know what happened to Kim Kardashian, right?' We all look around nodding, Simon puts his hands on Dominic's shoulder and I'm pretty sure by his reaction, it may have been a firmer grip than he had anticipated receiving. 'Dom is not Kim K. Sadly,' we laugh, Dom still looks in pain, 'but, he is in the public eye and this, as you all know, comes with attention and sometimes it is unwanted and potentially dangerous.'

We have an hour of security intel, which felt like we had gone from one extreme of a few security guards on hand to a full-blown army watching over us. We all walk out of the office and back to our desks and I'm feeling pretty jaded by it all. 'SO MUCH INFORMATION,' Michael sits down and rests his head in his hands.

'But at least we are prepared this time, right guys?' Seb walks over and pats Michael on the shoulder. 'We can't have a repeat of last time can we mate?' Seb drags a chair next to me and sits down.

'No Seb, obviously you are right. It Just feels like A LOT. I need caffeine, anyone?' We all raise our hands and with an eye roll, Michael sets off for his barista duties.

'Hey,' Seb gives me one of his gorgeous warm smiles and I try to act professional, even though the entire building, thanks to the tabloids, know we are together anyway.

'Hey,' I tap him on the knee trying to be inconspicuous.

'How was your first night in the new pad?'

'So good, I really like it and slept so well, but that may have been down to the second bottle of bubbles that Poppy opened. How are Lucinda and George?'

'They were good thanks. I just took them for a bite of food and went back to theirs. They live quite far out of town, near Epsom. It's nice, they have a cosy home in a nice area.'

'Did you find out much more, like what work they do or anything interesting?'

'Yeah, George is a Plasterer, but runs his own business now and Lucinda used to work in some kind of accounts, but gave it up to be a housewife after she had all her, well, struggles.' Seb looks a little uncomfortable and I realise this isn't the place for this chat.

'Shall we grab some lunch in a bit and catch up?' Seb pats me on the knee.

'That is a great idea. I have a quick meeting with Dom and Robocop,' he points to Dom and Simon, 'then I am pretty much free, just editing some photos later and that's me done.'

'Wow, it's hard work being the bosses best mate,' I tease, 'I've got, jeez, two hundred emails to check,' I say, scrolling through the highlighted and unanswered emails from the past few weeks, 'and then I guess we are location hunting for this next trip. In fact, guys, how long do we have?' All the team's heads shoot up over their laptops and glance over.

'Oh yeah, we forgot to tell you that bit. In ten days we leave,' Shauna says biting her lip.

Sitting next to Seb in the local cafe, I feel like the relaxed lunch I had envisaged, is now more of a panic sandwich with the news looming, that we have two weeks worth of shoots to plan in ten days.

'The good thing is, we have all the kit and no Visas are needed,' Seb tries to reassure me. 'We have two episodes from Brazil already in the bag. So it's the other eight that need shooting. Dom is adamant the final one should be in a cool location in Paris, his dream is under the Eiffel Tower, but I'm not sure how you would pull that one-off,'

'No me neither, not within this amount of time! Anyway, more importantly, you were telling me about your parents, did you send my apologies that I couldn't make last night? I felt really guilty about letting you go alone.'

'Don't be silly,' Seb puts a reassuring hand on my shoulder, 'I explained about your first day back in the office and new home. They totally understand, they are very excited to meet you, but actually, it's quite nice just getting to know them alone right now anyway' Seb pauses, 'oh I don't mean that in a bad way, you know that, right?' I giggle, my overthinking seems to be rubbing off on Seb,

'Of course. You need to get to know them first. Before I bound in and make a tit of myself.'

'Oh they are going to love you and you won't be a tit. As long as you meet them before we go away with work, that would be perfect.'

'We can definitely do that. What are you doing this evening, fancy dinner at mine? Well, I say dinner, it will be a takeaway, I haven't made it to any kind of food shops yet.'

'Sounds like a plan to me.' We finish our lunch in a rush, as it dawns on me that every second away from the office, is precious moments which I need to be helping to plan this extravagant shoot in T-minus ten days.

'Sophia, are you ready?'

We leave in a couple of days for France and the past week has become a blur of days morphed into the office and sleep. I have barely even had the chance to see Poppy, let alone have any form of a life outside of the Freedom walls, which seems ironic. My work is currently my life and even the voicemails from my parents are starting to get more impatient with my absence. To top it off, before we leave the country, Seb has arranged for me to meet up with, not one set, but both sets of his parents. Overwhelmed is an understatement and having changed my outfit at least four times in the last hour I have gone back to the first option of a simple dress, blazer and ankle boots. I have finally perfected my liquid eyeliner, even though it has been smudged three times already, due to hands shaking with nerves. I'm struggling to feel presentable with the thoughts of the afternoon racing through my mind. Not only is this the first time I will meet my boyfriend's parents, I am meeting two sets of them, who have never met each other. Well, officially if you don't count the years of random supermarket stalkings. I feel like this scenario sums up my past few months in a nutshell, it's great and it's a really positive step for Seb and me, but it also feels more complicated than life should be. I stand and stare at myself for a few more seconds in the mirror in my bedroom, making sure I look like a woman you would want your son to date. I take a few deep breaths to calm the speeding heart rate. 'I'm ready,' I walk into the lounge clutching my bag. 'How do I look? Good enough to meet the parents?' Seb turns to look me up and down, walking over to me and wrapping his strong arms around my waist and kissing me gently on my lips.

'You look perfect and they will all love you. I just hope they don't mind each other, that's my major concern!' Seb had met his adopted parents a week ago and apparently the news was received with a mixture of upset and relief. They were understandably upset at the idea of these new people stepping into Seb's life and in hand, losing their son to his biological parents. The son they had known from the first few hours of his life. The news, however, that they are normal people and a reasonable explanation of Lucinda's erratic behaviour had also managed to set their minds at ease.

We walk quietly down the London streets and I can't help but feel a little pensive. I have only met one of my boyfriend's parents before, so this isn't a regular occurrence for me. The fact they have most likely seen my face in not exactly the most flattering light, plastered on the front of the tabloids. I can't help but think that both sets of parents are bound to have a preconceived idea of me. Thankfully we are having afternoon tea at Fortnum & Mason, so if nothing else, the tea and food will be amazing, which is something I keep trying to remind myself as we get closer to the big meet.

'Hey over-thinker, don't you go worrying on me,' as finally the silence of our walk is broken by Seb.

'I know, sorry. I am fine. It's just, you know....'

'A LOT. Is that not what everyone seems to say now? "I had a busy full-on week and well, it's A LOT". It's like everything is now "sick" and "I'm dying", all these really irritating new terms someone like the Kardashians probably started,' Seb says in his overdramatic jokey manner, dipping in and out of a really dodgy American accent.

'Yes, exactly that, it's just A LOT!' I give him a playful dig to the ribs and he seems to have successfully distracted me. 'Actually, speaking of America, how are Arabella and the bump, have you spoken to her? I have been meaning to message her but have been so wrapped up with work.'

'Arabella is doing OK, she's actually back in the UK next week and staying here until the baby is born. Her parents and friends are in the UK and she said it was getting lonely out in LA alone. She's also considering not even putting Dom's name on the birth certificate, which I am pretty sure he is not aware of yet. So that's probably, well, definitely all going to kick-off.'

'Jeeez, it's quite intense then. Not surprising really, if you are going to be a dick and have an affair with your PA behind your pregnant wife's back, you get what's coming.'

'Anyway, let's not get wound up about it now. We will see Arabella when she is back and she was asking after you, she has taken a real liking to you Soph, which is not really like Arabella at all. She seems to have let her guard down with you.'

'That's really sweet, I really like her too. Maybe our bond formed over the dislike of horrible women. Well, one horrible woman.' Even though our chat has taken me back to the drama of LA and me being dragged into Dominic's mess, it actually helped my nerves for the few minutes before arriving at our destination.

We walk up the extravagant staircase to the tea room and suddenly the anxious butterflies return to my stomach.

'Good afternoon,' Seb puts on his most affluent voice and looks at me, giving a cheeky wink. I realise I have been so wrapped up in my own nerves, I hadn't given him the attention he deserves. I give him the once over, taking in the brown suede Chelsea boots, nicely cut indigo jeans, plain white shirt slightly unbuttoned with a navy pinstripe jacket over the top. He runs his floppy dark hair out of his face and I feel instant glee that he is all mine, wishing I had him to myself for the afternoon and I tiptoe up to his ear and whisper,

'You look fucking hot by the way' and kiss his cheek. A huge grin appears on his face.

'Straight back to yours after this then?' he whispers back.

'Sir, madam, right this way,' as the Maitre D directs us to our table as we giggle like teenagers behind.

I assumed we would be the first to arrive, but as soon as we are escorted to the opulent tea room table, I recognise Caroline and Martin straight away, but only from an afternoon I spent FaceBook "researching" Seb and had seen a few photos of him and his family. They are everything you would imagine of middle class Doctors eating afternoon tea at an upmarket establishment. They are the ducks and this is definitely their water. Caroline is incredibly put together, in a perfectly coordinated cream linen suit and soft pink blouse underneath. Her hair is perfectly blow-dried and she moves her Radley bag out of the way to stand up as we approach. Martin is equally as groomed and even though their genes might not be the same, he has the same dapper style as his son.

'Mum, Dad, I would like you to meet Sophia.'

'Hello Sophia. Finally, we get to meet you,' Caroline shuffles around the table to stand and hug me.

'Yes, I would like to say nice to put a face to the name, but we have already had the pleasure of seeing your face across the papers!'

'For goodness sake Martin. Sophia won't get your ridiculous humour, so please don't embarrass us.' Caroline is ironically worried they will be embarrassed as I stand, totally mortified. I grin, then find myself doing an awkward native Indian hand salute and wishing I have the superpower of teleportation right this second.

'Don't worry, he thinks he is funny,' Seb puts his hand on my lower back and whispers, which instantly comforts my nerves and I see Caroline elbowing Martin as they get back into their seats.

'Well done. In true Martin style, you have made that introduction more uncomfortable than needed,' she whispers loudly with a hint of anger. We all sit down and I grab the menu to use as a distraction and comforter.

'I'm sorry Sophia,' I just joke to try and break the ice, but obviously that hasn't worked this time.'

'Or ever,' Caroline says without even breaking her gaze at the menu.

'Oh no, it's fine. It's just not been the most ideal few weeks and as long as people know it's all lies, then it's history and I am ready to put it behind me.'

'That is the right attitude Sophia. Dom can be an absolute nightmare, we have known him long enough to be aware he is no saint. The affair is no surprise if I am being totally honest,' Caroline puts her hand on top of mine and gives me a reassuring look. I like this lady, I like her a lot already. It's obvious to me where Seb gets his care and compassion from. 'Speaking of Dom. Sebastian, how are Arabella and the baby? She is such a wonderful young woman, it cannot be easy for her right now.'

'She is fine. Obviously angry towards Dom, last time we spoke she was considering not putting his name on the birth certificate.'

'Oh dear, no,' Caroline responds in shock, 'please Sebastian, on her return can you ask her to pop and see us. I absolutely adore that girl, but totally disagree with that choice. I understand her anger, but not a healthy choice for an unborn child.'

'Right you are mother,' Seb rolls his eyes and I can see he has other things on his mind rather than discuss Dominic and the mess he has created.

As we all take a moment to scan the menu, it is blissfully calm and I find solace hiding behind the gigantic menu, filled with extravagant teas, sandwiches and cakes. This is until I peer over and see who I can only assume are Seb's biological parents, as they briskly make their way to our table. His description was perfect and I knock his knee under the table and he shoots out of his seat, the moment he sets his eyes on them.

'Hey, how are you both?' as he embraces Lucinda and George. I can't help but look to see Caroline and Martin's reaction as they watch on quietly and wait for their cue.

'Mum and Dad, I would like you to meet Lucinda and George,' Seb proudly introduces both sets of his parents. They all stand, hugging and greeting each other and I take a backseat and allow them to enjoy this moment. The mums are dabbing their eyes and the Dad's doing firm back pats and gripping each other's hands.

'This is the lovely Sophia I have been telling you about,' as he turns on his heels and holds his hand out to me. I stand, my cue to meet them is here and I scramble to my feet.

'Hi, it's great to meet you both,' George holds out his hand to shake mine.

'The pleasure is ours Sophia,' I look to Lucinda to acknowledge her, but she is clenching Seb's hand and smiling at him, staring up at his face and seemingly not noticing my presence. I feel instantly even more awkward than I had previously, but as we sit back in our seats, I try to remind myself how excited Lucinda must be to have her son back and to not take it too personally. It's only when Caroline taps my leg under the table and whispers in my ear,

'Don't worry, she's distracted right now.' I realise this snub by Lucinda wasn't just my paranoia.

'I'm glad you noticed that too,' I whisper back as she gives me a reassuring smile.

We put in our orders for six afternoon teas and the polite chat is flowing, I have attempted to catch Lucinda's eye a couple of times to shoot her a smile, but it seems she has very little interest in acknowledging me at all. That is until Seb sings my praises, 'so, as I mentioned, Sophia is an excellent Assistant Producer and is well on the way to Producing her own shows very soon.'

'Well that's lovely son, it always helps to be on the right side of the boss,' Lucinda smiles gleefully at me. Which is the first eye contact we have made and I am sure it's not just my insecurities that are making me feel like that comment was not meant in a flattering way.

'It takes more than that,' Seb defends me, 'Sophia is extremely talented and works incredibly hard. I am very proud of her.' Seb shuffles closer to me and finally gets to release his hands from his biological mother's grip, which by her expression, she is less than thrilled about.

'We are just so pleased to see Seb with a wonderful young woman who is making him happy. It's amazing that you get to work together and go on these adventures, especially the trip next week. Are you both ready?' Caroline has obviously clocked onto the negativity coming from Lucinda's direction and is doing her best to lighten the conversation.

'Going away, again?' Clearly, Lucinda is caught off guard and Seb has not informed her that we are imminently leaving the country for a few weeks.

'Yes, we are going away with Freedom to shoot the rest of Dom's TV show. I am sure I mentioned it.'

'You did Sebastian, don't worry, I am sure with everything that has happened over the past few weeks, it has simply slipped Lucinda's mind,' George strokes her arm, trying to appease her scornful look. Thankfully, two waiters have arrived with large trays covered with copious amounts of teacups, teapots and condiments to be passed around, I take my opportunity and ask to be excused to powder my nose and catch my breath.

Chapter Nineteen

The toilets are as lavish as you would imagine and I take my time and enjoy a moment to myself, as I look at my reflection in the mirror and reapply my lippy, shuffle my hair and straighten my clothes.

'Just so we are on the same page,' I turn around and out of nowhere, Lucinda has appeared in the entrance to the toilets, 'I have had too many years apart from my son and I certainly won't be letting a little tabloid tart get in between us.' I just stand, in shock, processing the aggression, the words and the anger on her face. 'You will be around for weeks, maybe a month, but I will always be his mother,' she continues and it confirms my worst fears that this is not going to be an easy ride. Part of me instantly wants to tell her to fuck off, but then I have a feeling that's how she wants me to respond and I refuse to give this woman any ammunition to hold against me. Before I even get a chance to respond,

'I think you need to calm down Lucinda.' Caroline walks around the corner behind her, startling us both, but I feel instant relief as she mouths 'it's OK' to me. I want to burst into tears and run to hug her, but I also don't want to show weakness to this woman who is clearly trying to upset me.

'This is between me and her thank you Caroline. You have been acting as my son's mother for long enough and now I am here and it's time Sebastian is looked after by his real parents.' I look at Caroline in shock and I can see the words have hit her as hard as they were intended. After a pause, I find myself staring at Lucinda, as she seems to enjoy watching Caroline taken aback by her nasty comments, I cannot stand and watch this woman be so vile.

'Actually Lucinda, I think you should be thanking her for the incredible job Caroline and Martin have done, raising Sebastian into an amazing man he is. I don't think it's fair for you to expect her to step aside now you are in contact with Seb. They will always be his parents too.' Oh, Jesus, I've really done it now. Lucinda's smirk fades but her piercing stare is now back on me. Before she even gets to respond, Caroline has grabbed my wrist,

'Come on Sophia, we need to get back to our men.' We are briskly walking through the restaurant and Caroline whispers, 'leave this to me. She is manipulative and whatever you say she will use against you.' I've totally screwed up, I panic as I slide into the seat next to Seb. He has a smile from cheek to cheek, but soon clocks on that something is wrong.

'You took your time, everything OK?' He says, darting back and forth from Caroline to me, but before we even have a chance to defend ourselves, we hear a loud sobbing, increasing in volume as Lucinda dramatically strides across the restaurant. The room falls silent and I look over to Caroline.

'See Sophia, I warned you, didn't I? That woman is unbelievable.' Within seconds, Seb has pushed past me and sped over to Lucinda with George on his tail. They have both wrapped their arms around her and are trying to calm her sobs. I take a look around the room and some onlookers seem to be enjoying the dramatics, with others rolling their eyes and continuing with their cakes and conversation. Which feels tempting as the food smells so good, but on the other hand I'm also looking for the exit and my escape route. I have two options right now, sit this out and listen to a barrage of Lucinda's bullshit which is due any second now, or grab my coat and bag and get out of here before I have to defend myself against this seemingly, very unstable woman. I look at Caroline and as if she is reading my mind, 'go Sophia, this is between us and you won't win with her. I promise to tell Seb the truth and I will fix this.' I see her eyes welling and I know she is right, I grab my things and mouth a thank you and goodbye to both Martin and Caroline and they send me off with a forced smile and a wave. Seb doesn't see me leave as I zig-zag around the tables and escape the restaurant. I reach the exit unscathed and vanish easily into the crowds of Piccadilly Circus. I aim in the direction of the Freedom Offices, I know there will be someone still working and I can find peace in the distraction of tying up the last few bits for the work trip.

It's taken an hour and one large coffee to walk across London and reach the offices. I had my headphones on the entire way and my phone is set to silent, but not before I had a quick chat with Poppy and she insisted on meeting me at the office to give me some much needed moral support. I walk into the building and Poppy is already there, sitting comfortably in the reception area with a coffee in hand and chatting to someone, I walk up to her, to see hidden around the corner, a very relaxed and poised Dominic.

'Hi Poppy, you got here quickly!,' she turns and jumps up to hug me.

'Yes, I was quicker than I thought, but Dom here let me in and kindly made me a coffee.' I look at him as he looks on at Poppy.

'Oh he did, did he? How lovely, I wonder if you fancy making me a coffee DOM? As I just had the world's worst afternoon tea with your best mate and nightmare of a biological mother,' I manage to break Dominic's gawking at my best friend and he finally looks in my direction.

'Oh no, Soph what happened? OK, I guess I can stretch to a coffee for you too. Let me say this though, I don't usually make the coffees around here,' he says, brimming with arrogance and reassuring Poppy of his boss status.

'No Dominic, Poppy knows that. She is fully aware that you are a very, very important man. Cappuccino please.' I roll my eyes at him as he finally clocks my sarcasm.

'Wow, really must have been a shit afternoon tea,' I hear him mumbling as he walks off, I watch Poppy as she looks on after him.

'Please don't Poppy. I have so much chaos already in my life and his PREGNANT wife is a brilliant human and he, well, hasn't got a great track record.'

'Sophia, please. As if he would be interested in me anyway!' Poppy is still looking in the direction that Dominic had vacated.

'Yeah, supermodel looks and a brain of a genius. Of course, he wouldn't be interested,' I roll my eyes and sigh. My best mate getting entangled with Dominic is really the last thing I need right now. 'Follow me through here and we can sit down.'

I walk Poppy through to the "Creativity Lair", which is essentially a room with bean bags, floor to ceiling blackboards and a Ping Pong table. It's the room where apparently our creative thoughts can run wild and we can develop TV gold. I slump on an oversized bean bag feeling totally uninspired.

'But Dom was saying they have broken up?' Poppy looks over her shoulder to check he is not in earshot.

'What part of pregnant and wife doesn't seem complicated to you? I know he is good looking, rich, famous and can cook,' Poppy rolls her eyes and laughs.

'You do realise you are just making him sound even more appealing, right?' I guess she skipped the major negatives, I sigh.

'Please Poppy, having my best friend and flatmate dating my boss will only make my life even harder right now. I know I'm being selfish, but after the day I've had, I have gone beyond caring.' Poppy drags her bean bag closer and puts her arm around me.

'I know, I'm sorry. This is definitely not about me and everything about you. Tell me it all, start to finish and we will work it out.' I love her optimism, but having checked my phone and no sign of Seb, I get the awful feeling that Lucinda's tricks have paid off.

Dominic finally strolls in with my Cappuccino and having filled Poppy in with all the details, she is now pacing the room and raging. 'Wow, what has rattled your cage?' Dominic tries to joke but is not aware that the less said, the better when Poppy hits this level of anger.

'Rattle my cage? Your best mates mum. Who is, by the way, an absolute cow bag bitch, crazy lunatic.'

'Breath Poppy' I laugh, but also grateful I have someone like Poppy on my team.

'Was it really that bad, Soph?' Dominic falls down onto the bean bag next to me and for once seems genuinely interested in my feelings.

'Yes, it was. It was actually horrific.'

'You don't think this will break you guys up?' His phone starts to ring, 'Oh, it's Seb, hang on, I will go out.'

'No stay,' I grab his forearm, 'please, I want to hear.'

'Hi mate, all OK?' Dominic answers his phone and all I can hear is the mumble of Seb's voice.

'Jeez, he hasn't grasped the concept of us wanting to listen, has he!' Poppy storms over to Dominic, grabs his phone and puts it on loudspeaker. Most people would definitely not be allowed to speak to Dominic, let alone grab his phone in such a manner, but Dominic looks at Poppy with a mix of surprise and seems to be in awe, which fills me with dread.

'Dom mate, are you still there?' His attention is drawn back to the phone.

'Yes, sorry Seb, just dropped my phone, I can hear you now. What's going on?'

'Is Sophia at the office? I just went to her flat and it seems no one is in. That or she is just ignoring me,' Dominic shrugs at us both obviously looking for guidance, but I don't know what to say, but thankfully I can rely on Poppy never being short of a plan.

'Ask why and what has happened, she mouths with a slight whisper and pointing at the phone, Dominic waves his hands and grimaces, I know he's in an awkward situation, but I also want to find out what he has to say.

'What has happened Seb? You sound stressed!' Dominic says, sounding so unconvincing, you would never imagine he spends most of his life on TV.

'Such a fucking nightmare mate, fucking, fucking nightmare. Pretty sure I've fucked it up royally with Soph. Turns out Lucinda has been bang out of order to both Soph and my mum. I just can't believe it, I feel the wool has been pulled over my eyes and now we are leaving for the shoot tomorrow and my mum is upset, Lucinda is on the warpath and my Dad and George haven't a clue how to sort this.'

'Meet me at the office, we will go to yours and get your bags and you stay with me tonight. I'm being driven to the office in the morning so you come with me. Few beers and some food will sort you out.' Poppy and I both stare at Dominic as he hangs up.

'Well that's a shit fucking idea, well done Dom,' Poppy waves her hands at him in despair.

'What?' Dominic looks genuinely confused, 'I thought I was helping you out, you don't want him to find you here, so I will take him to mine.'

'Yeah but now Soph doesn't even get to see him now, as you've hogged him away for the evening.'

'I can't bloody win with you women,' Dominic shakes his head and shrugs.

'Don't worry about it. I'm pleased he is wanting to talk to me, I was worried about how much damage Lucinda had managed to do. I will wait here until he comes to meet you. At least I will get to see him before we leave tomorrow .'

'Right, good plan Soph. I am going to head home and will make us some food and chill us some wine. You need it.' Poppy grabs her things and kisses my head.

'Thank you Pops, I really, really appreciate you coming here.'

'Anytime my doll. Nice to meet you Dom,' as she stands holding out her hand to shake his.

'Really good to meet you Poppy, I really hope I get to see you more. I am happy to cook for you anytime if you fancy it?' I glare at Poppy, my eyes pleading to avoid his charm.

'Thanks for the offer Dom, maybe once your wife has had your baby and your life is less complicated.' Dominic shuffles on the bean bag and looks a little uneasy. I take a deep and satisfying breath, I won't have to explain anytime soon to Arabella, that my best friend is now hooking up with the father of her unborn child.

'Hey you,' Seb walks into the office half an hour later and I have been perched over my desk, scrolling through the schedule one last time before we leave in the morning. I turn instantly at the sound of his voice and relief flows through me when I see him smiling and holding out his arms in my direction. I get up and throw myself into them. 'I'm so sorry you had to deal with that crap, not exactly the afternoon I had in mind.' He says and I squeeze into him so tight and I feel the reassurance I have been craving since running out of the tearoom.

'What happened after I legged it?' I sit down and twizzle in my office chair, feeling a warm glow of comfort to see that Lucinda's handy work has not paid off. Seb drags a chair over and sits down opposite me, his smile has faded.

'Well, mum told me everything that happened in the toilet. Lucinda denied it all, but obviously I will always believe my mum. She has never given me a reason not to. Can I get your side though Soph? It would really help me to get your perspective.'

Seb sits with his hands in his head after I retell my side of events with Lucinda, 'Maybe it's just all too much for her, she obviously loves you,' for some reason I find myself defending the witch, but part of me believes what I am saying too. I can't imagine what she has been through. I don't however, think I deserve to be the brunt of her frustration, anger or a multitude of other emotions she must have gone through.

'That Sophia, is sweet of you,' Seb finally lifts his head, 'but we both know she obviously has some mental health issues and what she has said to you and mum is totally unacceptable.' Seb stands and starts pacing, 'the ironic thing is, she pleads that it's because she is desperate to be closer with me, but it's actually having the opposite effect. I feel for George, he is trying so hard to get to know us and keep her stable. God, I just don't know what to do.'

'Well, the good thing is we are away tomorrow for a few weeks, so hopefully, that will give you time to work it out. It will probably be good for Lucinda too,' I shrug, trying to remain as positive as possible, but it doesn't feel like this situation will improve anytime soon.

'Guys, I have to lock up now, big day tomorrow and need to head off,' one of the many security team we now have, kindly ushers us out of the office, which is handy, as I still have everything to pack and it's already getting late.

'Sorry Jeff, we have held you up. See you tomorrow,' Seb says as he holds my hand and we walk out, into the Spring evening. I'm starting to realise how much I must really like this guy. I mean, I could have run miles after all the dramas recently, but instead, the safest place I feel is wrapped in his arms.

'What are you staring at little missy,' Seb laughs as he catches me gazing up at him, as we walk through the London streets in the direction of my home.

'Well, I was honestly thinking about how much we must really love each other. It's not like we have had an easy ride so far.'

'I know, I actually thought the same earlier at the office, when I realised you weren't going to break up with me after today.' I think for a second. I can't deny, the thought had crossed my mind, but there is a time and place to be that honest and Seb just doesn't need to hear about my second thoughts about our relationship right now. I hug his arm around my shoulders and tilt my head against his chest.

'Well, you don't need to worry about me Sebastian, it will take more than that   to   shake   me   off.'

Chapter Twenty

'SHIT.' I launch myself out of bed and I know instantly that I have overslept. 'FUCKETY FUCK,' I shout as I look at my phone and the battery is flat. I run out into the kitchen to check the oven clock. It's 6.30 am and I need to be at the office for the coach to leave at 7 am. 'FUCK YOU PHONE,' I run back to my room and my phone will take full responsibility and become the scapegoat for my total tardiness.

I jump in the shower and do my best to look as presentable as possible in ten minutes. My phone rings the moment it has any life charged back into it, 'SOPH, thank god I have been trying to call you for the past half hour, where are you? We literally leave in twenty minutes.'

'I KNOW Michael, I FUCKING KNOW,' I hang up as Michael wasting the precious little time I have, is definitely not helping. I grab my bag, have a rummage around and for the third time I confirm my passport is indeed, still in my tote and hasn't miraculously grown legs and done a runner, although, in my current state of panic, anything feels possible. I drag my bag through the flat and assume by now, I must have disturbed Poppy with my ranting and banging. Thankfully she seems to be sleeping like a baby as I peer around her door on my way out of the apartment. I swing the door open, prepared to run and catch whatever cab I can find.

'Good morning beautiful,' I look up and Seb is standing there. I feel surprise but instant relief, thank goodness I won't be the only one late. That's until I look over his shoulder and see the coach. The coach full of my colleagues and Dom hanging from the door.

'For fucksake, stop standing like dickheads and get on the coach, we need to get gone.' Seb kisses me on the cheek and grabs my bag, chucking it in the direction of the driver as he loads it in with the other piles of luggage. I climb on and feel the heat of embarrassment rising to my cheeks. Clearly, I have had preferential treatment and there is no hiding it this time. The coach is filled with an extremely sarcastic slow clap and everyone is staring and smiling.

'I guess that's the treatment you get if you shag the boss's mate,' Michael whispers loudly to me with a huge grin on his face, as I squeeze into the seat in front of him.

'Now, now, Don't be jealous Michael,' winking at him and trying to play down the fact I am actually mortified by the current situation.

We sit and watch the busy London streets go by, as we take a drive to the Eurotunnel. The next time I take a breath of air that hasn't been airconed, we will be stepping on to French soil. I sit and look at Seb, who is engrossed in the manual of a new camera he has purchased especially for this shoot. I feel excited, the last trip I was single and it was intimidating to take on such a huge shoot weeks into working at Freedom. This time I feel secure, I have Seb, the team I am with are fab and I

247

know France and love it. I lay my head on Seb's warm arm and pull my coat over my body and cosy in for the long journey ahead.

'Sophia,' I feel a gentle nudge and I am woken by a smiling Seb. 'Hey sleepy, we are in France. Just about to stop for a coffee break.' I sit up and squint out of the coach window, a little confused as to how I managed to sleep through the entire journey thus far.

'I can't believe I missed the entire tunnel and arriving in France.'

'Don't worry,' Seb kissed my forehead, 'most of the coach seemed to be asleep and I didn't want to disturb your dreams.' I take a swig of water to wash away my dry, sleepy mouth and grab my bag as the coach starts to off-load.

It's bliss to feel warm French fresh air on my face and I take a long stretch, we walk into the huge service station and I clock the toilets, 'Seb, I will meet you back here in a minute, I say as I interrupt Seb and Dom's conversation over what they are getting to eat and drink.

The daze of just being woken is still looming over me, as I look at my tired eyes in the brightly illuminated public toilet. I wash my hands and reach over to the paper towels, catching a glimpse of some long dark and quite scruffy hair rushing quickly into a cubicle on the other side of the toilets, had we been in London, I would have been absolutely convinced it was Lucinda.

'Hey, I got you a Cappuccino and a Croissant. Think we are taking them straight back to the coach and heading to our first location.'

'Thanks, you are the best. Quick question,' I promised myself I wouldn't keep bringing up Seb's parents, it caused enough drama in London and this was our time, our time to enjoy this adventure. 'So where exactly is Lucinda right now?' Seb laughs and rubs my back as we take a slow walk back to the coach.

'Don't you go worrying, she is fine. George promised me that she is going to receive the help and care she needs. There is a rehabilitation clinic that has been recommended and I think she was checked in last night.'

'That's all I needed to hear, thanks,' I kiss him on the cheek, feeling silly that my paranoia was getting the better of me.

I gaze out at the French countryside, one of my absolute favourite places. My parents used to bring us here every Summer and we had the most amazing holidays filled with camping, bike rides and trips to the local boulangerie where Charly, Margo and I used to fight over who got to hold the money and practise our basic French to buy our breakfasts. Our first shooting location is a place I recommended, as I had visited Château de Saumur a few times and remember it being stunning, the absolute perfect backdrop for "Cooking with Dominic" and everyone else seemed equally excited about the prospect of spending a couple of days in, what could essentially be a Disney castle.

'Right guys.' Dominic breaks my daydream as he takes the position of tour guide at the front of the coach. 'We are now only twenty minutes from our first location and I would like to hand you over to Harriet, who will let you know more info about the plans for the first evening and hotel.' He passes the microphone over to Harriet and she takes centre stage of the coach, her glasses perched on her nose and clipboard in hand.

'Thank you Dom. Right team, plan of action for today. Now, we are all shattered and as you know, the schedule for this trip is packed. We have an awful lot to get done and this afternoon is going to be one of your few opportunities to relax and get prepared. With that in mind, I suggest we all check into our rooms and freshen up. Feel free to explore the town or just relax. The hotel will have a buffet on for us from 7 pm. My personal recommendation is no late nights, but I am not your mother,' she pauses and gazes over the entire production team, 'thank god. So, I will leave it in your hands to make the right choice and not have a ridiculously late night. That also goes for you too Dom,' she peers over her glasses at him and he grimaces back. After the past few weeks and his PR team being worked overtime to clear up his mess, he has apparently been warned to be on his best behaviour and avoid as much tabloid gossip as possible. 'One more thing,' Harriet continues, 'on this occasion you are all lucky enough to have your own rooms. Please make the most of it, as the following locations will all require sharing,' the coach roared with a cheer which quickly descended into a boo. 'Well, it's fine as you will be on set most of the day working, so I shouldn't worry too much about that.' Harriet hands the mic back to Dom and makes her way over to us, perching in the coach aisle next to Seb and I and whispers discreetly, 'I have actually got you a separate room for this first location, but for the rest of the hotels you are sharing, is that going to be a problem? I can always rejig for you to share with others if you think this is an issue?' Seb and I glance at each other and I am just hoping he is on the same page as me.

'Thanks Harriet, but it makes more sense we share together than with other people. Everyone is fully aware we are a couple, so it would be weird if we didn't.' Phew, maybe it was my side eyes or grin, but Seb and I are obviously on the same page.

'That's what I thought,' Harriet seems relieved and puts her hand on Seb's shoulders, 'thanks guys. Also, Seb, can you do me a favour and just keep your mate out of trouble, please. I really don't have the time to keep diffusing the gossip and bad press he seems to make for himself.'

'Of course Harriet. I will do my best, I can't promise anything though.'

'Maybe if I chain him to his room? Might be an option thinking about it,' Harriet rolls her eyes and giggles as she sets back to her seat.

'I am so pleased I don't have to share a room with someone I barely know.'

'Erm, Sophia Williams. What I think you mean is that you are incredibly excited to be sharing a room with me,' Seb pulls a faux angry face at me.

'Sorry, yes, of course. That's the main bonus obviously. I would actually like some, well, you know, alone time,' I stroke his arm playfully, but feel my cheeks slightly blush unintentionally.

'You see, that is the sort of response I am needing from you,' he kisses my lips gently, 'straight to your room when we arrive' he whispers softly in my ear.

'OH MY GOSH, this is beautiful.' I walk into my hotel room for the next few nights and it's stunning. Very old and traditional, but well looked after and feels more like a bedroom of a castle rather than a hotel. I walk over to my window and Seb follows me, dragging my bag behind him.

'Wow, that is an amazing view,' Seb puts our bags to one side and we walk over to the floor to ceiling window and stare out to the Chateau. It stands high on the pinnacle of the town and as the late afternoon sun shines down on it, it glistens like a fairytale castle. 'Look, you have a small balcony,' Seb unlatches the window and climbs out, turning around and grabbing my hand to help me out.

'Are you sure it's safe?' I look down and being four stories up from the road below, I can feel my nerves kicking in.

'Of course it is. Look, there's Michael,' as he waves.

'Hey Seb, beautiful isn't it,' I can hear Michael shouting back, Seb gives him thumbs up and steps back in the window, realising it will take more than that to get me out there. 'This is incredible Soph, it's just a shame we have to work tomorrow. Maybe we can go out for dinner tonight, just the two of us?'

'I think that would be the perfect way to spend the first evening of the trip,' I lean in for a kiss and it turns into a long, passionate, clothes being ripped off kind of kiss. Seb lifts my legs around his hips and carries me over the bed, laying me down slowly and kissing me down my neck and to my chest and I can feel him unbuttoning my jeans. I take his hands, 'I think we should freshen up after our trip.'

'Oh OK,' Seb pulls away and I can see by his disappointment he has misunderstood me. I wiggle from under him and take his hand, directing him to the large bathroom with a double shower. 'Right, now I see. Yes, we both definitely need to freshen up.'

I lay back on the bed, wrapped in a towel and feeling satisfied and slightly smug. Rolling over and looking out to views of the beautiful French town, I take in a deep breath. 'Wow, that was a big sigh,' Seb appears from the bathroom with a towel tied low around his abdomen, highlighting his perfectly toned torso and another towel drying his hair with his arm muscles tensed and looking incredibly sexy.

'Well, I'm just enjoying the view.'

'It's mad isn't it, as Seb walks over to the window.'

'Not that view Seb,' as he turns and catches me grinning ear to ear.

'Oh I see, it's like that is it,' as he jumps on to the bed, hitching my towel off my bum and kissing it, 'I actually prefer this view.' I giggle and he rolls me over, pinning me down and kissing me. 'Right you, I'm going to find my room and drop my bag off. I will be back in twenty. Will you be ready to leave to check this place out and get some food?'

'Absolutely,' one more kiss and Seb throws on his jeans and t-shirt, drags his bag out and I lay back, finding some energy to get dressed.

Lipstick on, Eyeliner flick in place with a simple white t-shirt, skinny jeans and sandals, I give myself a once over in the full-length antique mirror in the room. There is a knock at the door and grab my clutch and rush to open it, 'Coming, one sec.' I swing it open, expecting to see Seb, full of excitement and even though it has literally been a matter of minutes since I last saw him, I feel giddy. He is not there, I step out and the corridor is empty in every direction, apart from one room service tray left outside a door waiting to be collected. I look up and down the opulently decorated hallways and I realise the sound must have been from outside and I shake my head at myself for getting so excited at the prospect of seeing Seb. Before I even get a chance to shut the door,

'Soph, wait,' it's Seb, running down the hall.

'So odd, I thought you knocked a moment ago.'

'Not me, I have just run down from my room. I'm not too far, but it is quite a trek,' he kisses me hard and passionately and everything before this kiss is wiped from my mind.

'Are you sure you don't just fancy some room service,' I raise my eyebrows at him, feeling the urge and desire to drag him back into the shower and keep him all to myself.

'Wow Sophia, you are really insatiable aren't you? Must be something in this French air' He teases, kissing my neck. 'Later, I have done some research and I want to investigate this town with you.'

It's magic hour and the skies of Samur are dusky pink and orange, the cool breeze is perfect in the warm temperatures and it feels like a dream. We walk down the windy cobblestone streets and the shops are still open with a buzz of locals and tourists taking in the evening. All the restaurants are busy and bustling out onto the streets, with tables on the pavements and the town square. People are enjoying wine and food in the last of the evening's sun and there is a low murmur of laughing and conversation.

'What about this place?' Seb gestures over to a quintessential bistro.

'Absolutely perfect.' Seb gestures at a waiter for a table for two and the waiter ushers us over to a small table on the patio area, with views up to the Chateau.

'Let me,' Seb rushes around to pull out my chair and I sit down.

'How very gentlemanly of you Sebastian,' I tease.

'Well, I do try. What would you like to drink mon amie?'

'Oh you speak française now? Impressive. Well in that case, I think a bouteille de vin rouge would be perfect right now.'

'I couldn't agree more with mademoiselle.'

We sit and drink wine, eating our way through three courses of delicious French cuisine. As we chat, we watch our fellow diners and compare ourselves to where we hope to be at all the various milestones in our lives.

'Being married at 28 has always seemed like the ideal to me for some reason. Then have a couple of years for fun before children at thirty. I don't know why, but those ages have always seemed like a good plan.' I sip on my wine and have a sudden fear I am being too intense. After all, we have been dating only a short time and bonafide boyfriend and girlfriend for the past couple of weeks.

254

'I agree, I think they are good ages too. Seems like an excellent five-year plan,' Seb takes a sip of wine and my grand scheme doesn't seem to faze him as yet.

'So, Seb, just to clarify. None of that scares you? You know I am only actually two years off my ideal marriage age? You seem very calm, unless, that's because you don't think you will be around that long of course,' my thoughts start to trail off and I already regret oversharing. Seb reaches over and holds both of my hands across the table.

'Sophia, stop worrying. I never had considered marriage before in my life, I have just never been that fussed about the idea. OK, I have always thought that one day I would like a family and children, but I have never really thought of it too much. Well, that is until now and we are talking about it.'

'Oh no, sorry. Maybe let's just change the subject, It's all a little intense anyway, probably just the wine talking.'

'I don't mean that I don't want to talk about it. I enjoy chats about our future. It's just, it's the first time I have thought I actually might want to get married at some point, because I have met you.' Seb looks around the restaurant and takes a sip of his wine, I can see the cogs in his mind ticking over. 'Sophia, you are the only girl I have ever loved. I want to protect you, make you happy and laugh. As far as I am concerned, there is no reason why in two years we aren't ready to get hitched.' He looks sincerely in my eyes and I gently squeeze his hands.

'Phew, I thought I might have scared you away for a second,' Seb rolls his head back and laughs.

'Compared to the first weeks of our relationship, talking marriage is like a walk in the park considering the dramas we have already faced together. If we can get through that, I am pretty sure we can get through anything.'

'That's true. Maybe we can just calm it down for a while and enjoy a normal, stress free life?' Seb picks up his glass.

'Let's make a toast Sophia. To a calm and happy life, getting married when you are 28 and then starting a family,' we clink our glasses.

'And live happily ever after, cheers.'

'Cheers to that.'

Chapter Twenty-one

Closing the door after a prolonged goodbye to Seb in the hotel corridor, I walk over to my bed and throw myself onto it. I gaze up at the glistening Chateaux which fills the hotel window. My brain is busy with thoughts as I run through the evening's events and chats with Seb. Feeling more secure than I ever have with the idea that I may have found my one. My future husband and quite possibly, the father of my children.

'You have a nice evening with my son?' I jump off the bed and turn to see a very bedraggled Lucinda, standing and staring at me with eyes red and filled with anger.

'GET OUT OF MY ROOM, WHAT THE FUCK ARE YOU DOING HERE?!' My heart is racing and I almost feel like I could be sick.

'Trashy little bitch trying to poison my son against me. Do you really think for a second you would win this fight?' I step back towards the window, she is blocking the exit to the room and I can only assume she had been waiting for me in the bathroom. I have no idea what this woman is capable of, all I do know is that she is unstable and she was supposedly seeking help. In actual fact, it turns out she is standing in front of me and is clearly in no mood for a nice chat and reconciliation.

'Lucinda I really think you need to leave, you are scaring me and Seb is down the hall, I am sure he would love to see you, I can call him if you like,' I go to reach for my phone.

'DON'T YOU FUCKING DARE, I know what the fuck you are doing, but it won't work. You and that bitch Caroline who stole my child are the ones who are going to pay for trying to poison my son against me.'

'So what are you going to do Lucinda? Can we not sort this out? We can chat and get to know each other. I'm not trying to steal your son, I promise.' All of the police dramas I have watched over the years come flooding back into my head and I try to think rationally of how someone would negotiate in this situation. Although my instinct is to scream and cry, I have a distinct feeling that approach will not work in my favour right now.

'No, I'm going to do to you the same as what I did to Caroline,' She then pulls out what looks like a fishing knife, I recognise the shape from when my Dad used to take us to the local lake and try to convince us that sitting in silence for hours was lots of fun. It wasn't, but if I had the choice of that, or being here now, with this woman waving a knife in my face, I would definitely be by the lake.

'Lucinda, what did you do to Caroline? Is she OK?' So many thoughts are racing through my head, Is Caroline alive? How has Lucinda managed to get to France? How did she know where to find us? Someone has surely noticed she is missing. Lucinda doesn't answer me, she just stares with the knife held out in front of her and aimed at me. Every thought is running through my mind, if I scream will anyone actually hear me in this old stone building, or will she just take that as an opportunity to attack me. She is going to attack me, I can see there is no reasoning with her. I start to panic and remember the balcony, all I have to do is try and get out and close the window. Hoping she doesn't manage to stab me before or push me over the side, with four flights down, I don't rate my chances. The pangs of feeling the need to vomit are rising through my body and I know I have to do something and quickly. Lucinda starts pacing and she is muttering under her breath, I have no idea what she is saying, it's totally incoherent. I take my opportunity and slowly step backwards, finding my back against the large window and feel for the hook closure. Slowly unhooking the lock and hoping she doesn't hear the metal of the latch clink together. I quickly decide my plan and find myself feeling considerably sober, considering not ten minutes ago I was in a fairly tipsy state. Lucinda doesn't seem to have clocked my movements and with a deep breath I swing the large window door open and step out onto the balcony, quickly closing it behind me and holding it closed, 'HELP ME, SOMEONE PLEASE HELP ME,' I scream at the top of my voice. Lucinda is at the window and staring at me with her face against the glass with the knife still in her hand, she's trying with all her force to push it open. Managing to hold her off, I continue to scream and I can hear windows nearby being opened.

'DON'T WORRY SOPHIA.' It's Dom, I can't see him, but I can hear that he is not far, 'WE ARE COMING, I HAVE SENT THE SECURITY AND SEB SHOULD BE THERE ANY SECOND NOW.' I peer over Lucinda's shoulder, praying someone will be there soon, she is not giving up and she has a surprising amount of strength considering she looks so tired and weak. I look at the sharp blade and wonder what the hell she has done to Caroline. Looking down at my feet I try to get a better grip of the balcony. The idea that I have just planned my life with Seb, now I am here, trying to stop my sandals sliding across the uneven surface and letting a knife be wielded at me is on a loop in my head. Panic runs through me, that all those dreams might be taken away from me in the next few seconds. Suddenly the weight against the door has gone and I look up to see Lucinda with two of the security team either side of her and she is being dragged out of the room. I kneel on the balcony in relief and burst into tears, burying my head in my hands.

'Sophia, can you move over slightly so I can open the door please?' I look up and Seb is standing there, his face is sheet white.

'Has she gone?'

'Yes, I promise you. I promise you she has gone,' I open the door and Seb grabs me, picking me up off the floor and carrying me back into the room. He sits down and holds me as we curl up on the floor. I sob into his shoulders and I can feel his heart racing, I suddenly remember what Lucinda had threatened me with.

'Shit Seb, is your mum OK? Lucinda said she was going to do the same to me as what she had done to her and I can only imagine what that was.'

'Sophia. I don't really know how to say this,' his eyes gloss over and I know instantly it's bad. 'She stabbed her, she stabbed her in the stomach. Mum is in hospital and she should be fine, but she lost a lot of blood. Thank god she is a doctor and knew what to do. That fucking crazy bitch stabbed her and she was going to stab you too,' Seb starts to cry and I hold him.

'Oh Seb, I'm sorry, your poor mum. As long as she will be OK though, right, she will be OK? How did you find out?'

'Dad is pretty sure mum will be OK, possibly a blood transfusion, I'm not sure exactly, I just started to panic. I got back to my room and had been ignoring my phone, it had been going a bit mad since arriving with loads of messages about French networks. So I put it on silent and forgot all about it. I went to set my alarm for tomorrow and listened to all the voicemails and rang my Dad. He was in bits Soph, total bits. My mum had asked him to warn me about Lucinda's threats towards you, as she had told mum that you were going to get the same and she would be done with "the bitches", which is apparently what she started to call you both. They didn't want to worry us before we left as they knew we were leaving the country and thought that would be the safest option for us. She also knew I would never have left had I known she was in the hospital, so decided to wait until we were far enough away. Little did they know that the crazy cow would follow us to a different country! I also had a voicemail from George who had only just been told this morning that Lucinda had managed to escape the psychiatric ward. Apparently she got out late last night and had made her way to Mum and Dad's, then straight on to follow us. George was only alerted to the fact we might be in danger when he saw her passport and an envelope of cash had been moved from their safe earlier today as he was putting the pieces of the puzzle together.' I try to process all the information.

'Wow, for someone not in their right mind, she has done a damn good job of putting this plan together.'

'I know. It's my fucking fault. I dropped in the fact we were coming here yesterday, didn't I? The moment it was mentioned that we were going away again, that's when she started to go funny at you and mum. I was hoping that she would understand how happy I am. With that and getting the treatment she needs, I had hoped she would become more accepting of you guys. I had no idea she would be capable of this, no idea. It's all my fucking fault.' Seb stands up and perches on the bed with his head in his hands and crying.

'It's not your fault Seb, none of it,' he sets me off into a flood of tears again. 'All you ever did was want her in your life and every single choice you made was selfless. You would have never, ever let your mum and I get hurt. Please don't blame yourself, I know Caroline won't and I definitely don't.'

'Jesus Seb, I don't fucking believe it,' Dominic bounds into the room, arms waving about manically, 'She has been arrested and will be taken to the station. No idea if they intend to keep her here or deport her at the moment. Sophia, thank god you are OK.'

. 'Sorry Dom, I can't believe she followed us here. It hadn't crossed my mind she would be capable of this.'

'Do not apologise ever again Seb. NONE of this is your fault, none of it.'

'I said the same Dom, I don't want him thinking for a second any of this is down to him.'

'Exactly Soph. You have no control over a psychopath like that. It's pretty fucking traumatic, a lunatic waving a knife at you like that, Jesus, are you sure you are OK?' Dom is as subtle as a sledgehammer as usual.

'It's definitely not ideal Dom, maybe the less said at the moment, the better,' I look at him, wide-eyed, attempting to subliminally make him understand that now is not the time to be so blunt. Before he clocks on to my less than subtle hints,

'Dom, can I have a word?' One of the security details walks in and Dom follows him out of the room.

'She is a psychopath, isn't she? What kind of human stabs someone and then stalks another and attempts the same. She's a fucking nutter Soph, I wish she had never found me or ever knew who I was.' Seb sits with his head in his hands and I can see the drips of tears falling to the floor. I hold him tight into me and wish I could think of something nice to say about Lucinda, but I can't. She would have happily, seriously hurt me, if not killed me given the chance.

'I really have no words Seb. All you do have to know is that your parents love you so much and me too. No matter what, you still have us and hopefully, Lucinda will go and be treated and maybe in the future you guys can be in a better place.'

'I will never forgive her Soph, NEVER. Stabbing my mum, trying to hurt you. I will never, ever forgive that woman.' We sit in silence until Dominic returns, entering the room more cautiously this time around.

'Seb, your mum is asking to see you before they take her away,' Seb turns around, his eyes are red and his face is wet with tears.

'She's not my mum Dominic. My mum was stabbed and I have absolutely no intention of seeing that crazy woman out there, ever again. You can tell her she has no son, so please do us all a favour and forget about me.' I have never seen Seb so determined or final about anything and I am pretty sure he means every single word of it too.

'Are you sure Seb?' I feel my eyes welling up and I'm trying my best not to cry. Obviously I don't feel a great loss at the idea of not having Lucinda in my life. I have heard some horror stories about mums-in-law, but none who have ever attempted murder.

'So, so sure Sophia, I will never, ever forgive that woman for this. We will all be better without her around.'

After a few minutes of confirming my statement to the police, I am standing in my hotel room and with my bags packed, I am ready to be moved and share a room with Seb. I gaze around at the trail of blood drips which cover the carpet. Apparently, in Lucinda's rage, she had cut her hands a number of times on the blade as she tried to get to me.

'Right, let me grab those,' Seb walks back in the room and picks up my suitcase.

'Is everything sorted now?'

'I just had to leave my statement and I have requested a restraining order for you, my parents and me. Hopefully she won't even be granted bail for her attempt to kill mum. Anyway, it's not something we need to worry about now.' I walk over and as I drop my bags, Seb wraps his arms around me.

'As long as you are happy with all of that, I am too,' I try to reassure him.

'I am going to do whatever it takes to keep her away from us forever. I promise.'

'Can we go to bed please? I'm not gonna lie, that two hours has really worn me out,' Seb laughs and kisses the top of my head gently.

'How, even in the crappiest of situations, can you still manage to cheer me up? Right, let's go.' Seb leads us out of the room and as I walk out, Michael is in the hallway,

'I have been trying to get in to see you, but nobody would let me come in the room,' he looks scornfully between the guards who I hadn't even realised were standing either side of the hotel room door. 'Are you OK, did she try to stab you?'

'Yup, I think that was her plan,' Michael grabs and hugs me.

'Thank god you are OK. Do you know who it was? There are whispers that it was Seb's mum?' I look over Michael's shoulder and Seb is in earshot, I don't want him to feel the brunt of the gossip. As if the past hour hasn't been bad enough, the last thing he needs is the entire team whispering about his "crazy" mum.

'Something like that, probably too soon and the wrong place for that chat.'

'Ahh OK, gotcha. Well as long as you are OK missy, I will leave you to it and see you tomorrow,' Michael gives me one last hug before heading back in the direction of his room.

'Right, Soph, let's get out of here, I'm sure you don't need to be hanging around the horror scene,'

'Indeed, I don't,' as I grab Seb's hand and he walks me to the safety of his room.

Finally, we arrive in Paris and the past few weeks, after the significantly iffy start to this trip, have seemingly gone to plan. Seb and I threw ourselves into work straight after the incident with Lucinda, as we had jointly agreed that keeping busy and focusing on our jobs was the best thing for both of us. We had managed to take a free weekend and flew back to the UK to see Caroline and check all was well. Caroline had been adamant for us not to change any plans but the surprise visit was definitely the right move as she was ecstatic to see us and it helped to ease Seb's worries that she was in good health and on a really speedy road to recovery. We also managed to meet up with George, who had been absolutely broken by the whole course of events and Seb had promised to still be in his life, but only on the premise that Lucinda will never play a part in their relationship. It was a hard pill to swallow for George, but ultimately, at least they can build a father-son relationship in some capacity. So, something positive can be salvaged from the nightmare. It was also confirmed that Lucinda was now in a secure unit and there will be no way of her escaping and trying to hurt any of us again, she has had charges brought against her and hopefully, this will see the end of any stalking or surprise visits.

Having spoken to my parents on a few occasions, I have managed to skirt around the details of the events and will share the full debacle when I see them face to face. I am safe, so ultimately that is all they need to know, for now. Especially as we had some incredible news that Charly is pregnant, which has thankfully overshadowed any of the negative events and just fills us with the hope that good times and happiness has arrived and is here to stay. Also, the fact that Margo, in a shock move, is now relocating to London in search of a career path has elated my parents so much, there was no way I could ever burst their bubble with another episode of "The Trials and Tribulations of Sophia Williams."

We are thankfully on schedule with all the shoots and the final few days will be filming the last episode below the Eiffel Tower. Which feels like the biggest hurdle is yet to come, but first, Seb and I have a day off in the French Capital. We sit in a cute Cafe a few doors down from the extravagant hotel. We are now living our best lives, sipping Cappuccinos and eating our pastries to our hearts content. We watch the Parisian characters walk by and take in some sunshine, life doesn't feel like it could get much better right now.

'Sophia, I have something I would like to do today, would you mind?'

'Of course not, what is it?'

'You will see.' I look at Seb over my coffee and by the mischievous look wiped across his face, I realise instantly that he is up to no good.

'OK. I'm a little suspicious, but as long as we can pick up some macaroons on the way?'

'Seriously Sophia, I really worry you are going to turn into one of those, I have literally never witnessed an addiction like it,' he laughs and downs the last of his coffee. In fairness, he has a point, I'm pretty sure not a day has gone by that I haven't eaten a macaroon since we set foot on French soil.

'How far is this mysterious destination, I know I said I didn't mind, but are we walking the length of Paris?'

'Quit your complaining, it will be worth it. Anyway, it's not far now, pretty sure it's just down this road.' I look around and this street is a row of high-end boutiques, we have left GAP and Zara long behind us and now I feel well outside of my credit limit.

'Here we are. Now, let me just say this Sophia. It's culturally unacceptable in France to question or decline a gift. So please don't embarrass me in this fancy shop.' Seb pleads and it's only then I notice we are standing outside of Cartier. I look at him and attempt to argue the case, 'NO. Not a word. Please Sophia, please give me this one request. It will really mean the world to me.' His pleas are so sweet, that against my better judgement I close my mouth and let Seb have his moment. We walk in and scan the shop which is filled with opulence and elegance, but it is clear he is looking for something in particular. 'Right Sophia, I have it from great authority. Who is also known as Arabella. That this is a perfect gift and you will absolutely love it. If you don't, that is absolutely fine and we can pick something else.'

'Well Arabella has amazing taste and we are in Cartier, so I'm pretty sure it will be fab. If not ridiculously expensive.' Seb gives me a glare and I mimic zipping my mouth.

'Bonjour madame, monsieur,' a gentleman who is perfectly suited and booted, walks over to greet us.

'Bonjour monsieur, I am looking for the Love ring for my girlfriend, please.'

'Fabulous choice, over here.' The Love ring, I have absolutely no idea what this is, but I'm in Cartier, so how could I not love the Love ring?

'Here madam, please let me take your ring size, which finger would you like this on?' I instantly hold out my right hand and wiggle my ring finger.

'That is the perfect choice. For now.' Seb kisses my head and holds me around my waist. After a brief moment away, the shop assistant returns with a few different options,

'Madame, would you prefer the yellow gold,' as he opens the iconic red box and presents me with a gold band, 'or the white gold.' He places them next to each other on the counter.

'Which one would you like Sophia?'

'This is too much Seb, I can't accept this. It is a gorgeous gesture, but far, far

too much.' I haven't even

seen a price tag yet, which can only mean that it's going to be incredibly expensive.

'No, it's not. Please just pick which one you prefer. Otherwise, you will leave me no choice but to pick myself.' I look at the shop assistant and he has a large, sparkling smile and shrugs nonchalantly.

'It's a wonderful problem to have, no?' I giggle at him, as far as our problems have been since we met, this is definitely far down the list.

'Which one would you pick Seb?' I gaze up at him, wondering how lucky got when our paths crossed and now here I am, in this shop, with this man.

'Well, I would pick the gold, because it goes with that other ring you always wear.'

'Yes, that is definitely what I was thinking,' Seb takes the ring out of the box and holds my right hand up, placing it on the ring finger.

'This my darling Sophia is a promise ring. I am promising you that I will always be here for you, no matter what. I will never let anyone try to harm you again and I promise that one day, before you are 28, I will be putting another ring on the other hand and I will make you my wife. You are my one Sophia and I love you,' wrapping his arms around me, he lifts my feet off the ground and kisses me softly on the lips, putting me back down onto my feet, I gulp back the pain in my throat of the imminent happy tears.

'Sebastian Simpson. You really are one of a kind and I am literally the luckiest girl to have you as a boyfriend. I will love you forever and promise to take care of you too. Thank you so much for this gorgeous gift.'

We walk back out to the sunny Parisian streets, I gaze down at my new ring and up at Seb. I feel tingles of excitement in my stomach. This moment is the happiest I have ever experienced in my life and I take in a long deep breath, inhaling the light warm breeze of the city and I know, all my dreams really are coming true.

Printed in Great Britain
by Amazon